I0631598

Wind Riders Zebra

Wind Riders, Volume 3

R.P. Wollbaum

Published by R.P. Wollbaum, 2023.

Marg, have I told you yet today how much I love you?

Chapter One

It had been a long six months. Duncan and his negotiating team had been constantly on the move for the whole of that time.

The Interplanetary Council had recognized his peoples skills in negotiating peace treaties, and over the past five years, his team had not only been instrumental in stopping conflicts, but also in resolving them before they escalated into shooting wars. Not that they could stop them all – the Mercenary Guild was kept busy.

At first, Karl and some of Duncan's officers had agreed to reorganize and run the Guild. Then Bishop tired of the constant bickering of the Oaken leadership and, resigning his commission as the overall commander of the planet's army, joined Karl in running the Guild's affairs.

The Marauders and the PIGs were constantly employed, and half of the Wind Riders were usually deployed with them. The Black Shirts were stationed at home in Stanista to provide security for the province and the planet, as well as to train the new recruits.

It had been five years since the province had been established. Peace had seen Oaken prosper, but Stanista prospered faster. The reforms that had been instituted had proven sound. The people were happy and prosperous. Now the first crop of colony members would be finishing their five years of mandatory service, and many would be starting their new lives with their new lands or businesses. Some would stay in military service full time, but most would not.

Despite the success Stanista was having, the other provinces refused to adopt Statista's methods. Losing many of their best minor nobles and common people to Stanista, they refused to allow any more of their people to move there, erected barriers across the border, and instituted export and import taxes for goods to and from Stanista.

People still found a way in, and despite the increase in price caused by the export tax, Stanista goods and foodstuffs were still in high demand. The import tax had risen so high that it was now cheaper to import raw materials and goods from other planets, especially the devastated Arial, which desperately needed not only the goods and foodstuffs, but also the market that Stanista provided for their goods.

Arial had participated in the rebellion that had seen the Wind Riders summoned to Oaken and had been punished severely for it. Not only had half the planet been scarred heavily by a short and decisive attack by the Wind Riders and the PIGs, but the residents had had to pay very high reparations for their participation. Arial was nearly bankrupt. The combination of loan payments, the loss of half of their transportation fleet, and the loss of reputation had hurt them badly. The trade with Stanista was a godsend.

Close links between Arial's leadership and Statista's had seen Arial adopt many of the reforms that Stanista had implemented. They had not only copied the manufacturing and agricultural reforms, but also the constitutional monarchy model of government. So now, while the other regions of Oaken stagnated due to their refusal to modernize, Arial and her people prospered. Other planets had noted the close ties Stanista and Arial were forming and, at first tentatively and then in droves, were demanding more of Arial's goods and raw materials.

The Interplanetary Council had noticed all of this activity and the success the Wind Riders enjoyed in not only stopping conflicts before they became problems, but in stopping them quickly and efficiently. They had asked the Wind Riders to take possession of a small planet located in the middle of the Federation. The Wind Riders gladly took this one, as it would reduce the travel time required to reach any part of the Federation.

The new planet was roughly the size of Earth's moon and was uninhabited. It was too small so nobody wanted it. That was the main purpose of this trip – to establish the new planet's status in the Federation. CT and half the Wind Riders were quickly establishing a base on the planet and were undertaking surveys of the land for resources. Now Duncan would have to negotiate their permanent release from Oaken. He did not anticipate any problems. He had a very good relationship with the ruler of Oaken, and, in any case, the move had been made at the request of the Interplanetary Council, which would overrule any local resistance.

Strangely, all communications between the new planet and Oaken had been cut off, except for the ones necessary for navigation. Duncan and his band of returnees from the new planet had been curtly told to land at the small landing area just outside of Statista's HQ instead of the much larger commercial spaceport or even the one at the military base. No communications with the troop of Wind Riders left on Oaken or with the Black Shirts had been possible, and the limited capabilities that CT or Duncan currently had, would not allow them to override any security measures in place. Now that he was a day out of Oaken, Duncan hooked his trusty laptop up to the transport's communications systems and tried to make contact with his people on Oaken.

He was unable to gain direct access to his people, but found an open link that got him in touch with a Black Shirt major on a training mission. Things had changed radically while he had been gone, and not for the better. All of the Wind Riders' communications and computer specialists were with CT on the new planet setting things up, and it would take Duncan far too long by himself to override things. So he contacted CT and had him focus all his efforts on regaining control of their systems on Oaken.

Then he activated a Trojan he'd inserted into the government's computer systems, and what he found was extremely disturbing. He called an immediate meeting with his people and the transport's officers.

"Tanya has been overthrown," he said. "Her oldest son refused to take over, and her youngest son has been made the ruler in name only. A regent and council of nobles is ruling the planet. All of our people have been arrested, and we will be as well as soon as we touch down."

Bedlam erupted in the wardroom as everyone started talking at once. Duncan let them go on for a few minutes, then slammed his hand on the table to get their attention.

"Our allegiance is to Tanya and her descendants," Duncan said, "not a regency council. Right now, we are on an embassy mission from the Interplanetary Council. That means we are not subject to any local rulings or laws. This vessel is subject to that immunity. I expect all of you to defend it to the best of your abilities. Any move to board or take control of this vessel is to be dealt with aggressively. Is that clear?"

"I have informed the Interplanetary Council of developments on Oaken, and they have appointed me their ambassador. When we land, I will disembark, alone, from this vessel. If I am killed, you are to leave immediately, using any and all deadly force to make that happen. Luckily, half the PIGs are on stand-down on Arial right now. They are being brought to active duty right now and taken out of Guild control. They should be in orbit in three days. The Marauders not committed are also on their way, but they are weeks away. Before you ask, no, I do not know the status of the Black Shirts at this time."

The rest of the day was spent in readying people and the ship for possible hostile action. Duncan spent his time trying to gain contact with the Black Shirts, to no avail. As they prepared for landing, the video feeds showed a battalion of heavily armed Black Shirts surrounding the landing pad. Duncan had no doubt the ship would survive, but the carnage on both sides would be great. As they came to a halt and the loading ramp began to lower, the Black Shirts assumed defensive postures, weapons trained on the ship. Duncan walked down the ramp alone and unarmed. Five Black Shirts, armed but not pointing weapons at him, approached.

"Nice welcome home for your commander, General Isabell," Duncan said. "Or is it Commander Isabell now?"

"My lord Kovaks," she said, "you are under arrest. I am to escort you and your people to the Supreme Leader and to confiscate this vessel."

"As I am the ambassador for the Interplanetary Council, you have no right to arrest me or to confiscate my vehicle," Duncan said. "You can try, though."

As he finished speaking, turrets and ports all along the ship's surface became active – high caliber cannon and machine guns pointed at vehicles and troop formations.

"You will lose an awful lot of good people if you do, General," Duncan said. "Now, you may escort me to the Supreme Leader, or I can walk. Your choice."

He started walking toward the nearby palace complex, and a hasty escort surrounded him . The general walked beside him.

"You disappoint me, Marlene," Duncan said. She did not respond, and not a word was spoken the rest of the short walk to the palace, where Duncan was handed off to a large group of local troopers who roughly grabbed him and shoved him along to the throne room. His feet were kicked out from under him, and he was forced to kneel in front of a very frightened teenager sitting on the throne. Leaders of the other provinces flanked the room.

"Duncan Kovaks," the man next to the throne said, "you have been convicted of treason. Your titles and lands have been confiscated. You will be held for execution at our earliest convenience. What say you?"

"As ambassador for the Interplanetary Council, I do not recognize your authority to arrest or punish me," Duncan said, still on his knees. He keyed his throat mike and gave the prearranged signal. A loud roar could be heard as the ship took off.

"Three battalions of PIGs will be in orbit tomorrow afternoon," he continued. "Three troops of Wind Riders are already on the ground and beginning operations as we speak. One battle group of Marauders will be in orbit in five days' time. Arial has pledged her full support, as has the Interplanetary Council. So, execute me at your own peril, gentlemen."

Duncan stood up and addressed the young boy directly.

"Your Majesty," he said, "I have been asked by the Interplanetary Council to negotiate a peaceful solution to this unpleasantness. I fear that any harm done to my embassy will result in disaster for Oaken and her people, Sir. If Your Highness wishes, he can put himself under my and the Interplanetary Council's protection."

"*Wind Rider One, Wind Rider Six Four One. Packages are secure, over.*"

"*Wind Rider Six Four One, Wind Rider One, acknowledge packages are secure.*"

"Your Highness, your mother and brother are now under my protective custody and are being moved to a secure location. You may join them if you wish."

"Exactly how are you proposing to do that by yourself?" one of the council members said.

Duncan spoke a code word, and all the monitors in the room came alive with a picture of him in the center of each.

"People of Stanista," he said, "the Interplanetary Council does not approve or acknowledge the change of government on Oaken. As such, all members of the active and inactive reserves are placed on active duty immediately and are to report to their barracks armed and ready for combat. All active duty members are ordered to secure all transportation hubs and critical infrastructure. All commerce is suspended with the rest of Oaken as of this moment. A Company, 1st Battalion Black Shirts is to report under arms to the throne room immediately to provide security for the crown prince and myself. Further instructions to follow. Wind Rider One, out."

"Does that answer your question, Sir?" Duncan said to the man, as one hundred heavily armed Black Shirts entered the throne room and dispersed around it.

As red dots from laser sites appeared on all the men's chests, the fifteen-year-old prince jumped off the throne and sprinted to Duncan's side.

Duncan turned and, with the prince beside him, walked up to the Black Shirt captain.

"Transport the prince directly to Wind Rider barracks," he ordered. "Then I want a meeting of all field grade officers in the Wind Rider boardroom immediately. Have a platoon take custody of these gentlemen. They and their staffs are to be transported out of Stanista immediately. To the border will be sufficient."

One platoon surrounded the prince and led him out, another the nobles. The rest followed Duncan out of the palace complex. The prince was already being driven away when Duncan reached the courtyard, and a command vehicle with an LAV in front and behind was waiting for him. Marlene and her staff were standing beside the center vehicle.

"I thought I issued orders, General," Duncan said to her. "I have a big enough escort thank you. See to your troops."

Duncan got in the front passenger seat of the G-Wagon. Two troopers got in the rear, one manning the roof-mounted machine gun. The rest of the platoon entered the LAVs, and they were soon driving toward the barracks complex on the edge of town. Everywhere, singularly or in small groups, heavily armed and uniformed troops were making their way toward the barracks complex. Different-colored berets and unit crests showed it was a full callup of every battle group. The defenses of the base were fully manned and armed, and units already deploying to pre-planned positions by the time Duncan stopped in front of the complex. Two troops of Wind Riders were manning the perimeter, and another was stationed in Cougars, blocking the entrance.

Duncan got out of his vehicle, and all three then headed back to the Black Shirts area. He strode directly to his room and changed into his field uniform, complete with loaded Sigsauer 1911 pistol in a shoulder holster, mounted high on his left side. Marlene and her people were just scrambling to their chairs in the board room as Duncan marched in and stood behind his chair at the head of the table.

He pointed at the Wind Rider major. "Report."

"Sir," Dianne said. "Her Majesty and both boys are in the married quarters, unhurt and secure, Sir. Communications with the rest of the division have been re-established. Release of incarcerated Wind Rider members has been effected and casualties are being treated in the hospital, Sir."

"General," Duncan said, addressing Marlene, "I want a full written report of what happened here by the time I return from the hospital. Major, you and one of those Cougars out front will take me to the hospital right now!"

"What the hell happened here, Dianne?" he said once they were in the Cougar and headed to the hospital.

"As near as I can tell, Duncan," she said, "they hit us right at breakfast time. We only had thirty troopers here, as you know. They hit us with more than a thousand troops. We got a few, but it happened too fast, Duncan. We didn't have a chance. I don't know what the story is with the Black Shirts."

By then they were at the hospital, and Duncan was being ushered in to where his people were. The injuries for the most part were minor, but there were two broken arms and one broken leg. Heavy bruising was still prevalent on almost every face, and some were nursing bruised ribs. Duncan made a few jokes about how the bent noses and black-and-blue faces actually enhanced the looks of them, and then he headed back to the barracks.

Reports were coming in fast and furious about deployments and areas being secured. Air defenses were fully operational. The PIGs were in orbit, and most of them were deploying to the border area to the west. The command group would be arriving soon to be briefed. A battalion of Arial troops would be in orbit the next day and the Marauders two days after that. The rebel leaders had been unceremoniously dumped off at the border. All border crossings were closed and armed. Troops were being deployed to the border as they talked. Only minor enemy activity had been spotted in the border region. There was enough ammunition and fuel to conduct full-scale operations for two months. Offensive operations could commence at any time.

"Until we ascertain the status of the Black Shirts, we will concentrate on defense," Duncan said. "Once the Marauders arrive, that will change. I will have to consult with Her Majesty before I commit to offensive operations, though. We have planned and practiced for this. I want preliminary deployments readied. Wind Riders are to be ready to deploy as soon as possible. Ah, I see my errant battle group commander has arrived. Clear the room and have General Isabelle report to me in my office."

When Diane escorted Marlene into Duncan's office, he was sitting behind the desk. His back was to the door and his head was down and his shoulders slumped. He stayed that way when Marlene reported.

"Major, stay put," Duncan said. His voice low, almost a whisper. After a few seconds he raised his head, squared his shoulders, and spun the chair around to face them. His face was calm, but his eyes were narrow and full of fire. Diane had seen this before, and when he began to speak, his quiet speech betrayed that he was not pleased. Not pleased at all. Marlene had never seen this in him before. Shelly was waiting at the door with a report, and she had seen this look before.

"General Isabelle, you are relieved of your duties as commander of the Black Shirts," he said. "You are confined to your barracks and will hold yourself ready for a court of inquiry by your peers. Major, inform Colonel Bonchance that he is in temporary command of the Black Shirts. He is to have them stack arms in the armoury and confine them to barracks. Reserve troops that have been called up are to assume the defense of the complex. Arial troops are to take control of the border posts until the Marauders return. PIGs are to prepare for possible offensive operations here at the base."

At that point, Tanya and her two sons came into the office, and she made to speak but Duncan held up a hand.

"Whatever loyalty I had to you, Ma'am, has been all used up," he said in the same quiet cold voice. "You disregarded intelligence that was supplied to you warning of this coup attempt well in advance of it. Then you used your influence to have General Isabelle break her oath of allegiance to her overlord. You placed yourself, your sons and the people of Stanista in jeopardy, to prove a point, knowing the Wind Riders would take care of the problem for you. As such, my oath of fealty to you is broken. I, and whosoever of my people who wish to join me, shall be leaving Oaken as soon as possible.

"Major, take a fire team and escort their highnesses and the general to the Black Shirts barracks. Dismissed." He swung his chair around, turning his back to them` all.

With two armed Wind Riders in front, another two behind, and Shelly and Diane on each side, the three royals and Marlene walked through the barracks, every eye on them. Jane followed them outside and moved up beside Diane.

"I've seen Duncan angry before, but not like that," Diane said.

"I have," Shelly said, and faster than anyone could react, she shoved Marlene hard against the barrack wall, grabbed the lapels of her tunic, and held her up as high as she could.

"The last time I saw him like that, he scared the hell out of me, and I didn't see him for two years," she said. Jane came to stand beside her.

"The only time I've seen him like that was when he had that Sig of his pointed at my daughter's head, ready to blow it off," Jane said. "He thought she had betrayed him and gotten a bunch of his friends killed. Lucky for you, nobody got killed, or you would be dead, Isabelle, and not one of us would have lifted a finger to help you."

"Let the dumb shit go, Shelly. She's not worth it."

Shelly slammed Marlene against the wall again, then let her go, but not before spitting on Marlene's boots.

Just before they walked into the Black Shirts barracks, Diane stopped both women. Many Black Shirts were watching.

"He gave both of you everything he had," Diane said. "He proved his loyalty to both of you, put his life on the line for both of you. No more so than today. He, and we, rescued your sorry asses, even after you had betrayed him. At least I was armed. He went into that throne room unarmed, willing to be killed for you, Tanya. He kept his word to you, even though you betrayed him."

Then she turned around, not giving a salute, and marched away, not returning the Black Shirt salutes she was given.

Duncan had an Arial transport ship and its troops take Tanya back to her own palace and, once she was in safe hands, he returned to the border. Tanya was on her own. She would have to use her own army to quell the rebellion.

A communique had been issued to all the people of Stanista outlining everything that had happened: that Duncan had renounced his oath to Tanya and Oaken, that he had relinquished control of Stanista, that anyone who wanted to come along to the new planet was welcome. Those who wished to stay would be released from their oaths to Duncan.

Once the PIG and Marauder contingents arrived, Duncan mustered them on the main parade ground, then had the Black Shirts marched in. They were placed in the center, flanked by the other two, smaller groups. All of them were in regular uniform. Then the one hundred Wind Riders on the planet marched in, armed and wearing combat kit. They formed up in their troops facing the Black Shirts.

Duncan marched up the stairs of the reviewing stand to the microphone. Like the rest of the Wind Riders, he was in full combat kit, his rifle slung across his chest, barrel pointed down, and his right hand on the trigger guard.

"All of you swore an oath to your commanders and through your commanders to me. In turn, I swore an oath to protect all of you, your families, and the people of Stanista. Some of you chose to ignore that oath. Chose not to protect the people of Stanista when they needed your help. It could be said that you were only following orders. That it was your commander and not you who chose not to protect the people of Stanista. Thirty Wind Riders, clerks and computer technicians, chose otherwise. Outnumbered and weaponless, they did their best for the people of Stanista. That all of them were not killed is a miracle."

He stood looking over the whole assembly for a few moments. There was not a sound on the parade ground.

"The Wind Riders," he continued, "all of the Wind Riders, will be leaving Oaken. I have renounced my oath to Oaken, as have they through me. You were told when you joined us that you could leave anytime you wanted. You still can. I will have no one with me who does not want to be. When we leave, we will be taking everything with us. There will be no ammunition or weapons factories. We will leave none of our communication equipment or facilities. Oaken will be just like every other planet in the Interplanetary Alliance. We will support any faction that pays us enough and that suits our ideals, just like every other planet in the Alliance."

"If you choose to stay, you will stay in your units. The only changes will be that you will no longer have the royal designations you have now. The PIGs may choose another name for themselves if they wish. We begin transport to our new home in two days. Make up your minds by then."

Without another word, he marched off the platform and, followed by the Wind Riders, marched back to barracks.

That afternoon, Marlene in her regular uniform was marched into the base's main officers' mess boardroom, where she came to attention. Jane, the general representing the Wind Riders, Bishop, the general of the Marauders, Kurt of the PIGs, and Bonchance representing the Black Shirts were seated at a long table before her. Bishop, as the highest-ranking of the generals, was seated in the center.

"My Lady General Marlene Isabelle," Bishop said. "The evidence against you has been reviewed and a decision made. Your removal from command of the Black Shirts is confirmed. All rank is stripped, and you are discharged from duty. At My Lord Kovaks' request, you will be given the choice to remain a member of our community as a common citizen or to renounce your oath. What say you?"

Other than to swallow several times, Marlene betrayed no emotion as she absorbed what she had just heard.

"I would stay a member of the community, Sir," she said quietly.

"Very well, Citizen Isabelle," Bishop said, "you start with a clean slate. All seniority is lost. You will leave this room and report to your barracks, where you will surrender all uniforms and equipment. You will then report in civilian clothing to the main transport facility, where you will join the rest of your recruit training group. Once you have arrived at our new home and are processed, your seniority will commence. Like every other recruit, you will complete basic training and evaluation and then be placed in whichever branch of the service you qualify for, except for the Black Shirt battle group. Once you have satisfactorily completed your initial five years, you will regain the monetary rights you were granted previously. Do you understand?"

"The recruit understands, Sir!" she said.

"Dismissed," Bishop said, and Marlene spun around and marched out of the board room.

"She'd have been better off if Duncan had shot her," Bishop said.

Chapter Two

Marlene was the only recruit with no luggage. She was just wearing the clothing she had on. The only difference between her and the rest of the recruits was that she was a little older and had a scar on the left side of her face. Where the others were excited and chatty, she was quiet, her shoulders slumped, and her hands in her pockets. Once they had taken off, she began to cry.

"Hey, what's wrong?" the girl sitting beside her asked. "My sister just finished basic, and she said it's not that bad."

Marlene just cried harder. The girl put her arm around her, pulling her head onto her shoulder and stroking her hair.

If I find out who that son of a bitch is that hurt her this bad, I'll beat the shit out of him, she thought.

Marlene let the tears flow when they cut her hair short, like most of the other women, but for a different reason. It was after the haircuts that the indoctrination began. As they left, they were marshalled first in groups of five, then ten, twenty, and finally one hundred. At that point, escorted by five drill instructors, they were marched over to a large warehouse where they were once again separated into groups of twenty. This is where Marlene began to stand out from the other recruits. She automatically walked in step with the person in front of her, walking erect, with her arms swinging freely. When they entered the warehouse, they were told to remove all jewelry, watches, and clothing down to underwear and to turn over all personal property to waiting clerks. Marlene had served co-ed for many years, and not having any outer clothing on around others was nothing special for her. This was not so for many of the other females and some of the males, who were self-conscious. She also had better muscle tone than all the other females and most of the males, and in addition to the scar on her face, she had a burn scar on her right shoulder, down the back of her left leg and across her abdomen from laser hits.

The drill instructor assigned to her platoon took notice of all this. He was an older veteran of the PIG battle group, with almost twenty years of service, mostly as a highly skilled and decorated member of the SAS back on Earth. If the scars on her body hadn't given her away, her body tone and the way she moved would have. While some of the young women were embarrassed and others angry at the rude comments some of the males uttered, this one ignored them. One of the men in her section was becoming aggressive in his comments, and as the drill instructor was about to intervene, the scarred women turned around and just looked at the mouthy man. That's it, just looked at him, right in the eyes. After ten seconds the man lowered his eyes and no more was heard.

The next stop after the physical examinations was the inoculation station. This was where the barcodes tattooed on each trooper just below where the neck joins the shoulders and over the spine would be scanned for the first time. The drill instructor positioned himself so he could read the computer monitor as her bar code was scanned. Her name was Marlene Isabelle, she was twenty-eight years of age, and her inoculations were all up to date. That was all the data on her. No place of birth, no educational background, no military background, no history at all. Yet she was clearly a veteran and had seen combat.

At exactly five the next morning, the drill instructor snapped on the lights in the barracks and blew constantly on his whistle. All but a few of the recruits tumbled out of their bunks, looking around dazed.

"Half an hour, in front of the barracks in PT gear!" he yelled, then walked back out.

Isabelle was at the line painted on the ground in front of the barracks at parade rest at exactly the half-hour mark. Some of the recruits were early and on the line as well. Most of the others were late. She was the only one kitted out properly. The latecomers were made to do thirty push-ups. Once they were finished, the drill instructor made the ones not kitted out properly do twenty, and that included the people who had just finished thirty. During it all, Isabelle stood at parade rest staring blankly in the distance.

Three recruits noticed how Isabelle was standing and copied her, sort of. One of them was the girl that bunked beside her.

"I am Master Corporal Conrad!" he said. "I am to be your drill instructor for the rest of the cycle. I am god. Your mommy and daddy cannot help you now! You will form up each morning equipped in PT gear, in line and at parade rest by five-thirty each morning. Now you are going to form two lines. When I tell you, you will face to the left. Then we will take a little run. I will tell you when to stride with your left foot. All of you will do that.

"Left face! By the left, march!"

Conrad kept the pace easy, and he ranged up and down the two lines haranguing almost everyone for being out of step or too close to the person in front. Isabelle was the only exception. She was at the proper distance to the recruit in front of her and matched that trooper's pace, no matter how erratic it was. He only ran them around the block this time, a total of half a mile, yet over half the recruits barely made it, and most were out of breath. Again, except for Isabelle, who was not even breathing heavily.

"Ten minutes!" he yelled once they were lined up in front of the barracks again. "Back in line in ten minutes in fatigue uniform! Move it!"

Marlene was already dressed, her PT gear neatly folded and in her footlocker, while the girl next to her was still trying to figure out what to wear. Marlene tossed the proper gear on the girl's locker, and as she clothed herself, Marlene quickly packed her locker in the proper manner, then made her bed properly. Both of them made it to the line in time – just. Now there were two of them not doing push-ups. They formed up in two lines, then were made to trot to the mess hall.

"Match my pace," Marlene said only loud enough for the girl running beside her to hear. "My left foot, your left foot; my right, your right. Keep your strides as long as mine."

"Do I hear somebody talking in my line?" Conrad yelled. "No talking! If god wanted recruits to talk, he would not have given them a drill instructor to do their talking for them!"

They were given twenty minutes to have breakfast and told which bench they would occupy for meals. Marlene shepherded her bunkmate through the line, showing her what and what not to eat. Then, by example, how to shovel the food as fast as possible into her mouth and be back in line outside on time. Then they were marched over to the parade ground and, along with the other raw recruits, were shown how to properly line up. Over and over again for two hours.

After that, they were taken to a classroom and shown how to properly make up their bunks and pack their equipment in their lockers. Then back to the parade square for more practice in lining up, now with rudimentary commands to come to attention or at ease. Left face, right face, about face. Conrad, with the three foot-long riding crop he kept under his left armpit, was quick to smack an offending body part not conforming to his command.

It was almost dark when they left the mess hall after supper, and they were given half an hour of free time before lights out.

"Thanks for the help today. My name is Shandra Kensky," Marlene's bunkmate said. She stuck her hand out for a handshake.

"Marlene Isabelle," Marlene said shaking the hand. Then she started polishing her boots. "The DI will be inspecting our gear tomorrow. Make sure your shit is stowed away properly and your bed made properly before we hit the line in the morning. He'll go easy on us for a couple of days, then the punishments are going to be worse. Get in the habit right now."

"Ya, my sister warned me about that," Shandra said. "What are you doing here? It's obvious you've done this before."

"Different army, different place," Marlene said. "Most of the stuff is the same, but they do things a little differently here. Don't worry, I'm going to screw up at some point, too."

"Why are you helping me?" Sandra asked.

"Because you helped me," Marlene replied.

Then the lights went out.

As Marlene predicted, after breakfast the next morning, the DI inspected the barracks and dumped lockers and beds on the floor, scattering the contents of any that did not meet his approval. All but two. Three other recruits noticed that the two women never got "special" treatment and started to copy what they were doing. The bully from the first day did not like the way everyone was deferring to Marlene, and he and his two buddies decided to do something about it.

An hour after lights out, Marlene heard them get out of their bunks and start walking her way. She slipped out of her bunk and softly went across the hall and crouched down beside the two beds across from hers. The three men had a sock with something in it swinging from their right hands. They surrounded not Marlene's bed, but Shandra's, and as they swung the socks over their heads, Marlene sprang into action.

She rapid-punched the man at the foot of the bed in the kidneys, then vaulted across the bed and slammed both feet into the belly of the man on the left, knocking him on his back on the next bunk. Then she spun around and grabbed the last one's arm as the sock was descending and twisted it as she punched him in the solar plexus.

The one on the bunk sprang up. He was the bully and a good twenty pounds heavier than Marlene. The lights came on just as she punched him in the belly, knocking the wind out of him and dropping him to the floor.

Conrad and two of his DI buddies blew on their whistles and yelled for everyone to come to attention.

Conrad came right up to Isabelle, who was standing at attention in front of her bunk, and started yelling at her as loud as he could. He called her every name he could think of and made her drop and give him fifty.

"Get those three idiots over to the infirmary and have them checked out," he ordered the other DIs while Marlene was doing her push-ups. He made Marlene's job harder by pushing down on her back with his right foot.

"There will be no fighting in my barracks!" he yelled. "My recruits will only fight when I say they fight! Is that clear Isabelle?"

"Yes, Master Corporal!" Marlene gasped out as loud as she could.

"The only discipline handed out will be mine, is that clear?" he yelled.

"Yes, Master Corporal," she yelled again.

"When this idiot has finished her push-ups, she will be taking two laps around the camp perimeter," Conrad said. "The rest of you idiots will do push-ups until she returns. My friend Corporal Jenkins will stay and make sure you do. All right, Idiot Isabelle, out the door! Move it, move it!"

She was barefoot and only in her underwear as he made her run to the fence line and then stopped and come to attention.

Nose-to-nose with her, he asked normally, not yelling, "What the hell was that all about, Isabelle?"

"Must have been dreaming, Master Corporal," she said. "It won't happen again, Master Corporal."

"Ya right," Conrad said, then he moved back from her. "At ease, relax, Isabelle."

She came to parade rest, and he shook his head and shrugged his shoulders.

"We were waiting for those three knuckle heads to do that," Conrad said. "We didn't figure you would handle it yourself. You going to be a problem for me, Isabelle?"

"No, Master Corporal," she said in a normal voice.

"I don't know what your story is, Isabelle," he said. "It's pretty clear you know your shit, so you must have pissed off somebody pretty high up to get here. Your records are not just sealed, Isabelle, they have been wiped completely. The people in charge obviously think you are savable. That being said, this will be the only time you get off easy. I'm going to ride your ass, Isabelle. You and the whole platoon. You screw up, they all get punished. They screw up, you get the same punishment as the screw-up. Clear?"

"Yes, Master Corporal," she said.

"Next time you discipline that idiot, I want to see him pissing blood, not those little love taps you gave him. Is that clear?"

"Yes, Master Corporal," she said.

"All right, get your ass back to bed," he said.

True to his word, the next morning Marlene had to do as many push-ups, and other punishments, as often as others in the platoon were given. Not only that, but the three bullies, along with Shandra, were assigned as her fire teammates.

She never had to discipline them, and the rest of the platoon soon got the picture and started coming to her for advice on how to do things. There was always some minor detail that was overlooked, but in a short time, the punishments were few and far between. Conrad started handing out platoon leader duty on a rotating basis, but never to Marlene.

In their time off before lights out, the other platoon members bitched about it, but Marlene quieted them all down. She didn't want it, she said.

One morning Brock was handed the duty, but he refused it.

"Master Corporal," he said, "I believe Recruit Isabelle has missed her turn, Master Corporal. I have already had mine. Master Corporal."

"When I give an order. I expect it to be carried out. Recruit Brock!" he yelled. "Drop and give me fifty! Isabelle, give me a hundred."

Brock sat beside her at their mess table.

"Shit, sorry, Isabelle," he said. "It's not fair. You need your turn, too."

"Nothing fair about the army," she said. "Follow your orders as best you can Brock. I am."

Rapidly, their platoon became the best in the company. Then their company began to match them, and they were the best company in the training cycle. That became very clear when they were issued their rifles. Their platoon qualified on the range by the second day, and Marlene's fireteam all qualified expert, as did more than half of the platoon.

All of her section and two-thirds of the platoon were selected for advanced infantry training, and the five of them were kept together as a fireteam. Conrad joined them as their section leader.

It had been a long and tiring eleven weeks. This was their last week. Each fireteam would have a week to complete a task, on their own, with only the equipment they could carry on their backs. The fireteam leader was handed a sealed set of orders to be opened the next day, and they were sent off in different directions at different times.

The next morning, Brock, the designated team leader for this exercise, opened the sealed package. It had a map, a compass and a printed order sheet.

"Fan-fucking-tastic," he said. "We have a week to go thirty miles in this shit and take out whatever observation posts we can find."

He handed the orders and map to Marlene. She took a fast reading on the compass and placed where they were on the map.

"Piece of cake," she said. "Two days max to the area. The hard part is going to be finding them without getting our asses handed to us."

Two days later, they were sitting under some trees a mile short of the operating area, which was dominated by three large hills overlooking low flat lands. There was little cover once they broke the tree line.

As the designated sharpshooter for the fireteam, Marlene had a rifle with a scope, which she used to scan the hilltops. It took her an hour to spot the first observation post. It was located at the crest of the hill on the right. Shandra spotted the next one on the left hill, also at the crest.

The one on the center hill was located just below the crest overlooking their side. Now they sat and watched the targets. Mapping out where each team member was located. Each night they crawled out on the flat land and came back with armfuls of vegetation. On the fourth night, they started crawling toward the center outpost.

By daybreak, they were halfway up the hill and concealed in a formation of boulders. Shandra, scanning their back trail, spotted another fireteam at the edge of the tree line, half a mile from where they had been. Just at dusk, Marlene broke radio silence and reported in.

"We will be in position in five hours," she said. "Have our assets prepared by then."

She took a fast reading of the other fireteam in the treeline, then they started crawling up the hill again. The hint of dawn was on the horizon, but it was still dark when they reached their point of attack. Everyone but the one sentry at the observation point was asleep, and the sentry kept nodding off.

The sentry was sitting on a rock, huddled close to a fire. Marlene crept silently behind him, then sprang, placing him in a chokehold and dragging him onto her. When he passed out, she let the chokehold go and rolled him off quietly, making sure she had not killed him.

The rest of the team picked a sleeping bag, and at a signal, punched the bags with their rifle butts.

"Bang," Brock said. "You're all dead."

They used lengths of cord to secure them all in their sleeping bags, then Shandra glassed the other positions and saw they were still asleep, as was the other fireteam down on the tree line.

"Base One, Charley Five," Marlene said into the radio. "Fire mission. What assets do we have?"

"Charley Five, two fast movers and four 105s."

"Roger, Base One. Two painted targets on ridge 805, copy?"

"Two painted targets on ridge 805, copy."

"One gun target. 111.1 by 906.93 GPS actual."

"Copy, Charley Five, one gun target 111.1 by 906.93 GPS actual. Fast movers, six mikes, guns eight mikes."

"Copy, Base One. Fast movers six mikes, guns eight mikes. Charley Five, out."

"Shandra, paint the left target, John the right. The rest of us, form a perimeter and shoot anything that approaches."

Shandra and John lit up their targets with their laser devices, and five minutes later, high-speed engines were heard and flares popped over both targets right in the center of both camps. Two minutes after that, artillery-fired flares erupted around the fireteam camped on the tree line.

"Contact rear," Brock whispered. All five of them formed a fire line to the rear and waited. Marlene tossed a flash bang, which not only illuminated the advancing fireteam but blinded them, as they all had on night vision goggles. All five of Marlene's people opened fire, the blank rounds masking the laser hit designator noise temporarily.

They all heard swearing coming from the attackers. After ten minutes of no further activity, Marlene turned on the radio again.

"Base One, Charley Five," she said. "Three outposts and two fire teams eliminated."

"Repeat, Charley Five."

"You heard me," Marlene said. "Any more surprises for us?"

"Crappy radio discipline, Charley Five," A different voice on the radio said. "Extraction team is on the way. The exercise is finished."

"Nice work, Isabelle," Conrad said. "We didn't spot you until it was too late."

As they walked into the firelight, the fireteam saw the attackers were five DIs.

"Okay, cut those idiots loose," he said. "They can walk back. After they retrieve your gear."

Not surprisingly, their fire-team graduated at the top of the class. Instead of being allowed to pick what regiment they wanted to join, they were assigned to the PIGs and their reward was to be placed on immediate active duty and sent on their first mission the next day.

Chapter Three

A company of recently graduated recruits made up a part of the eight hundred troop battalion that was being sent to quell a rebellion on a minor planet. Marlene's fireteam was part of this new company. Sort of. On paper, they were part of the company, but they were billeted separately from the company and the rest of the battalion. They had a whole cargo bay to themselves and were told to stay there during transport.

For the first few days, it was fine. It had been a rough sixteen weeks, and all of them needed the rest. But then things became boring. Marlene had been promoted to corporal and the fireteam leader, so she started breaking their days into training regimes. Each team member soon knew how to do each other's jobs and how to use their equipment. Marlene showed them some tricks on modifying their personal pistols and rifles, and much time was spent on personalizing the weapons and other pieces of equipment to suit themselves.

In addition to her regular rifle with a grenade launcher under the barrel, Marlene had been issued a long-range sniper rifle. She spent much of her time familiarizing herself with the weapon and its sighting system and working with Shandra who, in addition to being one of the laser targeters, would be her spotter. The only interaction they had with the rest of the ship was at meal times, when members of the ship's crew would drop off their meals.

Even when they made landfall a week later, they were billeted by themselves off by the machinery repair facility, not the main barracks complex, although this time they took their meals with the rest of the company in the mess. They were all told they would have three days to acclimatize themselves to the new planet.

The planet was semi-tropical – hot and humid, with lush, dark green vegetation that was very thick outside the cleared areas the base occupied. It was valuable for the rubber-like plants it had, as well as rare earth metals and lithium. Other plants were cultivated and harvested for medical purposes, and there was an emerging farming culture providing local foods. It was the farmers who had first started to rebel, and they were soon joined by the manual laborers who harvested the rubber sap and the medicinal plants. The battalion had been sent to put a stop to the rebellion, which had been going on for better than five years now.

Marlene and her fireteam were to be sent as forward observers behind enemy lines to report on any movement or troop concentrations. They would be inserted by air and would be relieved after three weeks at the most. They would be landed in a valley at the foot of the mountain they would occupy, then make their way on foot to the top. To draw enemy eyes to other areas, the transport would then do fake insertions on the tops of five other mountains before leaving.

After the noise of the transport, the little valley clearing they had been inserted into seemed deadly quiet. It was anything but, though. Birds and small animals called out and made their way about their daily routines. Once the fireteam bulled their way through the heavy underbrush and under the cover of large trees, the undergrowth disappeared and the walking became easy, or as easy as could be with eighty pounds of equipment on their backs. It took them two days to climb the mountain and find a good spot to set up their observation post.

They spent their days looking for movement in the area and identifying places that could be used as trails and camping areas. The nights were spent looking for campfires. By the end of the week, they had identified several areas of concern, which were dealt with by air or artillery strikes.

It didn't take long for the enemy to figure out they were being observed, and that it was from the ground. No drone aircraft had been flying. The enemy began to explore the mountaintops the transport had made landings on. There were surprises waiting for them in these locations, as they had all been boobytrapped. Once the boobytraps had been sprung, Marlene called in artillery fire, which saturated the mountaintops.

There was little chance that they themselves would be discovered. They had set up their quarters in a large cave and had camouflaged the entrance. That was proven when, a few days later, an enemy patrol came up their mountain. The patrol was quiet, but not quiet enough. There were twenty of them, armed with crossbows, long bows, spears and long blades. A few had laser weapons.

The fireteam's job was to observe, not fight, and while they were prepared to defend themselves, they spent the two days the enemy explored the area quietly hiding from view. At one point, a five-man patrol had come within feet of discovering them. But after that, the enemy withdrew back down the mountain. For a time.

Then they began to concentrate below the mountain. The team soon found itself cut off, as the mountain was ringed by the enemy camp. They were told to hold position and wait. Other areas of concentration were hit when spotted, but not this one. Early on, the team had supplemented their rations by hunting and fishing. Clear clean water was never an issue, and much of the vegetation was edible. Even so, they had been in place for over a month now and were running low on supplies.

The enemy was becoming increasingly suspicious, and daily patrols were being conducted on the mountain looking for them. The first patrol that found them was small, only five men, and they were killed quickly and silently. But the patrol's disappearance triggered a big response. Again, they were told to hold, so the fireteam constructed defenses in layers and prepared for an assault. It was not long in coming.

A full company was sent up after them but soon found their way not unobstructed. The first scouts tripped a spring-loaded trap that shot two foot-long sharpened stakes, impaling both men. The next was a large, heavy tree trunk that came out of a tree bordering the trail. The tree trunk had spikes attached to it and took out four troopers. The next trap had been set up on the opposite side of a small clearing, and, once it was tripped, Marlene started picking off the exposed troops in the clearing, one-by-one, with her sniper rifle.

The first soldier she shot was at random, but then she began to shoot anyone who looked like they were giving orders. By the time they broke and ran back the way they had come, she had killed ten of them. The enemy tried that same tactic three more times, probing them from all four directions, each time with the same result.

Again, they were told to hold. The next day, three companies were sent up after them. This time they kept coming, and the fireteam had to fall back to their next position. Everyone but the machine gun was firing their weapons, not on full-auto but slow, aimed, single shots. Again the enemy was sent back suffering losses. And again, they were told to hold. The next day, they were hit from a different direction, and this time the enemy had learned and were not rushing them in one mass, but in platoon-sized rushes, spread across the front. The fireteam beat them back, but not before they had to pull back to their next line of defense.

Again, they were told to hold. The next day, they were hit on two sides, and while they were able to hold the enemy off, they were pushed back to the top of the mountain on their last defensive position. This time the enemy did not pull back down to the foot of the mountain. The team was now surrounded, and ammunition was running low.

"I don't think you understand our position, Sir," Marlene said on the radio. "We are completely surrounded. There are only five of us and we have enough ammunition to last maybe one more assault. At least give us some artillery cover, Sir."

"Negative, Zebra One. You are to hold." Then the radio was cut off.

"Fuck!" Marlene said, throwing the radio from her. "If we can drive these assholes off one more time, we are getting the hell off this hill the next night. Fuck them."

Just after dawn the next morning, the next attack started. Marlene used her sniper rifle, killing anyone that looked like an officer until she ran out of ammunition. Then they started shooting single shots, but the enemy kept coming, and they started firing in three-shot bursts.

Brock opened up with the machine gun, but nothing was stopping the enemy this time. They knew there were only five of them by now and kept coming at them. Not even the claymore mines stopped them. Brock was out of ammo for the machine gun, and now the enemy was close enough for their bows to be in range. Marlene started using her grenade launcher, but she only had ten grenades. Still, the enemy kept coming. They could sense the victory. The fireteam was down to using their pistols. Marlene had a crossbow bolt in a leg, Shandra one in an arm. John had gone down with one in his chest. The enemy was screaming now, coming on with spears and swords.

Marlene attached her bayonet to her rifle and charged their line, but then everything changed. Explosions erupted all along their lines, close enough to blow her off her feet. Then heavy machine gun and rifle fire erupted. Men were flung off their feet all along the attacker's lines, and then they broke and ran, right into a storm of rifle fire from the advancing battalion coming up behind them on all sides.

Gerry, the only member of the fire team not wounded by arrows, started first aid on the rest of them. John was dead. Even though wounded, they set up a perimeter. Each of them had a full clip of pistol bullets and maybe five rounds of rifle bullets left. They could still fight, but not for long.

"Hey Zebra, don't shoot us, we're friends," Conrad, along with ten other troopers, came into their position. Gerry was looking at the arrow in Marlene's leg, and a medic took over for him.

"What the fuck, Master Corporal!" Gerry said. "What kinda bullshit was this? Fucking suicide mission!"

"That would be Captain Conrad, Private," he said. "You got anything to say, Corporal?"

"Fuck you," Marlene said. "Sir." Then she stood up, came to attention and saluted. The rest of Zebra joined her in a line, all of them saluting.

"Zebra team reports position held, Sir!" she said. "One dead, three wounded, Sir!"

Even though he knew she was being disrespectful by saluting him and reporting in that fashion in the field, there was nothing he could do about it. She was following proper procedure. He would have done the same thing in her position.

"Okay, Isabelle, well done," Conrad said. "Medivac is on the way. Stand down."

None of the arrows had hit anything vital and they had been shot at long range, so had little power anyway. John's had been a lucky hit. Even so, they were all a little stiff and Marlene was walking with a bit of limp. They were still left alone in their bivouac area and in the mess. But this time, it was out of respect, not because they were different.

All of them had been promoted, Marlene to sergeant and the others to corporal. They had all lost weight and spent most of the first two days back at camp sleeping. The rebellion was over, and Zebra team was on the first transport ship home. This time, they were given two officer's cabins to share for the trip and their own table at the mess. The first day out, Conrad and two of the other original DIs joined them. All of them were captains, not corporals.

"I know you're pissed at us," Conrad said. "Hell, I'm pissed about it, too. But the locals would not let us mount an attack. Finally, the colonel launched it anyway. Good thing, they had you guys that last attack. If it is any consolation, all of you are getting hefty bonuses."

"Lot of good that does John," Marlene said. "He can't spend his."

"I'm sorry Marlene," Conrad said. "We look after our own. His family will be well looked after."

"We should never have been sent out there!" Marlene said. "Raw goddamned rookies! Where the hell were the big shot Wind Riders? That was their job, not ours! Christ, these kids have not even figured out how to march properly yet, and you had us out doing deep recon. Bullshit! Sir."

Her outburst had drawn attention, and everyone was looking at their table. One person wearing Wind Rider patches on his shoulder stood and looked at her.

"Ya, you asshole!" she yelled. "Where the fuck were you guys? One of my people was killed and two wounded doing your job! God-damned rookies right out of boot camp! This is bullshit! Arrest me, kick me out of the army. I don't care anymore!"

Then she stalked off.

The first thing that happened when they returned to base was that they were all taken over to the hospital. Blood tests were done, the three with wounds had those looked at, and all of them had to answer questions from psychologists. It was right after that that Marlene was stripped of her sergeant's stripes and her bonus for her outburst on the ship. Two days later, they were on a small, fast ship headed for a new mission.

They were given an information packet and studied it the whole trip. The head of a criminal gang was living in a remote area of the planet. They were to take custody of the man and extract him for trial. There were extensive files on his home and its grounds, the amount and type of security, access roads in and out, and his weekly schedule. The man was very regular in his routine, so it did not take very long to come up with a plan.

They would be inserted on Friday night and make their way five miles to a position overlooking the large complex, where they would verify the information they had and confirm that the man was indeed there. A perfect ambush site was located two miles away from the complex on the road to town that the man took every Wednesday afternoon. The road climbed a small hill at that point and made a hard right turn, which would force the vehicle to slow down. Marlene would take out the driver/guard, and they would commandeer the vehicle and drive it another five miles where they would be picked up.

They were given rations for two weeks in case they missed the first window. They would just have their personal rifles and, in Marlene's case, her sniper rifle. The squad machine gun was not needed for this mission, and, in any case, the barrel had been burnt out on the last mission, and they had not been given a new gun before they left.

It was after midnight planet side when they exited the small, stealthy landing craft and started making their way toward the residential complex. They had little trouble making their way, their night vision goggles lighting the area nicely for them, although everything was grey instead of color. The night was calm and quiet, the only sounds coming from their soft footfalls or a pant leg brushing a small bush.

By daybreak, they were concealed on a brush-covered hill overlooking the complex and glassing the area. Everything had been as they had been briefed, and after the initial look, three of them rested while the fourth kept watch. This area of the planet was dry and hot. It was just outside the forested areas, where the plains that stretched for hundreds of miles started.

The man had done well for himself. There were two tennis courts, a large swimming pool and even a nine-hole golf course on the grounds. There were also immaculate stables and six horses in a well-groomed pasture. The main house was a huge two-story affair with covered patios on all four sides and well-groomed gardens with ornamental trees and shrubs everywhere.

Several spacious guest houses adjacent to the main house were connected with shrub-lined pathways. Half a mile away from the main house were servant and workers houses, as well as machinery shops and a corral complex.

Cattle dotted a huge pasture across from hay and grain fields. As she glassed the area, Marlene was reminded of her family's holdings back on Oaken and wondered if she would ever see them again. She was just about to put the glasses away and grab the breakfast being cooked over a small portable stove when her radio crackled to life.

"Zebra One, Whiskey Charley One, sit rep."

"Station calling Zebra One, authorization code," Marlene said. She did not recognize the call sign.

The voice gave the proper response and asked for a situation report again. Marlene recognized the voice now and hit record.

"Whiskey Charley One, Zebra One, situation as briefed."

"Zebra One, monitor and hold, Whiskey Charley One out."

"What the fuck?" Brock said. "This was supposed to be a comms dark mission."

"He had the proper authorization codes," Marlene said. "I am just a lowly rookie corporal and have no need to know."

The next day was more of the same. Normal everyday activity, and at exactly the same time as the day before, Whiskey Charley contacted them again wanting a situation report and once again telling them to hold and monitor. The next day he said the same thing.

"Whiskey Charley One, confirm hold and monitor. If we miss this window, we have to wait another week," Marlene said.

The order was confirmed, and the next afternoon, right on schedule, their target drove away and returned the next afternoon. The next week was the same. Charley One called at the same time each day and told them to hold and monitor. They were out of rations and very low on water by Tuesday night, so Marlene decided to up the timetable. They left after dark and were in position at the ambush site by daybreak.

They dragged a large tree trunk to lay across the road after the curve, making it look like it had fallen down that day and sat back and waited. Once again, they were told to wait by Charley One, and once again Marlene acknowledged the order.

"Uh-oh," Shandra said. "They've got company this trip. A second vehicle with four guards is following."

"Right," Marlene said, thinking quickly. "Shandra, you and Gerry take the lead driver. I should be able to get three of them before they figure out what is going on. Brock, you take the fourth."

Shandra and Gerry were located twenty yards to the left of the road, Brock and Marlene two hundred further away. The two vehicles came around the corner and stopped. All six men got out of the vehicles and walked toward the tree trunk. Marlene hit the first two men with her sniper rifle before anyone knew they were being shot. As the rest of the men turned toward the sound of the shots, they joined their two friends on the ground, leaving just the target standing there.

Shandra and Gerry stood up and advanced, seemingly out of nowhere, on the target, who just froze where he was standing. They roughly kicked him to the ground and secured his hands and feet, while Marlene and Brock rolled the log to the side of the road. Then, tossing the man in the backseat wedged between Brock and Gerry, with Marlene covering him with her pistol from the front seat, Shandra hit the gas and headed for the extraction point.

"Charley Echo Five, Zebra One, how copy?" Marlene said.

"Zebra One, Charley Echo Five, send traffic."

"Charley Echo Five, target is secure and en route to primary extraction point. ETA fifteen mikes."

"Zebra One, copy target is secure, ETA primary extraction point fifteen mikes."

The small transport craft was just landing as they sped into the small clearing, coming to a dust-flying halt. A mile away and coming hard were four vehicles loaded with guards. As Brock and Gerry carried the target to the craft, Marlene sighted her sniper rifle on the driver of the leading vehicle. It was a long shot, and she waited the two seconds it took for the bullet to reach the vehicle. She must have at least scared the driver, as the vehicle lost control and went sideways across the road, rolling twice before it was T-boned by the vehicle following it. Marlene sprinted to the transport, which took off while the landing ramp was being closed.

A large contingent of heavily armed planetary council members were waiting when they landed back on base and took custody of the prisoner. Zebra fireteam came off the transport, unnoticed by the heavy news media presence, and made their way on foot to their hut. They were all tired and looked it. Their uniforms were dusty and sweat-stained, the men all had two-week beards and all of them smelled. Seeing heavily armed troops returning from a mission was nothing new on the base, but the state the Zebras were in was unusual and drew a lot of looks.

A pristine G-Wagon was parked in front of their hut when they arrived, and two sharply uniformed troopers, a sergeant and a private, were waiting for them. The sergeant gave them a frown when they lined up at attention in front of him.

"Which one of you is Isabelle?" the sergeant asked.

"That would be me, sergeant," Marlene said.

"You are to report to Captain Conrad no later than 13:00 for debrief," the sergeant said. "If I see any of you out of proper uniform again, you will be on report."

"Admin asshole," Shandra said as the sergeant and the private drove away. "The only ribbon that jerk had was the five-year good conduct medal."

"Which is one more ribbon than you have," Brock said and they all chuckled. None of them had a year of service yet.

Marlene had to hurry. She only had two hours to have a shower and prepare her uniform, plus walk the mile to the Captain's office. While the three other team members had long and hot showers, hers was rushed and she made it just a few minutes before the meeting time. Her dark green uniform was perfect. The buttons, belt buckle and crests were gleaming, her boots highly polished. The crossed rifles on her right sleeve denoting her status as an expert marksman drew the sergeant's eyes, as did the scar on the left side of her face. Now that all the dust, grime and cammo paint had been removed, the scar was very visible.

Conrad was smiling when she entered and put her at ease before she could even report in properly.

"Another job well done," he said. "One thing my boss and I are wondering is why you did not take out the target on the first Wednesday."

"The situation was not optimal, Sir," Marlene said. *Something's wrong here*, she thought.

"Well, no matter, you cut it a little close though," Conrad said. "During interrogation on the ship, the prisoner told us they had been tipped off that you were there. That's why he had extra guards with him. He was going to bring back a company of troops to smoke you out when he returned. Can you think of any way you could have been spotted?"

"Anything is possible, Sir," Marlene said. "But I don't think so."

"Well, the guy has tentacles everywhere, so anyone anywhere could have told him about the operation," Conrad said, and he tossed her a set of sergeant stripes.

"Do try to keep them longer this time, Isabelle," he said and smiled. "Now get the hell out of my office and get some sleep."

On her way out, she nodded at the sergeant, then made her way over to stores and was issued the correct number and type of sergeant stripes she needed for her uniforms. She was also given a star to put above the crossed rifles for her work on the first mission.

When the rest of the fireteam woke up from their naps, they found Marlene putting the final touches on cleaning her weapons. She was dressed in the green work uniform, and sergeant stripes instead of corporal's stripes were attached to the Velcro strip on her shoulder.

"All is forgiven then," Brock said, and he punched her on the stripes. Gerry followed suit as did Shandra, who also gave her a hug.

"Right, you mutts," Marlene said. "Off to the junior ranks we go, where I think I have enough cash to buy two and only two beers for each of us."

Luckily, the other team members had not had their pay docked like Marlene had and they paid for her meal and a few more beers. At first, they had the place to themselves, but as the regular work day finished, troops began to trickle in. The first were the support troops on the base coming in for a quick beer before going home for dinner. Then came the combat troopers, and the place was soon full of talk and laughter. Nobody took notice of the four troopers sitting by themselves in a back corner by the door. That is, until Brock made a whining impression of Marlene giving the Wind Rider what for on the previous mission and their table erupted in howls of laughter.

Just at that point, the admin sergeant from earlier in the day walked in and gave them a dirty look. As he continued on his way to a table of his cronies, Shandra made a credible impersonation of him giving Marlene hell, embellishing it heavily.

"But Sergeant," Brock said in a high-pitched voice, "We haven't been paid yet. I promise to get my nails and hair done up as soon as I get paid."

That remark got laughs from a few more tables and smirks from most of the rest of them.

"Let's get out of here," Marlene said. "I want to keep these stripes until at least the end of the week this time."

"Hey!" a voice yelled at them as they walked away down the street. Five large men were walking toward them. All were original PIG members and were Master Sergeants. They gave them a once over when they came up to them.

"You those Zebra people?" the biggest one asked. He was at least six foot five and well over two hundred pounds. The other four were not much smaller.

"You got a problem with that, Master Sergeant?" Marlene responded. She wasn't about to take anything from these guys, even if it meant a severe beating.

"Hell no," he said. "All of us were in charge of platoons that saved your asses a couple of weeks ago. You guys did a hell of job. We just wanted to tell you that. The Captain was some pissed about what happened. So was the Colonel. Somebody higher up the food chain called the shots, guys."

"I haven't seen anything like what you guys did since Iraq," another sergeant said. "There were ten of us on that mission, and

I was the only one who got out. Ya, your bad guys had inferior weapons, but hell, there was more than two thousand of them. No way you were going to win. If you had been given the support you asked for, you would have clobbered them all by yourselves. As it was, you had put a big dent in them by the time we got there. I'll serve with you guys anywhere, anytime. All of us will."

Three days later, they were on another fast transport. A full division of Marauders was involved in a major conflict between two large countries on a large planet. They desperately needed a good reconnaissance team, and the Zebras had been selected. This time they would be issued a G-Wagon with all the toys instead of having to pack everything in.

They were to proceed to the front lines located on a valley floor, then, the following night, they were to make their way to the top of a high point and set up their observation post. They were to report any troop movements and concentrations and, above all, to remain concealed.

At the appointed time, they made their way down the valley to where they were to break off and head for the hilltop. The G-Wagon was overloaded. Every spare inch of room, even the roof, was crammed with supplies. An hour after they had left and were about to turn off, Marlene's radio came alive.

"Zebra One, Whiskey Romeo Charley One, sit rep."

Well at least he is using the proper radio call sign this time, Marlene thought. It was the same voice that had been on the radio the other two times. Once again, she hit the record button on her radio.

"Station calling Zebra One, repeat with proper authorization," she said.

"Zebra One, Whiskey Romeo Charley One, 8670. Sit rep."

"Whiskey Romeo Charley One, Zebra One, am two clicks short of cut-off."

"Zebra One, you are to establish your post at the cut-off, hold and observe."

"Roger, Zebra One to hold and observe at the cut-off out."

"Shit," she said. "Did you guys hear that?"

The rest of the crew shook their heads.

"Only heard your side of it, just like the last two times," Gerry said.

Something was wrong. All of them should have received that call, not just her. Marlene played the recording back for them.

"What the hell are we going to see on the valley floor?" Brock asked. "Not to mention we are sure to get spotted the first day."

"Who is Whiskey Romeo Charley One?" Shandra asked.

"On the first op he called himself Charley One," Marlene said. "The last one Whiskey Charley One. He always has the proper authorizations codes, and he always changes our orders. This time he is using a Wind Rider designation. All I know for sure is that he is Charley troop, but not what regiment or company. I think it's the asshole from the transport. Something is not right here."

She thought frantically while they made their way to the cut-off point, and by the time they reached it, she had a plan.

"Right," she said. "Give me the spare headset."

She pulled the memory chip from hers and put it in the spare headset, then made a few adjustments to it and tossed the original out the window.

"Okay," she said. "We stick with our original orders. I think that guy compromised my comms somehow. This should buy us a few days until I figure something else out."

It took them two days to creep up to the mountaintop, driving at slow speed at night. Each night she reported no activity and was told to hold and observe by Charley One. This time the conversations were heard by all of them.

"What the fuck?" Brock said. "The enemy can vector in on those transmissions!"

"Ya, I think that's the point," Marlene said. "They are using us as bait."

They were fully camouflaged by morning and had their spotting scopes and high-powered binoculars set up and observing. There were four enemy patrols out scouring the area where they were supposed to be. Marlene waited until the time they were to report and sent a high-speed encrypted message back to headquarters reporting the activity. A short time later, two pairs of attack aircraft hit the patrols.

The next day, two companies were out in full force, along with anti-air defenses and covering aircraft. Marlene sent another radio burst and the area was saturated by artillery fire. That night, Marlene didn't respond to Charlie One's request, other than to tape it. The next day, the enemy came again, but before she could report it, the artillery rounds came in, many of them right on the position where her headset had been left. That night she got no message from Charley One, and using the more sophisticated gear in the G-Wagon, could pick up no signal from her original headset.

"That son of a bitch vectored that arty right on us," Gerry said. "What the hell is that?"

Marlene had a pretty good idea what was going on but didn't tell the others. Instead, she had them move a quarter of a mile away leaving the G-Wagon where it was. She changed all their headsets to frequency hop and the G-Wagon's receiver to match the pattern. They would make their reports from the new location, and the G-Wagon would relay them back to headquarters.

The first few days were boring. Nothing was going on in their sector now. Then the enemy began to build up, bringing up large numbers of troops and heavily armored vehicles. Marlene reported what they were seeing, but the buildup was too far away for artillery to hit and the airstrikes were beaten back by the enemy's massive anti-air defenses.

The enemy's next move was to probe along the lines, but Marlene was able to vector artillery strikes, and each probe was repulsed. That night, the enemy sent a whole company at their hill, and once again, artillery sent them back. The next day, a full battalion made its way, spread out across the valley floor. They were met by two companies of Marauders, and the fighting was heavy.

"Shit, Marlene!" Gerry said, and he was pointing to the bottom of their hill.

Three armored vehicles and two companies of infantry were advancing on their position.

Marlene didn't use the high-speed data transmission this time.

"Marauder Base Five, Zebra One, two infantry companies and three armored vehicles attacking my position."

"All assets currently committed Zebra One. Do what you can. Help is on the way."

"Ya right," Marlene said to her mates. "How the hell can help be on the way if all assets are committed? Okay, never mind observing now. They are headed right for the G-Wagon. We'll let them get close, then I'll start picking them off. Brock, concentrate your fire on those armored vehicles. That ceramic armor is no match for you."

Marlene started shooting officers as soon as they were in range and Brock opened up with his machine gun, blowing each armored vehicle to bits in turn.

"Sarge," Shandra yelled. "Three more companies and ten vehicles!"

Shandra and Gerry opened up on the first two companies, and Marlene shifted her fire to the new attackers, who were in range of her sniper rifle.

"Marauder Base, if that help doesn't get here pretty soon, there will be nothing left to help. Three more companies and ten vehicles have joined the party."

"Zebra One, Marauder Two, hold on, kid, we are on our way."

"You better hurry then, Marauder Two; two more companies look to be joining the party. They want this hill bad."

She was down to her last twenty rounds for the sniper rifle and used them all in two minutes. She then shifted to her assault rifle. The enemy had not spotted them yet and was still advancing on the G-Wagon. The assault was too far away for her grenade launcher, but not for the five rocket propelled grenades they had. She blew apart five of the ten new armored vehicles that were coming with the two new companies, then joined her teammates hitting the enemy assaulting the G-Wagon.

Finally, artillery rounds started impacting on the enemy advance, but, try as they would, the Zebras could not stop the enemy from overrunning the position. Shandra still had an RPG round left and she used it to blow up the G-Wagon and the sensitive radio equipment it had, taking more than a few enemy troops with it.

Then five LAVs came screaming up the hill, their 40mm cannon and machine guns creating havoc through the enemy lines. They came screeching to a halt, the ramps opened and fifty Marauders started firing at anything that moved. The enemy broke off and ran back down, followed by the massed fire of the Marauders, the LAVs and the Zebras. Not many got away.

Looking back down the valley, the Marauders had broken up the main enemy attack and were advancing into enemy territory. The enemy was suffering badly and in full retreat. Dead bodies and smoking machinery littered the valley floor.

Two more LAVs, one of them a command vehicle, made their way up the hill and stopped by the destroyed G-Wagon. The Zebras got out of their defensive positions and walked over. Other than the

"If the Sergeant may be permitted?" she held out the thumb drive that held all the communications she had received.

Duncan motioned to CT who took the thumb drive and inserted into his tablet. The whole string of communications was heard.

"My lord Duncan," Marlene said. "I have every reason to believe this Charley One was instrumental in denying us aide in the first action and leaking our intentions on the second. I also believe he planted a tracking device on my personal communication device, and his constant demands for reports allowed the enemy to locate that transmitter. Then he personally vectored artillery fire on that location. When the main enemy attack commenced, he purposely overstated the situation to the Marauders and denied my team much needed assistance. Had we not planned for that occurrence, we would have indeed been overwhelmed. Sir."

"Kill me, don't kill me, make up your mind, Sir," she said that last with as much sarcasm and scorn as she could get away with.

"CT?" Duncan said.

"Already on it, Boss," CT said.

"Very well," Duncan said. "Sergeant Isabelle, thank you for reporting this to us and keep up the good work. Dismissed."

Marlene was shown out the front door where all her teammates were waiting just outside. As she was adjusting her beret on her head, the Wind Rider captain was rushing up. He had to stop to return their salutes.

"Nice knowing you, asshole," Marlene said. "Next time I see you, I'll kill you. If my lord Duncan doesn't kill you first."

"I take it you keep your stripes?" Shandra asked as they walked away.

"For now," Marlene said. "Come on, I just got paid and I'm buying."

"Marlene, can I have a minute?" a voice in the shadows asked.

The fire team was feeling no pain at that point, but became instantly alert seeing five figures in the dark alleyway.

"Go ahead guys," Marlene said. "These guys used to be my buddies. I'll be with you in a bit, so leave some beer for me, eh?"

"Well, well," Marlene said as the five women came out of the shadows. "The whole gang is here. The mighty Wind Riders coming to gloat?"

Barb, Megan, Diane, Amanda and Anne came out of the shadows.

"Come on, hon," Barb said. "You know better than that. What else could Duncan do? You left him no choice."

"Typical Barb," Marlene said. "Always sticking up for her long-lost brother. I don't want to hear about how great the almighty Duncan is from any of you. For anybody else he would have checked his facts first. He just outright condemned me. You know what, he did me a favor. I like it here. I don't have to prove anything, and I have some real friends for once. So, get stuffed, Sirs!"

She saluted them and joined her comrades in their hut.

"Well I guess she told us what's what," Barb said. "Too bad, I really liked her."

The next day, Katerina tracked her down at the internet café.

"Sit your ass back down!" Katerina said as Marlene stood to leave. "Be an adult for once, instead of a spoiled aristocrat!"

"My aunt did wrong by you, not Duncan, Marlene," she continued. "Your first loyalty should have been to Duncan and not only because he was your overlord. At the very least, you should have explained yourself to him at your board of enquiry, instead of acting like what you are – an over-privileged former aristocrat. You didn't just let him down, Marlene, you let us all down. Being pigheaded about it in front of the whole board, you left him no choice, Marlene, none at all. Did you really expect my aunt, your cousin, to stand up that these people, especially the nobility, have a different mindset. This individual was from a high noble house. He was well-versed in how to manipulate the system to his advantage. At best, he should have only been a corporal. But again, we were short of officers."

"Okay," Duncan said. "Let's start looking at all our new officers and see if any more of them have slipped through the cracks. We'll figure out what to do with them afterward. As far as new recruits, at this time we can start to be picky. Priority should be given to combat veterans who have some recon experience. We should also be on the lookout for good rookies. We were all rookies at some point. Give a shot to the top performers of basic and advanced infantry training. We can use Isabelle's bunch as an example. She was able to take raw rookies and mold them into one of the best recon outfits in the army. Definitely on par with most of our people.

"Alright, Jane and I have a conference call with the other commanders. Let's nip this in the bud, people."

The boardroom cleared and Jane activated the large video screen, which broke up into three separate screens, one for each of the generals.

"Gentlemen," Duncan said. "Thank you for taking time out of your very busy days for this call. I know I have several important things I need to do myself today. The most pressing is my afternoon round of golf."

That got the requisite laughs. All of them knew each other and classed each other as friends.

"Right," Duncan continued. "We have just identified a problem in our ranks and are taking steps to rectify the situation. All of us have come up from the lower ranks and have seen this type of thing our whole careers. I just never thought to see it in my own organization. In our rush to expand and do to our mandatory service commitments, some – how should I say this – undesirable or misguided individuals are taking advantage of the system for their own gain. We called them Ticket Punchers where I come from: people who do as little as possible and use every trick possible to further their own advancement. On paper, they will have done nothing wrong. It will usually be the fault of an underling if something does show up. We need to start policing this up, guys. Identify the weak links and get rid of them if they don't shape up."

"It not just the officers, Duncan," Hans, the PIGs' general, said. "One of my captains caught a service corps sergeant playing games. The man has been demoted and reassigned. We have already started to investigate all sectors of our organization."

"Due to our past," Jacques, the Black Shirt commander, said, "we have an ongoing system of evaluations. So far, we have only had to expel three members."

"I've been at this a lot longer than the rest of you," Bishop, the Marauders commander, said. "We identify weak links right away. Then they are given a choice to smarten up or they are tossed out. Plus, while I don't condone this behavior, the ones that sneak through the cracks generally end up being casualties depending on how badly they have pissed their troop mates off."

"Yes, I have heard of that type of thing," Duncan said. "*I swear to you I will hunt that asshole Captain down and kill him*, I think is how Sergeant Isabelle phrased it."

"Sergeant already?" Jacques said. "She is doing well and toeing the line I take it."

"Yes, she and her team are progressing nicely," Hans said.

"Ah, that's bullshit and you know it," Bishop said. "She and her three buddies wiped out three complete companies of highly trained troops, plus ten armored vehicles. Not to mention I don't know exactly how many troops killed and wounded by her very accurate fire direction. Progressing nicely, my ass. Let's call a spade a spade. She is exceptionally good at her job."

Nobody said anything for a few moments.

"Ya," Bishop said. "I know. She was damned good at her job before, too."

"I would have her in a second," Jacques said. "But I know that would be a bad idea, for her and the Black Shirts."

"Early days yet," Duncan said. "Keep an eye on her, Hans. No undo attention or special treatment. Let her do her best and don't get in her way. But step on her hard if she gets out of line."

"Already have," Hans said. "She got busted back to corporal and lost a bonus already. I think she set the record for that. She was a sergeant for all of about ten minutes. She forgot she wasn't an officer anymore and called out that captain of yours in the ship mess. Bad for discipline for a sergeant to call out a captain, especially in front of a mixed mess."

"Ya, she always had a problem with her mouth," Jane said before Duncan could say anything. "She mouths off when she should shut up and keeps quiet when she should mouth off."

"Well, I have a very good man in charge of her," Hans said. "You remember Conrad, Duncan? Ex SAS. I put him in as her DI, then promoted him to captain so he is her company commander."

"I bet that went over like a lead balloon," Duncan said. "The man is a career noncommissioned officer like myself."

"Ya, he bitched like crazy about it," Hans said. "But then I told him I would keep his pay grade the same and he settled down. He hasn't figured out her story yet, but he knows something is not right. He really likes her, Duncan. Hell, so do I. She's one hell of a trooper, and she pushes those kids hard. Her training class was the best class I have had for a lot of years. She pushes herself, which makes her teammates push themselves, and everyone else scrambles to keep up. We need more like her, Duncan."

"Yes, well..." Duncan said.

"I know, I know," Hans said. "But I really think serving in the ranks is teaching her a lot of things. She and her teammates have bonded well. It's something like you and your team, Duncan. We need somebody like her to set an example of what we want."

"Well," Duncan said, "for obvious reasons it can't be her. All of you, on your next training cycles, start identifying high flyers like Marlene. Even with our little setback, the Wind Riders are still everyone's ideal to shoot for. You guys need to be doing that among yourselves. Push the high flyers hard right at the start. Just like Marlene and the PIGs. The high flyers will drag the others along in their wake.

"We are trying to break the mold here, people. Promotion and accolades due to deeds, not birth status. What we achieve here in the military will carry on in civvie street. We are building a new society here, people, not based on aristocracy, but on meritocracy.

"All right, Jane has promised to buy breakfast and all this talking and thinking has made me hungry. Have a good day, gentlemen."

"Are you ever going to let up on her?" Jane asked. They were seated in the back corner of a small breakfast café in town dressed in civilian clothing.

"What?" Duncan asked. "I already have. I gave her a second chance and she seems to be making the best of it. I am not interfering in any way."

"That's not what I mean, Dunc," she said. "Are you ever going to forgive her?"

"I forgave her a long time ago," he said. "She has her life to live, and I have mine." He reached in his pocket and dropped more than enough money on the table to pay for both meals and quietly walked out of the café. Jane knew better than to go after him.

Duncan wandered the streets for a while, hands in his pockets. He was dressed in blue jeans, sneakers and an open-necked polo shirt with a ball cap jammed on his head. He looked like any other guy his age, walking around on his day off, looking for something to do. A shopping mall had been built, and it was a favorite meeting spot for a lot of the single people on the planet. He went in.

Like most shopping malls everywhere, the majority of the stores catered to women, but there was a huge sporting goods store that Duncan and every other male liked to browse through. Not that he had any time anymore to do anything, but it was nice to dream and look at the boats, the fishing and camping gear, and dream. As usual, the food court was filled with young mothers and their small children. He got a coffee and sat at an empty table and watched them until the memories got too strong, especially when he saw a young couple and their children and another young couple, very much in love, walking hand in hand. He stood up and walked away. The memories of what he had lost, twice, were too strong today.

More for a distraction than anything, he walked into a video game arcade and found an off-road racing game he liked. It was a two-position game, but as there was no one in the other station, he contented himself with playing against the AI cars. He was really just competing against himself, concentrating on bettering his times each time he did the course. Suddenly he had some competition. One of the AIs was doing well and pushing him. He had to work hard to keep ahead. Even so, it beat him twice. That just made him try harder. His feet, hands and eyes were all coordinated, and he lost himself in the game, pushing ever harder to stay ahead of the AI, and he won twice. On the fifth one, somebody, Duncan or the AI, made a mistake, and they both wiped out and could not finish. It was a draw. The five races were finished and Duncan sat back trying to decide if he should have another go. That's when he noticed there was another person in the next position. He had been playing with a real person.

Somebody pounded him on the back.

"Holy shit, man," a male voice said. "Nobody has beaten her ever, man! If you hadn't taken each other out, I think you might just have beaten her again."

"In your dreams, Brock," Marlene said, and Duncan's heart skipped a beat.

"Tell you what, sport," Marlene said. "I'll let you by me a beverage for me letting you beat me."

She turned toward him and stuck out her hand.

"Marlene, fake driver extraordinaire," she said.

Duncan took her hand and looked up into her sparkling green eyes and saw the shock hit her.

"Duncan, wannabe off-road racer," he said. "Sure, I'll buy, if you still want to, that is."

"Why wouldn't she?" Shandra asked. "Nobody ever even comes close to beating her. Shandra, wild driver's wingman."

Brock and Gerry introduced themselves.

"So, where can we go to get a decent beer around here?" Duncan asked. "I don't get into town much."

"We have just the spot," Shandra said, and they led the way out of the mall and down the street a few blocks to a nice neighborhood bar. They sat down, making sure Duncan sat next to Marlene, then the server came over. It must have been their regular spot, as she already had their orders on the tray. Duncan ordered a beer.

He stayed quiet as the others talked and made jabs at each other.

"So, you're just in town for a bit then?" Brock said.

"Yes, my job keeps me pretty busy," Duncan said. "I don't get much time off."

"Tell me about it," Gerry said. "We are in the army. Just finishing our first year. We are always busy."

"What unit are you in?" Duncan asked.

"We have the privilege to be members of the PIGs," Brock said. "Not that we have served with them yet."

"Still in training then?" Duncan said.

"Hell no," Shandra said. "We're a recon team and have been serving with everybody but the PIGs."

"Wow, you guys must be good then," Duncan said. "I thought recon was Wind Rider territory."

"Hey, what do we know?" Brock said. "They tell us to grab our gear and go, so we go. Right Sarge?"

"That's what soldiers do," Marlene said. "They say jump, we jump. We don't ask how high, we just jump as high as we can."

"So, you in the army too?" Shandra asked.

"Sort of," Duncan said. "I've already done my five-year term. I do a lot of what you might call consulting now. Trying to iron out problems and putting round pegs into round holes instead of square ones. It's a bit of a challenge at times. Some of those commanders are pretty stubborn."

"Ya, we just ran into a Wind Rider who should have been doing anything but what he was doing," Brock said.

"It's not our job to criticize officers, Brock," Marlene said. "Especially to people we have just met."

"That's alright, Marlene," Duncan said. "Maybe if more subordinates spoke up at the right time, misunderstandings could be avoided."

"Got that right," Shandra said. "Marlene beaked off at the wrong time for the right reasons and got shit for it."

"Well seeing that she is still a sergeant, I guess the bosses have forgiven her then," Duncan said. "I have heard that writing a complaint out to your commander is an effective way of gaining support for your cause. Enough to get somebody looking at the problem, anyway."

"Now why didn't I think of that?" Marlene said with more than a little hint of sarcasm.

"Enough shop talk," Shandra said. "What else do you do besides work?"

"I haven't really had much time to myself ever since the boss decided to come here," Duncan said. "I'm actually a pretty boring guy. I grew up on a farm and joined the army early. I really enjoy being out in the wild. I used to go horseback riding and camping with a girl back on Oaken."

"So you have a girl then?" Shandra asked.

"Used to," Duncan said. "Some things happened, things said at the wrong time and not said at others, so we split apart."

"Ya, that happens sometimes," Brock said. "Hell, I screwed up big time with Marlene back in basic. She clued me in right quick. We are the best of buddies now, right boss." He leaned over and gave her a kiss on the cheek.

"Only if you keep your hands to yourself, you big goof," Marlene said. "I keep telling you, you aren't my type."

"So what's your story, Marlene?" Duncan asked. "What do you on your time off?"

"Hang around with these guys mostly," she said. "Until they decide to go clubbing that is. I'm not much into that meat market stuff. Get a little older, get a little wiser, I guess. I enjoy a quiet drink like this, or I go and have a quiet coffee someplace. I don't have enough money to buy my own wheels yet, but soon I would like to explore this new home of ours. I don't plan on going further than my five-year commitment. I'd like to find a nice guy and have a nice quiet family life."

"Well, thanks for the beer and the conversation," Duncan said. "Maybe I can link up with you and beat you some more at that video game, Marlene."

"Hey, don't run off so fast," Shandra said. "The three of us are heading to the club in a couple of minutes and spoil sport Marlene won't be coming with us. Why don't the two of you go out for dinner or something?"

"Shandra!" Marlene said.

"What? Two lost and bored puppies. Go on, it'll be good for the both of you."

Duncan looked over at Marlene and shrugged his shoulders.

"I'm in if you are," he said.

"Oh, why not," Marlene said. "It's only dinner, not like we are getting married or anything."

"Well, I have to go get all prettied up for all the hunks at the club," Shandra said. "Coming?"

"Oh, he is really cute," Shandra said once she and Marlene were in the ladies' room. "He kept looking at you out of the corner of his eye when you weren't paying attention. Hell, I wouldn't say no if he asked me back to his room tonight. Only for the night though. He's too old for me."

"But just right for me?" Marlene said. "Thanks a lot, buddy."

"Ah hell, who said you have to marry the guy?" Shandra said. "Get laid tonight, hon. It'll take the edge off."

"Jesus," Marlene said. "Is that all you ever think about?"

"Until we go back on duty, or I meet Mr. Right, you bet," she said. "Now go out with this guy. I am really worried about you. Get back on the market, girl. You've got a lot to offer."

"OK kiddies," Marlene said when they got back to the table. "Off you go to the kiddie show. We adults will go for a nice quiet dinner, and then maybe I'll beat his ass some more on the video game. Come on, bub, it's time to go."

"You think that's the right thing to do?" Brock asked. "Maybe we should tag along?"

"Oh, let her be," Shandra said. "Besides, if that chair-warming goof tries anything, she will chew him up and spit him out."

"You don't have to do this, Marlene," Duncan said. "They don't know we know each other. They will never know if we go our separate ways."

"But I would, Duncan," she said. "I like those kids, a lot. I don't want to lie to them. Honestly, until next payday, I don't have any spare cash to go have a really good meal. I lost my whole month's pay for that little outburst on the ship, plus my bonus, plus a big fine. This will be the first pay day where I have it all to myself."

"Well, that will never do," Duncan said. "Megan tells me there is an excellent pizza joint downtown. Never been myself, but I hear they have the best pizza in town and the best steak."

"I've eaten enough pizza with those kids to last me for a few months," Marlene said. "But I think I might kill someone for a good steak."

They spent the meal talking generalities, and while Duncan was attentive and cracking jokes, he was not the Duncan she remembered. He was working hard to make her feel comfortable and to smile, but both of them were working at it and they both knew it.

"Would you mind if I walked you home?" Duncan asked when they walked outside. It was a nice night, and there was no wind. "I know you are more than capable of taking care of yourself, Marlene. I would just like some company tonight. I don't get much time to be a normal person anymore."

"Sure, why not," she said. "It's a nice night for a walk."

They walked a few blocks in silence, and then Marlene looked over at him. He was walking with his hands deep in his pockets and looking at his feet, the ball cap pulled low over his eyes. This was not the self-assured and confidant Duncan she knew. They came to an area of empty lots, and she stopped. After a few steps he realized she was not with him anymore, and he stopped and turned around. She just looked at him and he at her, neither saying anything. Finally, Duncan swallowed a few times and began to talk.

"I didn't send that guy after you, Marlene," he said. "I would never do something like that to you. I did all I was going to do. A lot of people wanted me to do more, but I even felt bad doing what I did. I hope someday that you will understand. Hans and a few of the original PIGs know who you are, but as far as I know, nobody else does. Your captain doesn't. Conrad is a good man. I worked with him a lot in the old days. He says nothing but good things about you and your kids, Marlene. If you ever need anything, I mean anything, you let me know, okay?"

Now she was looking at her feet. She was trying to find the right words.

"Well, I could use a new sniper rifle," she said. "Mine is a little worn out. One of those nice fifty cal jobs you guys have would be nice. They make ever-so-nice big bangs."

Duncan chuckled. "You sure you can handle it? Sucker kicks like a mule."

"Can't be any worse than that squad weapon Brock uses," she said. "That thing is a bear."

"It's almost as heavy, too," he said. "Ya, I can make that happen. Anything else?"

"I'm sorry, Duncan," she said. She was looking right in his eyes now. "I am sorry not for what I did, but for not letting you know what I was doing. Tanya told me she had everything under control and that you didn't need to know. By the time I figured out what was going on, it was too late to do anything about it. I do understand why you did what you did. You didn't have a choice, and I didn't give you one. It wasn't my pride that kept me silent, Duncan. It was my shame."

She saw his eyes get moist, and she forced herself to say what she had to say.

"The shame of letting my commander down. The shame of betraying the man I loved. My teammates see me crying and vow to kill the one who makes me cry. And I wish they would. Take this pain away from me, please, someone take this pain away. How can anyone stand to be around me?"

Duncan made to come to her and comfort her.

"No! Don't you dare! Stay away from me! Don't you see? I am poison for you. First, I kill your unborn child and your wife, then

I make you love me and I betray you. I can and never will forgive myself for this. I am crying not for what you did to me but what I did to you. All I have ever given you is pain and sorrow."

Then she ran from him.

She was still sitting on the step crying when they came home.

"God dammit," Brock said. "that's enough of this shit. Who is the asshole? If you don't tell me now, I swear I will leave no stone unturned until I find the fucking guy that hurt you like this."

"No need to go looking, Brock," Duncan said walking out of the shadows. "I'm right here."

He took his ball cap off, stuck it in his back pocket, and put his arms out to his sides.

"Come on then," he said walking toward them. "There are three of you and only one of me. Come ON!"

Brock came at him at a rush and he made no attempt to protect himself. Duncan had taken several hard hits when Marlene swung Brock out of the way. She pointed her finger at Duncan.

"Don't you dare!" she yelled at him. "Don't you dare take this on yourself! Don't you dare add to my shame and guilt!"

She turned and looked at her friends.

"You leave him alone! He didn't do anything but love me and give me his all. I'm the one who broke his heart. Me! You want someone to punch? To kill? Punch me. Kill me. I deserve it, not him. All he is guilty of is loving the wrong person."

She saw Duncan was going to come to her and she ran.

"Holy fuck," Shandra said and took off after Marlene.

"Ah, shit!" Brock said. "Sorry man. You okay?"

"I've been hit harder," Duncan said. "By a 7.62 in the chest. No hard feelings?" He stuck out his hand. Brock took it and slapped Duncan on the back.

"Got some beer in the fridge if you're interested," Gerry said. "Sorry man, we really like Marlene. She's tough as nails most times and when she gets like that...well, we kind of get over-protective. You know?"

"Ya, I do, if you hadn't noticed," Duncan said, shaking Gerry's hand as well. "Tough lady to love. But I'll keep working on her. 'Till she shoots me or something."

"So you weren't always a chair-warmer then?" Brock said tossing a beer to Duncan.

"Hell no," Duncan said. "Got the callouses on my feet and shoulders to prove it, too. I'd love to be back on a fireteam, man. Nothing better than to be on some hilltop in the back and beyond away from all the chicken shit BS at camp. But us peons got no say where the big shots put us, eh?"

"You were a recon guy as well?" Gerry asked.

"Something like that," Duncan said. "Not exactly what you guys do, but close."

Shandra caught up to Marlene a couple of blocks away. She was walking in a circle and swearing to herself.

"Why can't he just let me be?" she asked. "I was just starting to think I could live with myself, and there he is, right in my face again. Shit!"

"It can't be that bad, Marlene," Shandra said. "He stood up for you back there."

"That's the god-dammed point. He always sticks up for me! No matter what I do to him, he always sticks up for me! God dammit! Shit! Why can't he just hate me like a normal person would?"

"Did you know that was him in that video console?"

"Hell no!" Marlene said. "I would have walked the other way before he saw me."

"And I suppose he has never hurt you, or done anything to hurt you?"

"Nothing more than being the regular pain in the ass guys get to be," Marlene said.

"Well, you couldn't have hurt him that bad, or he wouldn't still be lurking around."

"You don't get it," Marlene said. "He has the biggest heart of any man I have ever met. Not just with me, with everyone. But with me, it was more, and I let him down, more than once. I can't seem to help myself. Before you say anything, it has nothing to do with sex or other guys. We are both old enough and soldiers. We understand sometimes shit happens. You wait. I bet when we get back home, he will have Brock and Gerry willing to do anything for him.

"God help me, but I love that man. I can't stand it anymore."

"Well," Shandra said. "It seems to me that God has already helped you. He put you next to him today. We all make mistakes, hon. We are all human. It's clear to me he still loves you and for sure you love him. Christ, I would do anything to get a guy like him. Go to him. He wants you to."

"I know," Marlene said. "We both want it. But you really do not understand. No matter what we both want, it can never be. I made sure of that the last time. Me and my stupid pride. Fuck!"

Then she sank to her knees and started crying again.

"Well guys, I had better be going," Duncan said. "I am on duty in the morning. I'll be planet-side for a while. Maybe I'll catch you for beer sometime?"

He walked away, head down and hands in his pockets, and a few blocks later he let the tears flow freely. Man, how he loved her. He should have just slapped her on the wrist and given her a big fine, protocol be damned! Both their stupid prides had gotten in the way. Now he had to figure a way out of this mess.

Megan saw him coming back to base and caught up with him.

"My, my, don't we look like a forlorn puppy today," she said.

"Ya, I guess," Duncan said. She grabbed his arm and made him stop.

"Come on, Uncle Duncan, this is me. remember? Your goddaughter. I know your shit stinks and that you are a human being, not a god. What the hell is going on?"

"I met her today," he said. "We went for dinner." Now he really did break down.

"God, I miss her," he blurted out.

"So, what happened?" Megan asked.

"We talked it out," Duncan said. "She knows I still love her, and I know she loves me. But God help us, our stupid pride and sense of loyalty to things bigger than us are getting in the way."

"So, fix it then," Megan said. "You are the lord and master. You can do anything you like."

"Hell no!" he said. "How would you like it if I made you a general just because you are my goddaughter?"

"Well, for one thing, you would never do that," Megan said. "I would take the job because you ordered me to – well I can use the extra money, too – but I wouldn't be happy about it. I would know I hadn't earn it."

"All along, Marlene has felt I have given her special treatment," he said. "She was right, but not for the reasons she thinks. She had a lot of potential and she proved it. She's proving it again. Those kids of hers will do anything for her. Conrad even likes her."

"SAS Conrad? Shit, it takes a lot to impress him."

"Shit," Duncan said. "I've got to figure a way out of this mess."

"Well, my dear lost puppy," Megan said. "My lord and master Duncan really has other things to worry about. I am sure someone will find a way out for you."

She didn't tell him she already had and that the plan was in action already.

Chapter Five

Zebra team was standing at parade rest in front of Conrad's desk. They were all in their dark green regular uniforms, with all their ranks and awards showing.

"So," he said, "ready to go back to work then. Normally after one hundred and ninety days of active service in the field, you are given a couple of weeks off, which you have just had. It is also normal to be given at least a week to recuperate between operations. That, you were not granted. We will tack that onto your regular annual leave. You are also usually awarded a ribbon for serving in a theater under arms for one hundred and ninety days. Unfortunately, you were not in any one theater that long. However, at the request of the Marauder's commander, well, he actually insisted on it, you will be awarded a ribbon for that theater. Sergeant Isabelle, you have also been mentioned in dispatches and will be awarded accordingly."

He handed each of them a small box and Marlene two of them.

"So, your time in service and the added leave days are cause for concern at this point. We can't put you in the field for another deployment because it would run into your leave time. Instead, Corporals Brock and Gerry will report for advanced artillery and air spotting training. Your skills are somewhat lacking. Sergeant Isabelle, the brass has decided that you require expert sharpshooter status. As such, you will be issued a new long-range rifle and sent to sniper school. Corporal Shandra will join you as your spotter and backup sharpshooter. By the time your training is complete, it will be time for your annual requalifications, and after that you will go on your annual leaves. Questions?"

"Yes, sir," Marlene said. "Will we be assigned new barracks or will we keep our own?"

"For reasons known only to themselves, the brass wants you knuckleheads to stay together, so yes, the Zebra house is still yours. For now. I might change my mind if you piss me off. So now, get the hell out of my office, grab your orders on the way out, and you have the rest of the day."

Once outside, they opened the boxes. Inside were two medals and a ribbon. Marlene pinned Sandra's on in the right place on her tunic and showed Shandra where to pin the Mentioned in Dispatch ribbon on hers.

"The real medals are only to be worn on formal military parade," she said. "The miniatures are for formal gatherings. The rest of the time, we just wear the ribbons. They are called "I was there ribbons." The ones that really matter are the ones on our sleeves and our cap badges." She pointed to her crossed rifles.

"Lots of people get the cap badges and this other stuff." She continued. "But these rifles, that is a whole different story. I want the crown that goes on top of them real bad. So you better not fuck it up for me, Shandra. I've got my eye on a nice SUV and need the money."

She had more or less gotten back to normal the last few days. Getting back to work would help a lot.

"God damn, Isabelle," the instructor said. "I know damn well you hit that target. I've never seen anybody hit the same spot five times in a row at that distance. Okay, you've passed expert. But let's see if that was just a fluke. There is a tree, sixteen hundred meters down range. There is a man-sized target on it. You hit that target once in the kill zone, and I will be impressed. Five shots only."

They had never shot that far before. Nobody in the class had. The rest of the class focused their spotting scopes on the tree.

"Crosswind about halfway there," Shandra said. "Looks to be about two miles an hour. Target itself is calm. Range is 1606."

Marlene dialed the range, wind speed and direction into her scope and settled her breathing and heartrate. She gently stroked the trigger, and the big gun went off, raising the barrel a couple of inches. She automatically jacked another round in the chamber and started sighting again.

"One inch high and to the left," Shandra said. It took two seconds for the bullet to hit the target.

Marlene compensated and fired again.

"Target zeroed," Shandra said.

Marlene fired her last three shots at three seconds apart.

"Son of a bitch!" the instructor said shaking his head. "Five goddamn bulls, all in the kill zone. Never even seen a Wind Rider do that."

Marlene removed her clip, opened the bolt, made sure the weapon was empty, and then closed it again. Then she stood, folded the bipod back up to the stock and brushed the grass and dirt from the front of her uniform.

"That's because I am a Zebra, not a Wind Rider, Master Sergeant," she said. Then she started picking up her brass casings and put all but three in her pocket. The other three she tossed in a barrel there for the purpose.

"You keeping those things for souvenirs?" the Master Sergeant asked as he gave her her expert sharpshooter badge and framed certificate.

"Nope," was all she said. "Come on rookie, I have a beer with my name on it waiting for me. See ya, Wind Riders."

Shandra blew kisses at the rest of the training class, all Wind Riders, as she walked away. She had a sharpshooter badge too, just not a master sharpshooter like Marlene's.

"God damn," the instructor said. "The only one I have ever seen shoot that good was Ghost himself. God damn."

"You hear that?" Shandra said as they were packing their gear into the back of the cheap four-year-old SUV that Marlene had purchased the week before. "He just said you were as good as Ghost himself."

"Oh, I doubt that," Marlene said. "The man is a legend. If he even exists."

"I heard during that mess on Oaken he regularly hit moving targets at that range," Shandra said. "Then he took out a bunch of those Arial yahoos after he had run two miles and been hit in the chest with a 9mm Glock."

"Sounds like tall stories to me," Marlene said. She didn't know about the moving targets, but she had seen him do the other things.

"My dad says he saw the second one, Marlene, and my brother was with the Oaken troops that were training with him. He said the guy is amazing. All of them were."

"You are kind of confusing me," Marlene said. "Your brother was with Tanya and your dad was in New Paris?" This could be trouble, she thought.

"My dad was a fitter on a transport ship," Shandra said. "His ship just happened to be there when the shit hit the fan."

"Well, you know how stories tend to grow over time," Marlene said.

"Are you kidding me?" she replied. "I saw you doing the same stuff with the 7.62 on that last hill, and you took out the driver of that SUV when he was on the move."

"More luck on that last one. I was just hoping to scare him."

By that time, they were back at their hut. They unloaded their rifles and gear, had a shower, and dressed in their regular uniforms. Then they unstitched the marksman badges from their tunic sleeves and stitched on the sharpshooter ones.

"Off we go then," Marlene said. "Hey, I just remembered, a sharpshooter gets promoted to Master Corporal. That means you owe me a beer."

"Ya, well, an expert sharpshooter gets promoted to Master Sergeant, so you owe me a beer."

"Okay, I guess we're even then," Marlene said.

"Oh no we aren't," Shandra said. "You qualified expert. You owe me a beer for that."

"Okay, you got me on that one," Marlene said.

This time they thought they would live it up and go to the All Ranks Mess, which is why they were dressed in their regular uniforms and not their normal work uniforms. Brock and Gerry were waiting for them.

"A round for my friends and me," she said to the waitress when she came over. "Put it on my tab."

"Wow, look at the fancy arm candy," Brock said. "Not one, but two sharpshooters in my team. I am impressed, guys."

"The instructor said he's never seen anyone as good as her but Ghost himself," Shandra said.

"Ya, I bet he says that to all the top grads," Marlene replied.

"Are you kidding me? She put five in the kill zone at sixteen hundred meters with a crosswind. Shit, I can't even see that far."

"There you go, Sergeant," the waitress said. "And the boys over in the corner there said all the booze is on them tonight."

Marlene looked over to the corner and saw Conrad and five of his buddies. She raised her glass in his direction, then pointed at the badge on her sleeve. The whole table raised their glasses to her. Then she raised Shandra's arm and pointed to her badge, and the glasses were raised again.

"So, how did you boys do?" Marlene asked.

"I passed," Brock said, "but Gerry was ahead of me by one."

"Outstanding," Marlene said. "So, what was your ranking?"

"I was only second," Brock said deadpanned. "Sorry, Sarge."

"What?" Marlene exclaimed. "I've got the number one and number two grads on my team?"

She reached over and gave them both an enthusiastic hug.

"Hot damn," Gerry said. "Number one and number two in both classes."

"No, you've got that wrong," Shandra said. "Technically, I was in the spotter and assistant gunner class, so I am number one as well."

"Ah shit," Brock said. "that means the next round is on me."

"Nope," Marlene said. "You're off the hook. The boys in the corner are buyin'."

The waitress came with another round.

"They said to keep them coming, Sergeant," she said.

Marlene raised her glass.

"Who are we?"

"Zebras!"

"What do we do?"

"Kick wolfhound asses!"

"Hoorah!"

It was Monday, and all they had to do was their qualification on Friday and they had a full month off. Once again, they were in front of Captain Conrad at parade rest.

"Well done, all of you," he said. "We have never had PIGs qualify that high, ever. Not only that, but beating Wind Riders. Outstanding! As to the quals, as recon, you have to qualify with every weapon the team has, except the fifty cal, that is. Isabelle is the only one who has to do that. You need to finish the course in under eight hours to stay in the army. Under six to keep combat status and five to keep the recon status. It's a five-mile course. You will be issued the same loads as you had for that snatch operation. One clip from each weapon, minimum of five in the kill zone. Except the grenade launcher, one shot only, close to the target is good enough. Both of your promotions have been confirmed. Dismissed."

"Five miles on a road in daylight, piece of cake," Brock said.

"Don't get cocky," Marlene said. "There will be a thousand of us on that course. Shit happens."

"Not if we are out front, Boss," Gerry said. "We are Zebras, and Zebras are born to run."

In addition to their battalion, there were a hundred Wind Riders qualifying. The Zebras were given a start time just after the last of the Wind Riders. They all would be running in their section size. For the Zebras, that meant four of them. The rest were in groups of ten.

"All set, then?" Conrad asked. "Come with me. Some people want to meet you guys. Leave your shit here. My aide will watch over it for you."

He walked them over to a group of about forty PIGs. Somebody called them to attention, and they lined up in two rows. The lowest grade of officer in the group was Conrad. The rest ranged from a general to majors. None of the non-commissioned officers were lower than a Master Sergeant.

The Zebras came to a foot-stomping halt in perfect line and saluted. The general returned it.

"We, all of us, just wanted to say, we will serve anywhere anytime with you Master Sergeant Isabelle, if you will have us," the general said.

"PIGs, attention!" he ordered. "PIGs, present arms!"

All forty of them saluted. Marlene had tears in her eyes as she returned the salute.

"I meant it, Marlene," the general said. "Anytime, anywhere, you ask and I'll come running. Now go show those god-damned Wind Riders what Zebras are made of!"

"Holy shit, Boss!" Brock said. "Those were all original PIGs. Holy shit!"

"Don't let it go to your head, Brock," Marlene said. "We owe those Wind Rider assholes. I want to beat their asses. Come on, we've only got twenty minutes to share out the loads."

"Hey, Amanda," Megan said, poking Amanda in the ribs with her elbow. "Look what they're doing. They're splitting up the loads."

"She always was sharp," Amanda said. "How much you want to bet they just toss the rifles to each other?"

"No bet," Megan said. "I'd lose. They'll shave a lot of time doing that. Okay, let's go, gang. I want a good spot at the finish line."

Twenty-five Wind Riders walked by them, each nodding at Marlene as they went by. The oddest one had on long combat shorts and a pair of sandals instead of boots. And he winked at her.

"Hey, that's the same guy who winked at you that other time," Shandra said. "I think he's got the hots for you."

"Get your mind out of the gutter, Shandra," Marlene said. "He was probably winking at you anyway. Okay, I want to give those Wind Riders something to think about. You ready?"

The first group of ten Wind Riders was just coming up to the start line.

"Who are we?" Marlene yelled out as loud as she could.

"Zebras!"

"What were we born to do?"

"Run!"

"What do we love to do?"

"Run!"

"What are we going to do?"

"Kick Wind Rider Ass!"

"I can't hear you!"

"Kick Wind Rider Ass!"

"Zebras! Zebras! Zebras! Hoorah!"

All the Wind Riders and the rest of the groups were looking at them now. Each of the Zebras was ready to go. The two snipers and the squad gunner had their primary weapons strapped across the packs on their backs. Assault weapons were slung across their chests pointing down and away, weapons harnesses loaded with full combat loads of clips and grenades. The only one without a secondary weapon had an aerial sticking out of his pack. Unlike the rest of the qualifiers who only had minimum loads, the Zebras were ready for action.

The Zebras had passed the first half of the Wind Riders by the second mile. They passed on the left in single file and in step.

"How many is that?" Marlene asked as they passed each group and formed up in line abreast again.

The rest of the Zebras would shout out the number of Wind Riders they had passed every time. They had caught them all up but the first two by the time the gun range came into view. Marlene had lost track of the time. She just wanted to beat them all. Now she slowed down their pace to match the two groups in front of them.

"Shit, what we slowing down for?" Gerry asked. "We could catch those guys easy."

"We've already got them on time," Marlene said. "Shooting scores are more important now, especially for me. I've got to hit that six hundred meter target. I need to get my heart rate and breathing rate down or I'll never make it. Stick with the plan."

The Wind Riders were still catching their breaths, hands on knees, when the Zebras skidded to a stop in front of their targets and pulled equipment off their backs. Marlene shot her clip from her personal weapon from one knee first, then fired a grenade at the grenade target. Brock had already finished with his squad weapon and was tossing it to Gerry. Marlene tossed her rifle to Shandra, then dropped her pack and sniper rifle. She pulled out her pistol and shot the whole clip at the pistol target. Shandra had tossed her sniper rifle to Gerry and taken the squad gun from him. She fired her assault rifle while she was waiting, then tossed Marlene's rifle at him and opened up with the squad gun. Marlene had extended her bipod and taken a preliminary look at her sniper target, checking the wind direction, then put it aside and pulled her clip for the squad gun beside her.

It took only seconds to dump the empty clip out of the squad gun and load hers in it. Then in three-round measured shots, she emptied the clip in the target. Now she took up the sniper rifle and jacked a round into the chamber. Shandra already had her spotting scope on the target.

"Range, 598," she said. "Angle wind from the right, not heavy. Ready."

"On the way," Marlene said and caressed the trigger. She had another round in the chamber by the time the first one was on target.

"Half inch low, to the right," Shandra said. "Ready."

"On the way."

"Zero, Ready. Zero ready, zero ready, zero ready, zero ready."

"Clear," Marlene said. She dropped the clip and ejected the spent round.

"Zebra is range clear," the range officer yelled out.

Marlene picked up all her brass and put it in her pants cargo pocket. They all gathered up their packs and rifles and headed over to where some benches were set up and dumped everything. They took off the weapons harnesses and grabbed some bottled water out of their packs.

"That looked like fun," Megan said. She had Amanda, Ann and CT with her. "Not bad for rookies. The boss looks like he's impressed."

"He better be," Marlene said. "These kids worked hard for this."

"I hear some naughty girl has been sending nasty messages to someone," CT said.

"Can it, CT," Marlene said, "before Diane thinks you're flirting with Shandra here and drags you away by the ear."

CT grabbed his ear, but not because of that. "Yup, the boss is impressed. Come on Zebras, the boss wants to congratulate you himself."

"You guys go ahead, I'll catch up with you," Marlene said.

"Nope, you're coming too," Megan said. "I didn't set this all up so you two could fuck it up again."

"You know these guys?" Brock said.

"Ya, we've met before," Marlene said. "Another time and another place."

All the original Wind Riders were lined up, including Duncan. Marlene knew what was coming and took two steps back. Jane, Barb, and Dave came forward, removed the berets from the Zebras' heads, and put the black berets of the Wind Riders on their heads. Then a bottle of vodka was given to each of them.

"All in one go or you can't keep the beret," Jane said.

"Hey," Shandra said after she finished coughing. "What about Master Sergeant Isabelle, where's her beret?"

"I've already got one," Marlene said and she walked away.

Shandra grabbed her arm.

"What, you're already a Wind Rider and you're walking away? What kind of shit is that? Are you kidding me?"

Marlene hugged her. "You deserve it, kid. All of you do. I am damn proud of all of you. You come and see me when you want to do some slumming. Hell, I might even buy."

"Master Sergeant Isabelle!" Duncan roared out. "Just where in the hell do you think you are going?"

Marlene came to attention and saluted.

"Back to my barracks, Master Warrant Kovaks!" she said.

"Like hell you are, Isabelle!" he said. "My people and your people worked damn hard to give you this shot and you will damn well take it!"

"Only if you meet my conditions, my lord Duncan," she said.

"Still as cheeky as ever, my daughter," Magdalene said, coming up from behind Duncan.

"State your case," Duncan said.

"The Zebras stay together," Marlene said. "We expand to troop size. I command the troop and you don't make me no stinking officer. Master Warrant."

"I can live with that," Duncan said. "Jane?"

"Hey, you're the boss Duncan, not me." Jane said. "But ya, fine by me. If she can train up a troop as good as these yahoos, I'm all for it. Hell, I just want her back is all."

"Okay," Duncan said. "Two conditions. First, you guys move out of that shithole you're living in. Second, you give me a hug."

"Come on Marlene, please!" The vodka was already hitting Shandra. "They've got way better booze over here and nicer toys. Come on, Boss, give him a hug already."

Duncan came right up to her, and she reluctantly put her arms around him. All the memories of that smell and that touch coming back in rush.

"Welcome home, love," he whispered in her ear.

"Don't push it, Duncan. Please don't push it. For both our sakes."

"Whenever you're ready, Zebra, whenever you're ready." He let her loose. "Now go greet your mother."

"Fuck me," Shandra said. "You're the fucking Ghost! Holy shit. Wait till I tell my brother. I met the fucking Ghost. He worships the ground you walk on."

"Yes, he does, sister," her brother wearing a black beret came up to her.

"Holy fuck! Brock, Gerry, this is my brother Jim. He's a fucking Wind Rider too." Then her brother had to catch her as she passed out.

"Never could hold her booze," Jim said. The three of them dragged her over to a soft spot and laid her down.

"She really come in first at sniper school?" he asked.

"Well, technically second," Brock said. "Marlene was first overall, but ya, she finished first in the secondary gun class. One tough girl, your sister."

"Not as tough as fucking Marlene," Shandra said coming to. "What the hell am I doing on the ground, and where the hell is my booze. Oh, hey Jim. Hey guys, have you met my brother Jim?"

Then she passed out again.

Chapter Six

It was dark now. The qualifying was done, and except for the Wind Riders' partying, it was quiet. Marlene was sitting silently listening to friends she had not seen for over a year. She realized how much she had missed them all. As usual, the women and men were at opposite sides of the fire. The ones with partners would be pairing off soon, but for now, she was just enjoying listening to her friends. But they didn't have her full attention. She kept looking over at Duncan, willing the longing for him to go away. She so very much wanted to rush over to him and drape herself around him. To feel his arms around her once again.

"He's a little better now," Amanda said. "Once we sprung this scheme on him, he has almost been normal again. First Karen and then you. I don't think I could have stood even one of those. I think he loves you more than he loved Karen. Shit, I think I would have drunk myself to death by now."

"You know, I don't think I have ever seen Uncle Duncan drunk," Megan said. "A little tipsy, yes, drunk, no."

"Oh I have hon," Shelly said. "It was not pretty, let me tell you."

"You were with him then?" Marlene asked.

"Ya, it was right after he came back from Africa. Man was he messed up. I think he was trying to drink himself to death. I was scared he was going to do the same thing when you left. Lucky for all of us, he didn't."

"He'll never admit it, Marlene," Barb said, "but he needs you. More than you need him. Yes, sorry Jane, but I believe he loves you more than he loved Karen."

"Who is this Karen?" Magdalene asked. "And where is she?"

"She was my daughter," Jane said. "And she was Duncan's wife. Yes Barb, I agree, God help me and Karen forgive me, but yes, I really believe he loves Marlene at least as much as he loved Karen. Maybe more."

"But where is she? Did she not come with you from Earth?

No one made to answer.

"No, mom," Marlene said almost in a whisper. "I killed her and his unborn child."

Then she got up and walked away.

Shandra had just walked up to the fire and made to go after her. Amanda held her back, and Jane went after her.

"We are all friends. Old and dear friends," Barb said. "Everyone here but Magdalene came here from earth with Duncan and his wife Karen. Duncan and I grew up together. Jane was Karen's mother. Amanda, you tell the story. You were there. We were not. Shandra is Marlene's friend, and we are Marlene's friends. She should hear this."

"Holy fuck," Shandra said after she heard the story. "No wonder she is all messed up. She cries damn near every night we are back on base."

"Shelly?" Barb said. "I think this is your territory."

"No kidding," Shelly said. "I didn't think it was that bad." She took off in the direction Marlene and Jane had gone at the run.

She found them just outside the firelight. Marlene was sitting on the ground with her arms wrapped around her knees. Jane was squatting down beside her, gently rubbing her back.

"So this is where you two got to," Shelly said. "Care for some company? I brought a friend." She held up a bottle of vodka.

"Oh God, not you too," Marlene said, and she sunk her head between her arms.

"Okay Jane, I've got it," Shelly said.

Jane gave Marlene a quick squeeze and kissed her on the neck, missing the shudder Marlene gave when she did it.

"So," Shelly said. "do you know what I am?"

"One of Duncan's oldest friends come to witness my shame," she said.

"I am a trained and certified psychologist," Shelly said. "Do you know what that is?"

"Yes, a doctor of mental disorders."

"Close enough," Shelly said. "Whatever you say to me, I am not allowed to repeat, do you understand that?"

"Yes."

"So, from where I am standing, you are about six months past a complete and total mental breakdown. Back home I would probably dope you up with all kinds of happy drugs and hope the problem went away. I can't do that here for a lot of reasons. The biggest one is that I like you. So now I am going to talk and you are going to listen. I am probably not going to be nice to you like the others were. Do you understand?"

"Yes."

"Okay, you killed his wife and his unborn kid, so what? Get over it. He has. Did you betray him? Yes, you did. Did he overreact? You bet your ass he did. Get over it. Shit happens, especially with pigheaded idiots like you two. These people are not like you, Marlene. You are just learning that. The country they come from is as big as this planet. It is very hot in the summer and very cold in the winter. The winters you had on Oaken? They just laughed at the rest of us. I come from a country just south of theirs. It is not as big but has ten times as many people in it. We tried to invade them twice and twice they beat us.

"Duncan's people? Barb and her family? They are not like other people in their country. They come from long lines of military people. They were bred for this shit. The rest of us just muddle along. So yes, he can try and kill you one day and be your friend the next. Real professional soldiers are all like that. His people more than others.

"He understands you need time, Marlene. Just don't wait too long. Duncan is a survivor. He has to be. You wait too long and he will shut you right out like he never knew you. He will hate it, but he will do it."

"Maybe that would be for the best," Marlene said. "I will just hurt him again."

"Ya, you probably will," Shelly said. "And he will probably hurt you, too. That happens when you are in love and try so hard not to hurt the other person's feelings. It gets all bottled up and eventually explodes. I can't make your choice for you, Marlene. You know he loves you. I don't have to tell you that. You have to make up your mind if you want to be with him or not before it destroys you."

Marlene jumped up and flung herself around Shelly.

"Oh, God help me, I want him so bad," she said. "I want him to love me. I want to have his babies. Oh God, I am so wicked."

"Well love, if God had anything to do with it, he put you two together for a reason." Shelly had to stop talking, she was crying too hard.

"Now what?" Marlene asked. "What do I do now?"

"Well, with guys like Duncan, you have to let them think it was all their idea," Shelly said. "You do remember how to flirt and play hard to get?"

"But you just told me I had to grab him fast or he would forget about me."

"I did tell you that, but there is a difference between grabbing him and throwing yourself at him. You don't want to be

Bitch-in-heat Marlene, but you don't want to be Ice Queen Isabelle either. None of us liked ice queen too much. Let your hair grow out a little. You've served in the field with longer hair before. Let him know you are not super trooper Marlene all the time. None of the rest of us act like that."

"I wish I could look as good as you," Marlene said. "Even before the scar, I didn't look as good."

"Ya, well, I can't run five miles in just over four hours with a full combat load and shoot perfect scores afterward like you can. Some of us have to get by on our looks to get a guy. Not you though, oh no, Super Trooper has to almost beat the Great King Ghost's record to get her guy."

"What do you mean, almost beat him? I am nowhere near as good as he is."

"Check it out if you don't believe me," Shelly said. "His best time was four hours thirty-five minutes. Yours was four hours forty-five minutes. You had identical shooting scores, though you used more ammo and he didn't have a spotter. He ran that same course the day before you did. We all did. He just made the time limit. He's been pushing paper for too long.

"Come on, I'm getting chilly out here in the dark, and there might be some mice or some other kind of nasty wildlife around that comes out after dark to eat us city girls."

They walked back to the campfire, and while Shelly went to her chair by the fire, Marlene stood just inside the area lit up by it. She looked around the fire at all the happy faces. Even her mother was laughing at something CT had just said. She felt her spirits rise and her heart become free. She was back home, among her friends, her family. She looked over at Duncan and saw he was looking at her, and she flashed him the *advance to contact* hand signal and walked back into the darkness.

"Are you okay?" he said when he came to her. "I am sorry if..."

She put her hand over his lips, and her hand trembled at the touch. She dropped her hand quickly, before he could grab it.

"We have both apologized enough," she said. "No more apologies. I have hurt you, and you have hurt me. Let's move on."

"Is that what Shelly told you to say?" he asked. She could see the hurt in his eyes.

"No, she told me not to be the ice queen," she said. "Then she told me not to be a bitch in heat. So confusing, those shrinks. Play hard to get, but not too hard to get. Flirt but don't be slutty. All these rules. No wonder once they get their hands on you, you never leave."

She was playing with his open shirt lapels now. Then she looked up into his eyes.

"I love you, Duncan. God help me, I love you, and I know you love me. But I need some time to let all this sink in. First Karen, then all the changes. Then us falling in love. Oh, I was never so happy in my life as when we were living together. I never wanted to leave that house. Then you had to go away and I had so much work to do, so much adjusting to do, and then Tanya happened. Oh God, my world came to an end. I lost everything, but most of all, I lost you."

He was stroking her scar now, the scar that had started it all. His hand was quivering, and she took it in hers and kissed it.

"Do you mean it?" he asked, his voice just over a whisper. "I think I might lose it if you leave again."

"Yes, Duncan, I mean it," she kissed his hand again. Her legs felt weak now. She would let him take her right then, right there, if he wanted it.

"Well, okay then," he said, grinning.

"Not so fast, buddy boy," she said, giving him a gentle push on the chest. "My sources tell me you only finished your qual with five minutes to spare. You're going to have to be a hell of lot faster than that to keep up with me, sonny."

"Shit, it was that slow? The bums never told me."

"We run five miles at five every morning. You want to catch me, be there tomorrow."

"I dunno," he said, a sly look on face. They were walking back to the campfire now. "Rumor has it Zebras like to kick the shit out of wolfhounds."

"Zebras!" she yelled out. "What were we born to do?"

"Run!" came from two campfires.

"Zebras, what were we trained to do?"

"Kill lions!"

"Zebras what do we love to do?"

"Kick wolfhound asses!"

"Zebras! Zebras! Zebras! Hoorah!"

"And don't you damn wolfhounds forget it!" Marlene yelled as they came into the fire ring.

"Oh my," Shelly said. "Is this the ice queen or the bitch in heat?"

"Neither," Marlene said as she sat next to her mother and patted the chair next to her for Duncan to sit down on. "This is the Zebra leading the wolfhound around by the nose."

"Ya, well, this wolfhound is a ghost," Duncan said. "Now he is here, now he is there. Always just out of reach."

"Shades of grey," Marlene said. "Like a Zebra, neither black nor white."

"Very good daughter, you are learning," Magdalene said. "Devie Devie, checkie checkie."

"Oh shit," Duncan said. "My mom used to say that to my dad all the time. Then she would laugh like hell."

"But of course," Carol said in Ukrainian. "Otherwise, you men would run all over us."

"Hey speak for yourself, Carol," Amanda said. "I just got my guy and I ain't letting him go." She was draped all over Jim.

"Can all you guys speak Oaken?" Shandra asked in the same language.

"We all understand it can," Shelly said. "Some of us speak not so well."

Then Marlene said something in French, and most of them laughed.

"Shit, Parisian too?" Shandra said.

"But of course," Marlene said. "I was born there. I am really a Black Shirt. Well, used to be. Then I was a Wind Rider, then a Black Shirt again, then a PIG. Now I'm a Wind Rider again. So confusing."

"Okay, this Zebra and that Wind Rider have a date at five tomorrow morning. Come on Shandra, time to go." She kissed Duncan's hand again, then stood, and she and Shandra walked into the darkness. "Zebras! Form up! Somebody better have a vehicle here. I'll be damned if I run this hill twice in one day."

"Yes, Boss," she heard Brock say. "Some cute little wolfhound chick drove your chariot over here. All the shit is already loaded, your bossness."

"Shit, I suppose I am the soberest and have to drive, then," Marlene said. "Alright, pile in, you boneheads."

She rolled down her window and started to drive away.

They heard her yell *Zebras love to kick Wind Rider ass* at the top of her lungs as she drove away.

"I'd better go," Duncan said. "I have a feeling she is going to make me pay tomorrow."

Chapter Seven

Duncan was sitting on the fender of his G-Wagon at ten to five in front of their hut. He had his track suit on, and his sneaker-clad feet were swinging in the air when the Zebras came out. His smirk vanished. They were in combat uniform, with boots in one hand and a rifle in the other. None of them said anything to him. They just looked at him. Then they lined up and began their half hour Tai Chi exercises. Duncan belatedly jumped off the fender and joined them. Without a word spoken, they stooped and sat on the grass, putting on their shoes and boots. Then, rifles in hand, they started to run. Run, not jog. A little over an hour later, they were back in front of the hut.

Duncan made it, barely. He was sweating badly and breathing heavily. His hands were on his knees, and he was gulping for air.

"I remember," Marlene said, "some smartass Wind Rider in full gear running around us in circles and backwards the first time I made that run. Remember what you told us afterward, Duncan? You are trained to ride around in vehicles and are sheepdogs, you said. We are wolfhounds, and we run down wolves and kill them. You were right, Duncan. I saw you guys take off and run two miles flat out with all your gear and engage an enemy five times your number. You saved a lot of lives that day, Duncan.

"Somewhere the Wind Riders have lost their way, Duncan. There is no way my rookie kids should beat your people. But we do. My Zebras beat you Wind Riders in everything we do."

"Well, almost everything," Duncan said. "You start learning on Monday what you have not been taught yet. Tomorrow, you guys move into your new barracks. Then, every morning, you guys kick my people's asses. Then your asses are ours for the rest of the day. We'll see what's what after a month."

Monday morning, all the Wind Riders on the planet were in front of their barracks in track suits doing Tai chi. The Zebras were in combat gear, this time with web harnesses, pistols, rifles, and packs. By the time they had donned all their gear, half the Wind Riders had gone by. By the end of the first mile, the Zebras were in front.

"Who are we?"

"Zebras!"

What are we born to do?"

"Run!"

"What are we trained to do?"

"Kill lions!"

"What do we love to do?"

"Kick wolfhound ass!"

Then they sped up. They had all their gear packed away and were sitting on the step of the barracks as the first of the Wind Riders showed up. They didn't say anything. They just watched.

After breakfast, they were in a classroom all day learning electronic systems.

The next morning, the original thirty Wind Riders were equipped the same way the Zebras were. They made a valiant effort, but at the halfway mark, the Zebras passed them and began their chant. Then they sped up again.

After the first month, they had to leave first in order to keep ahead of the originals. They only started their chant as they passed the rear-enders on their way back to barracks now.

The second month, the Zebras were introduced to the Wind Riders version of the G-Wagon. It had a lot more electronic goodies in it than they were used to, and they had to learn how to use them all.

By the end of the second month, all the Wind Riders were keeping up, and at the beginning of the third, the Zebras changed it up again. Now they were running with combat loads, including all their weapons and necessary gear. They still were in the lead. The next day all the Wind Riders were outfitted the same way. Not all of them had a second sniper rifle. More than half had no sniper rifles at all. By the end of the third month, the Wind Riders were back in shape. The Zebras knew their G-Wagons inside out, and things changed again.

Half the Wind Riders were deployed off-planet, and they were replaced by others who had just come back from deployment. The newcomers showed up the first morning in track suits, and the Zebras let them lead off in their jog. Then they took off, and after they passed them, the Zebras began their chant.

The Zebras were issued their Coyote that day, and the learning began again. The newcomers were equipped properly the next day and gave it a good try. They were better than the first group, but not by much.

Friday nights, Duncan and Marlene would go for beer with their friends. Half of the originals had been deployed, and the pizza joint they began to call their own was not as packed as it had been.

Saturday nights were their own. Dressed in civilian clothing, looking just like two normal people, they would go to the mall or to a movie. They were regularly holding hands now, and Marlene would let him kiss her now and then, but nothing more than that.

The fifth month they were training on the Coyote weapons systems. The last month was real life simulations with live weapons and realistic situations. They were as ready as they ever would be.

"Duncan," Marlene asked on their last Saturday together, "are we the only ones with anti-air capability?"

"As far as I know, why?"

"That job we did with the Marauders? Both sides were using air assets. Bishop was able to beat them off, but only because the bad guys were not that good. It's a weakness, Duncan. Others are going to pick up on it."

"I'll get CT and Bob checking into it right away," he said. "That's why I love you. You're always thinking."

"Oh," she said, "and here I was thinking you were just after this." She put his hand on her rear.

"Well, that is also very nice," he said.

"What these not good enough?" she stuck her chest out.

"Also very nice," he said. "You offering or just teasing?"

"Oh I want to all right," she said. "I have ever since I saw you sitting next to me in that stupid video machine. But it will have to wait, love. I haven't prepared, and I am at the height of my fertility cycle. I can't risk it."

"Drat, foiled again," Duncan said. "Ya, I get it. Let your kids get a few ops under them first. By the time you come back, I should have some new kids for you. We are only taking the best of the new kids now. No more right-out-of advanced training. They all have to have a least one deployment under their belts first. I think we are going to be very PIG-heavy the first go-round. But one Marauder battalion had some good people in it. How many do you want?"

"Send me twenty," she said. "I'll take the best four. I don't want to rush this like you guys did when you expanded."

"Gotcha," he said. Then he pulled her to him and kissed her. They were in front of her barracks by then. "You be damn careful out there. This is a nasty one."

"They all are," she said laying her head on his shoulder. "The nights are always the hardest."

"I know," he replied. They were not talking about combat.

They had been up early Sunday loading their Coyote. Truck after truck of supplies had arrived, and the armoured vehicle was crammed with food, water, ammunition, medical supplies, and spare parts. Most of their personal gear was strapped on top, along with their tents and camo netting. All of their personal weapons were stowed in racks next to their seats, and their web harnesses were draped over the seats.

Then they drove over to the landing field and waited, as all armies do, for their turn to load. This was a big deployment. A full battalion of Black Shirts, along with their artillery and support troops, was going. Marlene had not seen any of her old battle group for almost two years. Many were young and new. Their vehicles and uniforms were pristine. Like their smaller cousins, the LAVs were fully loaded, personal gear stacked on the outside. Each LAV had a crew of three and ten troopers, being several feet longer than the Coyotes. They had six wheels instead of the Coyotes' four, but the weapons cupola were identical. The only Black Shirts onsite were the LAV crew members. There was no need for the dismounts to be there today.

Twenty vehicles were waiting. Including the Zebras, there were five Coyotes and twenty G-Wagons. One of the Coyotes was their command vehicle, and Carol was their commander. Technically, each Coyote was responsible for four G-Wagons, but in the field, they operated independently. Each of the vehicles would cover a Black Shirt company. They had no need for support troops, as all their needs would be handled by the Black Shirts.

This was the third Black Shirt battalion to be sent to that planet. Originally, one was scheduled to go, but then the Planetary Council intervened and a second battalion joined the first. Once on the ground, the Black Shirt general had seen how bad the situation was and requested his third battalion. So here they were, waiting to load. They would be loaded last. Their transport held half the support troops and all of the artillery of the battalion. There were three large transports in all.

The three Wind Rider squadrons deploying for their regular rotation were waiting next to them. They had their own transport but had to wait for the supply-loading process. They would be stopping at three planets, supplies needed to be loaded in reverse of the travel pattern. The Wind Rider squadron would load second.

"So, now you can see why we need another squadron," Carol said to Marlene. "We are really stretched thin when we have to deploy an extra squadron like today. It makes it hard to conduct special ops. That's why we were tapping the PIGs. Due to their origins, they train some of their troops extensively for special ops, like you people were. The other two battle groups don't have that capability."

The artillery was starting to load now. They would be next.

"This is your final training mission, Marlene," Carol continued. "If I think you Zebras are ready, after this mission you will be doing special ops for us. I think you are ready, but we have to prove it. So, for this one you get to do my job, while I get to sit on my ass and drink vodka and tonic by the beach in my bikini."

Both of them had a good laugh at that. Then it was their turn to load.

"Four hours of waiting for ten minutes of work," Brock said. "What a waste of a nice Sunday afternoon."

"You were just going to sit around the barracks and sleep anyway," Gerry said. "Come on, I want one last crack at crappy mall food. We won't be seeing any for the next six months."

They hurried back to their barracks, changed into their civilian clothing, and drove to the mall in Marlene's battered old SUV. As they walked by a beauty salon on the way to the food court, Marlene caught her reflection in the glass and stopped.

"Go ahead," she said. "I'll catch up with you guys in a bit."

"Planning something special with the hunk tonight?" Shandra said.

"Yes, if it is any of your business," she answered. "No, I don't need the hassle of long hair out in the wild. Time for a major reduction."

"Oh," Shandra said. "I hadn't thought about that. Come on, I know a better place. They're better and a whole lot cheaper."

The guys saw where she was headed and tagged along. They ended up at the other end of the mall where there was a men's barbershop. All four of them walked in. There were four chairs, and all of them were free.

"I can't remember the last time we had a woman come in here for a cut," Marlene's barber said. "You want the full treatment? Wash, cut, style?"

"Nope," she said. "Same as those guys. Brush cut."

"That's a shame," he said. "You have such beautiful hair. Some kind of a charity deal right? Don't worry, it will grow back nice and lush again."

He took out his clippers and started chopping off her hair, which had grown down to her shoulders. Soon, large piles were laying all around the chair. He started on the left side, and as he brushed the hair back from her face, he saw the scar for the first time and stopped.

"You were in the army?" he asked. He had also seen her bar code tattooed to the base of her neck.

"Still am," Marlene said.

"I was a Marauder," he said. "Just got out last year. What unit you with?"

"Zebras."

"Never heard of them," he said.

"New unit," Marlene said. "First deployment."

"You'll be okay," he said. "Used to be, the new guys were thrown right up front. 'Cannon fodder,' we called them. Now they bring the new guys up slow. Much better for the health. I started off as a trooper and was of the survivors of that fiasco on Oaken. What a mess that was. Mustered out as a major."

"I was a Black Shirt," she said. "Like you, one of the lucky survivors. I am extremely happy to be a master sergeant. Same pay as a major, a lot less hassle."

"I should have done the same thing," the barber said. "'Come on Billy,' Bishop said, 'I really need you to be an officer. Better pay, better benefits, you get to order people around.' Like a dumbass I jumped on it. Same pay, mess fees, paperwork coming out my butt, troopers whining all the time, bosses yelling all the time. Believe me, you made the right decision, Master Sergeant. You must be close to your five years now?"

"I'm thinking about it," Marlene said. "I had three years in as a Black Shirt before. That time doesn't count though. Do you miss it?"

"A little, but I am on the active reserve, so I get to play soldier every Wednesday night and the last weekend of every month. I start my mandatory three months next month. That's enough for me. I was a Marauder for ten years before. Got married last year and the missus is pregnant, so I'll probably go inactive in a couple of years."

He was finished now and was brushing all the clippings from her shoulders. She stood up and looked at herself in the mirror. It was not as severe a cut as she had gotten during basic, but was very short. Brock gave her a wolf whistle, and she struck a cover girl pose, hand on a hip, head tilted up and to the right, and blew him a kiss. Then she was digging in her pocket for cash to pay and was laughing. All of them had the same haircuts.

"No charge, Master Sergeant," Billy said. "Your first deployment and I know you guys don't make much money."

"I got the same bonuses you did, Major," Marlene said. "Just don't say anything to those knuckleheads. They think I am dirt-ass poor like they are." She paid for all four haircuts and a hefty tip.

"Keep the shiny side up, Zebra," Billy said as they walked out.

"Still want some mall food?" Marlene asked. "We better hurry."

"Nice guys, those barbers," Shandra said. "They were all ex-Marauders. You didn't have to pay for us, Marlene. Those guys said it was on the house."

"They all have families to feed and rent and overhead to pay, Shandra," she answered. "It was still cheaper than that stupid salon would have charged me. Besides, it's Gerry's idea for mall food, so he is buying mine and you two are buying the beer after."

They parked the SUV behind their barracks and walked to the All Ranks. The dining room and lounge were full, as was the bar, so they headed to the Junior Ranks. A G-Wagon came up beside them and stopped.

"Hey," Amanda said from the front passenger seat. "Where you guys headed?"

"Junior Ranks," Gerry said. "All Ranks is full."

"All of us are going to the firing range," Amanda said. "The regulars all go to the clubs, so all of them will be full, and we kind of don't fit in anyway. Come on, the whole gang will be there."

"Might as well," Brock said. "We'll have to stop and pick up some booze though."

"Ah, so the mighty Zebras don't know everything then," Jim the driver said. "Which is why they are all still rookies. Come on, jump in. The four of you can jam in the backseat. It's not far."

"Whoa, nice wheels, Brother," Shandra said. It was the civilian version of the G-Wagon and had leather seats and all the bells and whistles.

"Boys and their toys," Amanda said. "I myself have a nice, super-fast sports car. I drive around in a G-Wagon all day every day."

They pulled into the firing range parking lot. It was full of fancy sports cars, G-Wagons, and luxury vehicles. Four bonfires were blazing and troopers were sitting or dancing all around. Music was blaring from a large portable stereo system that CT and an oddly dressed female were operating. Stacks of cardboard cases were beside each fire, which were obviously full of booze.

Shandra stuck with her brother, while Amanda, Brock, and Gerry headed to a fire where they knew some people, leaving Marlene on her own. She grabbed a beer from the closest fire, but no one she knew was there, so she started making her way to where Brock and Gerry had gone.

"Hey," Dianne said coming up beside her. "I almost missed you. Nice do. Almost as nice as mine."

Dianne had cut her hair short too. It was close cropped on the sides and back, but longer on the top. She and her team were going as replacements to another planet.

"The boss got hung up on some last-minute deal," she said. "He'll be here soon."

They were between fires and alone. Dianne put her hand on Marlene's shoulder to stop her from moving off.

"I know we haven't hit it off, Marlene," she said. "Two alpha females over-protective of the same alpha male. I love Duncan, Marlene, but not like you do. He is my father, my brother. He is all the family I have. He took me under his wing and gave me a chance when nobody else would. He made me who I am. I owe everything to him. Can you understand? I didn't see him at his worst like Shelly did, but I saw him at his fiercest. He was ruthless then. He really was going to kill Karen.

"I see how you have changed from a cold professional killer to a vibrant young woman. You mellow him, and he mellows you. Without you, Marlene, he is incomplete."

"He loves you too, Dianne," Marlene said. "He loves all of you. He'll never say it, but he does. He is doing all of this for all of you. Me? Well, he just loves me. It's different. It's hard to explain and hard to understand and accept sometimes. I have to share him with you all, when I want him to myself. But I am trying hard, Dianne. I am trying hard."

"I know," she said. "Friends?"

"Are all you guys this contrary?" Marlene asked after they broke off their hug.

"Nah, not all of us," Dianne said grinning. "Just us crazy Canucks. Well, Carol has a stick up her ass sometimes."

"Oh goody," Marlene said "Another ice queen. I am not alone then."

"I wouldn't call her an ice queen," Dianne said. "She has a chip on her shoulder is all. She's more like you than you know. She didn't really fit in with her people back home, so they sent her to us. She didn't come from a good family and had to fight hard to get where she is. She is tough as nails, but has a really tender heart that she shows once in a while. She fought Duncan tooth and nail for you, Marlene. She was going to quit and join you, change her name and everything so she could be with you. Now don't get all mushy on me. You would do the same for any of us. I know you would."

"Come on, the gang is waiting for you. It's our last night together, so let's make the best of it."

Chapter Eight

They had to report to the port by seven, and the personal gear they would need for the trip had been sent ahead. They had a choice – take the bus assigned for them or walk. It was only a mile and a half, so they chose the latter, almost.

At five, they were lined up in front of their barracks, combat uniforms on. The first of the daily runners passed them by. They were loaded with their combat loads and striding confidently. They went by, squadron by squadron, and then came the latest troops, in for their rotation. As normal, they were in track suits and running shoes.

The Zebras let them pass, then in line abreast, joined the run. They changed to single file and began to pass the track-suited newcomers. They reached the gap between the squadrons and slotted in front of the last squadron.

"Who are we?" Marlene yelled.

"Zebras!"

"What are we bred for?"

"To run!"

"What we born doing?"

"Running!"

"What were we trained to do?"

"Kill lions!"

"What do we love to do?"

"Kick wolfhound butt!"

"Zebras! Zebras! Zebras! Hoorah!"

Then the Zebras sped up, formed a single file, passed another squadron and turned left onto the road heading to the port. They formed a line of two and kept to the right side of the road, until they entered the marshalling area and spread out into line-abreast again. Most of the Black Shirts and all the Wind Riders were off the busses and grouped loosely in their companies or squadrons. Wind Riders were on the left, the much larger Black Shirt formation on the right, leaving twenty feet between both groups. The Zebras ran up the center of the gap.

The command groups of both regiments were at the far end of the formation, and the Zebras ran right up to them, came to a foot crashing halt in front of Carol, then came to attention and saluted.

"Wind Rider, Charley Squadron, Zebra, reporting for duty!" Marlene yelled. "All present and accounted for ma'am!"

"Very well, Zebra," Carol said. "Join the formation, Master Sergeant."

"Yes, Ma'am!" Zebras saluted again, then about-faced and double-timed to their position at the tail end of the Wind Rider formation. It was a quarter to seven. Amanda walked down to them from her section.

"Christ, Isabelle!" Amanda said. "I'm so hungover I could hardly walk off the bus. You guys ran here?"

"I remember some smartass female Wind Rider sergeant tell me once that if I could drink with the girls at night, I could damn well work with the girls in the morning."

"Ya, thanks," Amanda said. "Rub it in, why don't you? Now we get to stand around for a couple of hours."

"Could be worse," Marlene said. "Could be in an untrained support unit like those guys over there."

The Black Shirts across from them were the support unit that would be on the same transport as the Wind Riders. They had their personal gear stowed in duffle bags at their feet and had their personal rifles with them. Where the Wind Riders were all loose and making jokes, these were all nervous, many looking anxiously around them.

"First time off planet for them," Amanda said, "let alone going into a major hot zone. The whole battalion is like that. This could be interesting."

"Like you were not nervous the first time," Marlene said.

"Different story," Amanda replied. "Where I come from, being in the army is voluntary. After all the training and waiting, I couldn't wait. I was combat arms the whole way. Most of those guys over there probably thought they would get to spend the whole five years on planet, pushing paper or something."

"They'll be way behind the lines anyway," Marlene said. "Better get back to your people. It looks like we are starting to board."

The first of the Wind Riders formed up and marched into the huge interplanetary transport. The Zebras were the last, following behind a section of green and nervous young Black Shirts. They were billeted across from each other, separated by a hallway.

All of the billets were designed to hold a regular ten-person section and were comfortable enough for that number. There were only eight in a normal Wind Rider section, which meant more room for them, but the Zebras were only four. They had plenty of room. All of the duffle bags holding their uniforms and personal gear were stacked neatly in the center of the floor. They had half an hour to store their gear – plenty of time.

Then a series of bangs and clangs was heard as the ramps and hatches closed, and vibrations could be felt as the propulsion systems started up. This was followed by a klaxon sounding and a voice over the intercom telling them to strap in and prepare for takeoff. The Zebras had been through this enough times that it was old hat . They laid on bunks near each other and strapped in, with heads close to each other so they could talk.

The vibration of the engines increased, and they knew they were airborne as they heard and felt the landing gear retract. They knew they were in orbit when the few loose items in the billet started floating around in a freefall, no-gravity state. Once they were up to speed, the items crashed to the floor as the artificial gravity was turned on. All four of them were unbuckling straps and getting off the bunks before the klaxon sounded again and they were informed they could do so.

Marlene walked over to a video console mounted on a desk by the door, turned it on, and checked their timetable. With this many people on board, everything from eating to exercise time was scheduled. They were on the last shift. It wouldn't matter after a couple of days. It would take that long for their internal clocks to adjust. There was no day and night on a transport ship. The people across the hall had the same schedule. It was the beginning of their new eight-hour sleep cycle. None of them complained. They had not gone to bed the night before.

Their billet alarm went off, and it was time to wake up. They had a half-hour to shower and get dressed, then an hour for breakfast. After that was the mandatory safety session, which would take four hours. After one hour for lunch, they would be taken on a tour of the ship, which would take another four hours. Then an hour for dinner, a half hour for free time, and lights out.

Luckily, the trip would only be eight days this time. After the first day, things would quickly become boring. The recreation rooms and bars would be popular, as there would be a lot of free time.

Knowing they had a lot of time, the Zebras didn't rush. The noise level in the hallway increased greatly as the excited youngsters across the hall started making their way to the dining area. They waited until the noise level went down, then opened the door and walked into the filled dining area. One shift was having their supper, while they would be having their breakfast.

The Zebras joined the tail end of the line of excited Black Shirts and shuffled their way along the buffet line, overloading their plates. They would also be sharing a table with these people. They all wore the same uniforms. The only way the Zebras could be told apart was from the missing unit patches on their uniforms and by their close-cropped hair cuts. The service people had their Black Shirt unit crests on their shoulders, and their hair was as long as regulation would permit. Most of the women had their long hair pulled up and tucked behind their heads.

Their section leader was a master corporal. A corporal was in charge of the other fireteam, and the rest were privates. The Zebras nodded at them, then sat down at the far end of the table meant to hold twenty troops. The table went quiet as they sat down, everyone taking in their short haircuts. The Zebras ate their breakfast quietly and quickly, then went for seconds. When everyone finished, the master corporal decided it was time to go to the lecture and assumed he was in charge. None of the Zebras were wearing their rank badges on their chests.

The Zebras paid attention to the first hour of the lecture – the part about where the emergency exits and suits were. Then they slept through the rest. Lunch was pretty much the same as breakfast, but with different food choices. Then came the equally boring ship tour, which they couldn't sleep through.

They were more relaxed during supper, only going through the line once, and the Black Shirt section leader decided to come and talk to them.

"I hope you don't mind me giving orders," he said.

"Somebody has to," Gerry said. "Might as well be you."

"You guys are Wind Riders, right?"

"You could say that." Gerry had opened up his mouth, so he got to be the spokesman.

"Bet you've been off planet a lot, seen a lot of action?"

"A time or two," Gerry said. He looked at his watch. The section leader did, too.

"Okay, time to go," the section leader said.

The Zebras waited until they were behind closed doors to start laughing.

The first thing the Zebras did after breakfast the next morning was to head to the gym and begin their Tai Chi routine. They had the place to themselves, as the Black Shirts had decided to go exploring. Then the Zebras ran. They ran in single file down the right side of the hallway, passing on the left. They had to make ten laps of the ship to make their five miles. Then they had a shower and changed. By then it was lunchtime. After lunch, they went into the cargo bay where the vehicles were stored and went over the Coyote, making sure all their gear was still in place, that the Coyote was properly secured to the floor, and nothing was damaged. Then it was suppertime again.

After three days, the crew and anyone else walking the halls got out of their way when they went for their morning run. The afternoons were now spent watching a movie or hanging out in one of the lounges. Brock came for supper one day and said there was an excellent driving game in one of the rec rooms. The next afternoon found the Zebras in the rec room crashing and burning each other on the game, hooting and hollering and punching each other, trying to distract the other drivers. Soon they had an audience, and there was a lot of laughing and cheering going on.

"Attention!" somebody yelled out and everyone scrambled to line up and come to attention.

A Black Shirt major and his entourage wandered about looking everyone up and down. He stopped in front of the Zebras with a frown on his face.

"What unit are you people with," he demanded.

"Zebras, sir," Gerry said.

"Never heard of you. Once again, Trooper, what unit are you with?"

"Third Battalion Wind Riders, Sir."

"Where are your rank badges, Trooper? I better see them the next time I run into you, or I will place you on report."

"Yes Sir, sorry, Sir. Won't happen again, Sir."

"See that it doesn't."

He stopped in front of Marlene and looked her up and down.

"Do I know you from somewhere, Trooper?" he said.

"Not that I recall, Sir!" Marlene said.

"Where is your name tag, and what is your name, Trooper?"

"Regulations prohibit the wearing of name tags while deployed or the disclosure of our names to anyone not in our regiment, Sir!"

"Not in my army, Trooper. We will see about that," the major said. "Captain, schedule a meeting with the colonel. As you were. Keep it down. Other people than you are on this ship. Carry on!"

Marlene waited until he was almost out the door and then blew a very loud raspberry. The major spun around and marched back into the room, looking for an indication of who had done it. Not finding any, he strode away, but as he reached the doorway, Marlene started again, making it sound like he was passing gas with each step. A ship's officer happened to see it all, and he grabbed the major's arm and stopped him from re-entering the room. He whispered quickly in his ear, then guided him out.

"Fucking asshole," Marlene said.

"Oh man, are you in shit now," the Black Shirt master corporal said. "He is in tight with the colonel and the general."

"Not mine," Marlene said. "I don't much like his attitude. You should report this to your sergeant, master corporal. He has no right coming into our area like that. It's your warrant officer or master sergeant's territory."

"They are all scared of him," the master corporal said. "He had something to do with getting rid of our original general."

"Really?" Marlene said. "Why don't you tell me about it?"

They knew something would happen and, other than their early morning run and meal times, stayed to their billet. They heard the rumblings on the shipboard net she had hacked into, and she nodded. It was time. They had been waiting for this and were in their normal uniforms, all badging and rank symbols in place. The Zebras marched out of their billet to the rec center, where once again the Major was chastising the troops. This time he had a transport officer with him.

The Zebras spread out in a line just inside the door, Marlene in the center.

"What the hell are these officers doing in my territory, Chief Petty Officer!" she barked out. "I was not informed of this inspection!"

The officers spun around. They saw two master corporals with master marksmen badges on their sleeves, a sergeant with a sharpshooter badge, all three with a campaign ribbon on their chests and Wind Rider berets on the heads. The three of them were at parade rest. The fourth was a master sergeant. She had a master sharpshooter badge on her sleeve and to the left of her campaign ribbon was a mention in dispatch ribbon. She had a Black Shirt beret on her head.

"Since when does a master sergeant give orders to a major? I'll have..."

"You'll have me what, Major?" Marlene said. "You are out of order, Sir. Shipboard regulations state that permission from the ranking non-commissioned officer shall be sought and granted for any inspection of personnel off duty in authorized off-duty areas. My permission was not sought."

"We had the permission of the Chief Petty Officer," the Major said.

"The Chief Petty Officer is not the ranking officer over these troopers. I am," Marlene said.

"We'll see about that!" the major said. "What is your name Master Sergeant. I will..."

"My name is Master Sergeant Marlene Isabelle," she said. "What are you going to do? Falsify another report, have me thrown out of my regiment and reduced in rank to a common trooper like the last time? It seems it didn't work out as you had planned, did it, Major? Now get the fuck off my deck... Sir!"

"Attention, present arms!" Every trooper in the rec hall came to attention and saluted, including Marlene. Every single person in the room knew that, although it was frowned upon to salute indoors, it was not against regulations and that it was also a sign of displeasure of the enlisted troops when they did it.

The Major did not return the salute and marched out of the room, his entourage hurrying after him. The transport officer came to attention and returned the salute.

"Order arms," Marlene ordered. "As you were. Chief Petty Officer, Lieutenant, a moment outside?"

"Gentlemen, I am sorry you were dragged into this," she said once in the hallway. "These rear echelon people can be a pain at times."

"Not for long they won't," the lieutenant said. "Chief, make sure you coordinate with the Master Sergeant from now on. Carry on."

"Sir!" both non-commissioned officers said coming to attention raising their right knees high and stomping them to the deck, which was the normal procedure. The lieutenant nodded and walked away.

"Sorry, Chief," Marlene said. "We are supposed to keep a low profile, but that Master Corporal is just a kid and way over his head. Buy you a beer?"

They both walked in and made their way to the bar. The room was very quiet. Marlene took off her beret, opened the top two buttons in her tunic, and stuffed the beret inside. She took her bottle of beer in hand and turned around, raising the beer up high.

"Who are we?"

"Zebras!" her three troopers yelled holding their refreshments high.

"What are we born to do?"

"Run!"

"What are we bred to do?"

"Kill lions!"

Then she pointed at Brock.

"What do we love to do?" he said.

"Kick Black Shirt officer ass!" Marlene yelled out.

"Zebras, Zebras, Zebras, Hoorah!" Then they slammed the drinks back and laughed.

"See ya around, Chief," Marlene said. Then the four of them walked out of the room and back to their billet. There were no further officer incursions onto their deck, and three days later they were on the ground.

Chapter Nine

They went over their Coyote, making sure all systems were operational and tie-downs were removed. They had their weapons harnesses on with common loads attached to them. It was supposed to be a secure area, but it was a war zone. You never knew.

As she was doing her final walk around, she spotted the Master Corporal they had been quartered with doing the same thing, and she walked over to him. The whole section saw her coming and lined up in front of the LAV she was approaching. They all had flak jackets and helmets on. All of them were nervous, but none had a weapon on them or mounted on the LAV.

They saw a fully armed soldier, no flak jacket on and a camouflaged ball cap on her head, approaching them. Another was loading a belt of ammo on the crew gun mounted on the Coyote's cupola.

"This is a hot zone, people," Marlene said. "You always go armed and loaded. That includes those LAVs Master Corporal. I'll be counting on you people for support, and I can't do that if you are all dead, can I?"

"S-S-Sorry, Master Sergeant," he said.

She clapped him on the shoulder. "See ya around, Black Shirts."

"Fire the bitch up, Gerry! Let's get off this goddamned tin can!" then she went to the front of the Coyote and, walking backwards, guided Gerry as he drove down the ramp, jumping up and climbing in her commander's hatch.

They drove over to their marshalling area and shut down, waiting for everyone else to unload. She and Brock walked around the Coyote's hull, unclipping and letting loose the four aerials. A hydraulic noise began, and the large mast that contained the surveillance and detection equipment deployed to its full height.

"Comms check," Marlene said. All the Zebras checked in.

"All systems functional," Shandra reported. The surveillance tower retracted back into the Coyote body. The four G-Wagons assigned to them formed up around the Coyote, two in front and two behind, checked in and shut down. They also let their four antennas loose. The gunners were arming their roof-mounted crew guns, and the troops were loading their rifles. Unlike the Zebras, they all had helmets and flak jackets on.

"Nice fucking place this," Brock said.

It was mid-morning and already hot and very dry. Dust from the landing was still in the air and getting thicker as vehicles unloaded from the transports and moved to their marshalling areas. They had received their briefings on their billet consoles on the ship and knew where they were going.

They would normally have a week to prepare, but things were deteriorating quickly. The Wind Riders were needed desperately. They would be put in a quiet sector at first, but they needed to be in the line right away.

"*Zebra One, Charley One, copy?*" Carol's command Coyote had barely come off the ramp.

"*Charley One, Zebra One, copy.*"

"*Zebra One, deploy to area of operations. Copy?*"

"*Zebra One, copy, deploy to area of operations. Out.*"

"Crank 'em up gang. We're out of here," Marlene said.

All five vehicles started up and sped out of the huge camp to the operating location. It was a four-hour drive just to get to the gravel road on which they turned west, then another hour before the first

G-Wagon split off. They would be stationed five kilometres apart in more or less a north-south line. It was after dark when they came close to the position they were supposed to occupy. They stayed at the bottom of a small hill the first night. There was no sense in setting up in the dark. They would find a spot in the morning and occupy it the next night.

Shandra deployed the surveillance mast to its full height, but they had a good view of the area anyway. Headquarters confirmed they had a good feed and were receiving feeds from the remote sensors the G-Wagons had deployed, which were patched into the Coyote's more powerful communication suites and sent back to headquarters. Other than themselves, there was nothing in the area.

Daylight came early, and Marlene and Shandra climbed the hill, crawling the last few meters. They were on the edge of a deep river valley that was about a hundred meters deep and over a kilometer wide. The enemy held the territory on the far side, so it was important that they kept surveillance on this valley. It ran for hundreds of kilometers and could be used not only for river transport but also for out of sight land transport.

A perfect position was spotted about ten meters away. It was a large natural depression with a lot of scraggly trees in and around it. They could set up there and still have good clear sightlines all in all directions. They could see about twenty kilometres into the enemy territory. It was perfect.

By the time the sun came up the next morning, the Coyote was in position, camouflage netting draped over it, invisible even ten meters away. The sensor units covered about ten kilometers into enemy territory, across the valley and deep into the valley itself. Their support base was set up ten kilometers to their rear. It had a company of Black Shirts with LAVs and three artillery guns. The next few days, the Zebras gave prospective gun target coordinates to the support base. Then everything became routine.

They ran the Coyote engine for two hours a night to recharge the batteries, but other than that, things were quiet. Listening to the nightly reports, their whole sector was quiet. Further south, the other two Black Shirt battalions had some action now and then, but there was nothing at all going on around here. It was so quiet that deer and rabbits would come right up to them and graze nearby. Marlene attached her silencer to her pistol and shot a rabbit a week so that they had fresh meat to go along with their field rations. A small freshwater spring was located in the depression, and they had fresh water all the time.

Their three weeks were almost up, and they were due to rotate back to the main camp for a week to re-equip and replenish their rations.

"Zebra One, Whiskey Romeo Charley Five, how copy?"

"Zebra One, Charley Five, copy."

"Secure transmission, Zebra One."

Marlene hit the button on her comms device and waited ten seconds. The frequency would change to a pattern every ten seconds now.

"Whiskey Romeo Charley Five, Whiskey Romeo Zebra One, copy?"

"Zebra One, Charley One, sit rep."

"Getting a nice beauty tan on the beach, boss. Lots of wonderful scenery and wildlife, over."

"Sounds nice, Zebra One. You are going to have to extend. All other assets are committed. Give us some coordinates and a time, and we will have your support base drop off some rations, fuel, and water for you."

Marlene rattled off a time two nights hence and the set of coordinates for the base of the hill.

"Copy, Zebra One. We haven't been able to contact Echo. Any way you can help us out?"

Echo was two sectors over, and they were a rookie crew.

"Wait one, Charley One."

"Shandra, is Echo still moving around or what?" Marlene asked.

"Ya, somebody is moving over there," Shandra said.

Marlene switched to the local command tactical frequency they all used. It was low powered, but coupled with the Coyote's powerful radios, she could contact any of the teams she had under her.

"Echo One, Zebra One, copy?"

She tried twice more.

"Any Echo, Zebra One, copy?"

"Zebra One, Echo Four, copy."

"Echo Four, check your coms. Charley says they are out of contact. Where is Echo One?"

"Snoozing in the bus, Zebra One. Wait one."

"Zebra, uh One. Echo One."

"Wacky Wacky Echo One. Charley One wants to know if you have a comms problem. Do you have a comms problem, Echo One?"

"No, Zebra One, no problem."

"Echo One, wait one, then contact Charley, copy."

"Copy, Zebra One."

"Charley One, Zebra One. Echo One will report in one."

"Copy, Zebra One. Charley One out."

Marlene grabbed a coffee and waited five minutes.

"Echo One, Zebra One copy?"

"Zebra One, Echo One copy."

"The next time that happens, I am coming over there and kick your ass myself. Is that clear, Echo One?"

"Copy, Zebra One."

"Stay alert, stay alive, kid. Zebra One, out."

"Fucking rookies," Brock said.

"Coming from the yahoo who kicked off my comms yesterday?" Shandra said.

"Hey, I caught it and fixed it as soon as it happened."

The next morning, Marlene shot a nice deer buck. The four troopers carried half of it down the hill that night and gave it to the troopers in the LAV that had dropped off their fuel and rations.

"Thanks guys," Marlene said. "A little fresh meat to sweeten up your pots."

"You shoot that with that big gun of yours," one of the troopers asked. "The boss will be pissed if you did."

"Nah," Brock said. He pulled his hunting knife out of his boot. "Got it with this."

The Zebra legend grew a little more that night.

The enemy started patrolling the area early the next week. In fact, it was the day after the two fireteams located to the north were relocated to another area, leaving the Zebras alone on the northern edge of the sector. They set up their small camp just inside the ten kilometer ring that the Zebras surveillance suit could detect. They were positioned right in the gap between Echo and Fox. It had two sections of troops – two five-man teams in small scout vehicles and a ten-man team in a larger armored vehicle. After lunch, the two scout vehicles split north and south and headed for the valley.

"*Echo, Foxtrot, Zebra Two,*" Shandra said. "*Be advised, two Tango Sierra vehicles are approaching your area. Get under cover, observe, and report. Copy?*"

Echo and Foxtrot acknowledged, and their remote sensor units came online in the Coyote. Brock, the vehicle gunner, activated the main gun and swung the cupola to cover the advancing scout vehicles, putting the tracking system on automatic and standby. It would now compute firing solutions on both vehicles, and as soon as Brock highlighted one of them as a target and armed the system, it would begin firing. The big twenty millimeter shells would destroy the scout vehicles with ease to just over two kilometres out, and it would only take one shot each.

Unless it was a dire emergency, all transmissions would be sent by text in an encrypted data burst between the fireteams, as well as to the rear. While Marlene grabbed her sniper rifle and spotting scope, Shandra sent a data burst to the rear informing them of the enemy activity and that they were enacting security protocols.

There was a large stand of berry bushes on the edge of the canyon. The grove was thick and tall, and the team had spent many days hollowing out the interior. It would accommodate all four of them comfortably, and it had become a home. Over time, they had created homemade chairs and an eating table. An observation slit gave them a one-hundred-and-eighty-degree view of the canyon and surrounding area. They rigged up one of the two small solar chargers outside, and it charged the little battery enough to charge two of their personal comms units and a couple of low intensity lights for the interior. They rigged the other small solar cell to charge the Coyote batteries. It was unlikely the small charging unit would ever completely charge the Coyote's batteries, but it gave them an extra couple of days before they had to turn the vehicle on to recharge them.

After the first few weeks, they noticed the wind never blew toward the enemy, always away, so they set up a small campfire ring for cooking and to drive the chill off in the cool mornings. Today, while Shandra and Brock manned the Coyote, Gerry and Marlene headed into the grove. They quickly set up the two powerful spotting scopes and monitored the two scout vehicles as they made their way almost opposite Echo's position and stopped. Even with her powerful optics, Echo was too far away for Marlene to see, and she texted Foxtrot to have a look. They saw nothing unusual. Marlene assumed the scouts had gotten out of the vehicles to look things over. She could barely see the vehicles, let alone the people. After an hour, the two vehicles headed back to their camp, and they began to relax.

Just before dusk, the two vehicles were back again, and they stopped in the same positions as earlier. Marlene could tell that someone had gotten out of the vehicles this time, as the interior lights went on as they opened the doors.

"Must be rookies," she said to Gerry. "Who leaves the lights working in the trucks?"

"That's not all, Sarge," he said. "Take a look at the camp."

Not only was there a very large bonfire taking hold in the enemy camp, but they also had lights burning all over the camp. Even with the naked eye, the enemy camp was visible, and using the spotting scope, tiny figures could be seen walking around. Marlene was just about to call it a night when the interior lights of the two scout vehicles came back on, and the headlights and tail lights came on as they started the vehicles in preparation to move. Then stupidity once again reared its ugly head.

"Romeo Whiskey Charley Echo One, Bravo Charley Tango Six, over?"

Bravo Charley Tango Six, Romeo Echo Charley Echo One, copy."

Romeo Whiskey Charley Echo One, Bravo Charley Tango Six, be advised, airborne resupply en route your location. Please supply direct coordinates, over."

Marlene was furiously typing Echo and Foxtrot to disregard, when Echo transmitted his exact coordinates. The vehicle lights shut off, as did the interior lamps, as the enemy overheard the transmission.

"Fuck!" she said, then started typing to HQ.

"Romeo Whiskey Charley Foxtrot One, Bravo Charley Tango Six, over?"

Foxtrot did not answer, and Tango Six tried three more times before switching to the Zebras, who also did not answer.

Shandra, use Echo's comms to warn that airborne resupply off. Then, when he gets in range, light him up with a Stinger, Marlene typed. The Coyote had five anti-air Stinger missiles located in an automatic pod on the rear of the vehicle. The missiles would target the aircraft with radar, then switch to heat-seeking after launch.

"Aircraft approaching my location, be advised, you are approaching a no fly zone. Any unauthorized penetration of this zone will be considered hostile and you will be fired upon."

A faint whining noise could be heard as the Coyote's weapons systems went to anti-air and began to track the inbound aircraft.

That scared him off, Shandra typed. *He is rotating over by the forward base now.*

"Romeo Whiskey Charlie Zulu One, Bravo Charlie Tango One, over?" The call came twice more.

Enemy has transmitted Echo coordinate to their base, Boss, and that there are two more of us around here as well as a forward base ten klicks to the rear. They can see the transport.

"Shit!" Marlene said.

Echo, at first light, reposition your vehicle. I would recommend you reposition yourselves ASAP.

Boss, the enemy is coming in force. Shandra sent.

Echo has been compromised. The enemy has been informed that there are two more of us nearby and now know where the firebase is. Enemy is reinforcing forward operating post. Attack of my position imminent. Marlene encrypted the message and hit send. Then she typed another message, this one to the support base warning them to get the supply transport gone as fast as possible.

It was a long and tense night, and two hours before daylight, the enemy arrived. They came in battalion strength in an armored column that drove up the valley floor and stopped, deploying with the center of the column directly opposite Echo. At dawn, they attacked.

The whole enemy column advanced across the river, which was shallow at this point and the canyon bank was not steep. The gloves were off now, and they were completely compromised.

"Grab your shit and hightail it back to the Coyote," Marlene said to Gerry. She grabbed her sniper rifle and spotting scope and began to run to as well.

"*Echo, get the fuck out of there,*" she said over the tac net. "*Foxtrot One, Zebra One, prepare to withdraw. Charley base, Zebra One, copy?*"

"*Whiskey Charley Zulu One, Bravo Charley Tango One, you will provide your coordinates and accept my resupply. Is that clear, Zulu One?*"

"*Zebra One, Charley One, disregard previous. Bravo Charley Tango One, you are not authorized on this channel. Clear channel immediate. Echo, Foxtrot, Zebra, Tac One, secure.*"

Marlene was inside the Coyote by then and jammed her sniper rifle in its rack, grabbed an ammo belt for the crew gun mounted on the cupola, put it within easy reach, opened the hatch, and manned the weapon.

"Shandra, give a firing solution to that battery on the FOB and get them firing rounds to cover Echo's withdrawal," Marlene said. "*Charley One, Zebra One, full battalion strength attack Echo's position. Attempting withdrawal, request full response.*"

"*Zebra One, Charley One, Bravo Charley on the way, ETA thirty mikes. Will monitor your frequency.*"

"Crank it up, Gerry," she yelled down into the vehicle.

"*Zebra One, Echo One, dead battery, vehicle is a no go.*"

"Fuck!" Marlene said. "*Fox One, Zebra One, proceed to Echo and extract.*"

"*Copy,*" Fox said.

"*Zebra Four, get us out of here, Zebra Two, retract the mast. Zebra Three, anti-personnel for main gun. Load smoke in launchers. FOB Sierra copy?*"

"Sierra copy."

"Sierra, lay me a smoke in front of Echo."

"Sierra copy, smoke on the way."

"Uh, Zebra One, Fox One. Catastrophic vehicle failure, copy?"

"Copy Fox One, ETA five mikes, grab all weapons and ammo, copy?"

"Copy Zebra One."

"Zebra One, Echo One, falling back, requesting permission to open fire."

"Jesus! You should be doing that already Echo! Sierra, HE both guns, 800."

"Zebra, copy HE 800." A minute later, both guns roared out, and two 105mm shells exploded in the front of the advancing battalion.

The Coyote came rushing up to the disabled Fox G-Wagon, the four troopers waiting with all their weapons and ammo boxes beside them. One team member was finishing pouring the last of the fuel over the vehicle. The front right wheel assembly was laying two meters away from the vehicle. The rear ramp was crashing down as the Coyote slid to a stop, and Fox began to toss equipment and themselves in the back. The trooper who had been pouring the fuel on the G-Wagon tossed a grenade inside it, then pelted for the Coyote, flinging himself inside. The G-Wagon exploded in a ball of fire as the Coyote sped off, closing the rear ramp as it left.

Marlene dropped inside and motioned the Fox gunner to take her spot on the cupola.

"Get somebody in the commander's hatch with your crew gun!" she yelled. "Somebody else use the rear hatch!"

"They're gonna be overrun, Boss," Shandra said.

"Boot it, Gerry!" Marlene yelled. "Sierra, HE 600 and keep it coming. Brock engage with HE as soon as you're in range. Shandra?"

"I've got the anti-armor online and am bringing the 50 up. Echo just got overrun."

"Brock, hit that fucking G-Wagon as soon as you can. Shandra, keep their IFFs locked on. Please tell me the dummy at least had them on."

The Coyote was at high speed, and it was not comfortable in the now-cramped interior as they bounced over the rough terrain. The main gun fired twice, then the cupola moved and Brock began to systematically engage the enemy's armored vehicles. One second apart, the five anti-armor rockets they carried fired off. They were still a kilometer away.

"I'm isolating Echo from the rest of the battalion," Brock said. "They've only got about twenty enemy around them."

"You Fox guys, except the gunner, get ready to dismount and provide cover for Echo." Marlene said. "Gerry, drop the ramp and keep the nose pointed at the enemy a hundred meters downrange. Shandra, pick off the four smoke from the right side then rearm with frags. Engage with the fifty when in range."

She grabbed her rifle and loaded a grenade in the launcher under the barrel. Now the machine gun on the cupola and the one the Fox trooper was manning at the rear hatch opened up. The big 50 caliber chain gun began firing in three-round bursts. Shandra put it on automatic and grabbed her rifle.

"No," Marlene said. "I need you here. Those guns are going to need ammo. You two Fox guys, with me. As soon as the ramp drops, we go left and start laying down fire. Hopefully, those Echo guys can come to us, otherwise we have to go get them."

Brock had the main gun on auto, and he began to fire the coaxially mounted machine gun. Marlene cursed as a hot expended shell casing from that gun landed on her neck. Then the ramp dropped, and she was sprinting off to the left of the Coyote, the two Fox troopers right behind her. The enemy was easy to spot because they had green uniforms on and the Wind Riders had on tan desert camo. She fired her grenade at one group, then hit the dirt and began to fire her rifle.

She fired single shots, one by one taking out the enemy holding Echo. Then Echo fought back, overwhelming their guards and retrieving their weapons, and joined the fray, making their way to the Coyote. Two were walking backwards, firing as they went. Another was supporting a trooper with a leg injury. Then sparks started joining the laser strikes on the Coyote as one of the enemy started using Echo's machine gun. He didn't last long as all the Wind Rider weapons took him out.

Sierra was using the telemetry from the Coyote to vector their fire, no longer needing Shandra to provide it, and artillery rounds were impacting every thirty seconds.

"Zebra, they are spreading out, and I can't cover them all. Reaction force has just passed us at high speed, but I would advise you get out of there ASAP," Sierra said.

The main gun on the Coyote went silent as it ran out of ammo, and the four grenade tubes on the right side fired their fragmentation grenades. Marlene sprinted for the dead enemy trooper who had used the machine gun, grabbed it and started running back to the Coyote.

"Everyone inside!" she yelled. Lasers were firing all around her as she ran. "Gerry, get moving. I am on my way!" She let her rifle dangle on its sling across her chest, both hands on the machine gun as she ran as fast as she could. Both light machine guns were firing rapid three-round bursts, tracers going over her head. Then the main gun and the coaxial gun started firing again as the Coyote turned and started slowly driving away. Marlene was the only one still running. She stumbled just a few feet from the ramp as a laser hit her right thigh, but kept her balance and waiting hands dragged her inside.

"GO! GO! GO!" Shandra yelled, and Gerry booted it. The cupola was pointed to the rear now, and the main gun fired its last rounds while the final four smoke grenades on the left launchers were fired. The ramp slammed shut, and they were safe.

"LAVs are in range and engaging," Shandra said. It was overcrowded in the Coyote now. The vehicle normally held four, but there were nine inside and two up in the hatches.

"What the fuck!" Marlene cried as Shandra opened up the seam of her right pants leg to the crotch with a knife. She had a four-inch gash in her thigh, blood was pouring down her leg. Shandra grabbed bandages out of the aid kit.

"How's Echo?" Marlene asked.

"Sprained ankle and a bunch of bruises," Shandra said. "We are ammo critical. All main gun ammo is expended, and we are down to ten rounds for the coax. Fifty is all gone, and we are using rifle clips for the crew guns."

"Ah shit! That hurts," Marlene said as Shandra poured some medical adhesive on her wound and pulled it shut. "*Charley One, Zebra One is disengaged and proceeding to firebase. Two casualties, both ambulatory. Two light vehicles destroyed. Main armament, zero ammunition, all secondary ammunition expended except for anti-air. Light ammunition below critical. Enemy attack is battalion strength, reaction force is engaging. Copy?*"

"*Copy, Zebra One. Air reinforcement in ten mikes. Have Echo, Foxtrot, and casualities return by air. Zebra to RTB, another section will be rotated in.*"

"*Copy Charley One, Zebra One out.* Fuck, Shandra, take it easy will you. That hurts worse than the fucking wound does." Shandra was wrapping a tight bandage across the thigh. The bouncing was less severe now as they were back on the road.

"*Zebra One, are you one of the casualties?*"

"*Ah, just ruined my best party pant suit, Charley One. Nothing serious.*"

"Well I have made an appointment at the salon for you guys when you get back here, keep the shiny side up, Zebra One. Charley One out."

"Ok guys," Marlene said. "Now you know why we don't talk on the radios and why we keep our vehicle batteries charged up. What happened with the Fox truck?"

"Goddamned rabbit or badger or whatever-the-hell hole collapsed on us," the Fox commander said. "Busted the goddamned whole front wheel assembly off. Jesus, can you run fast, Sarge."

"She's got lots of practice running from all you horny guys," Shandra said getting a bunch of laughs.

"Getting tickled by a laser helped a lot," Marlene said. "Nothing better than fried air whizzing by your head for motivation."

"Shit, you were hitting everything you aimed at," one of the Fox troopers who was on the ground with her said. Then his stomach growled loudly. "Hope they got some rations in camp. Haven't eaten in two days."

Brock reached into an overhead rack and brought a carton down. "Here ya go. We got two more cases left."

"What the hell?" the Fox man said.

"It seems as though I had to expend two clips of pistol ammo during the attack," Marlene said. "Or was it killing those rabbits and two deer. I get so forgetful at times."

"You assholes," one of the Echo guys said. "Why didn't we think of that?"

"Which is why we are Zebras and you are Wind Riders," Brock said. "Think outside the box, our boss does."

"Got a bucket of fresh berries here if you want," Shandra said, opening up a plastic bucket full of them. "Here, Boss." She handed Marlene a roll of duct tape.

Marlene took a look at her wound, saw the blood was no longer soaking the bandages, pulled the edges of her pant leg together, and wrapped the leg with three rows of duct tape, one just above the wound, one below, and the last at her ankle.

Chapter Ten

The Coyote slowed down and turned into the firebase at last. The two artillery pieces were firing as fast as they could, filling the compound with noise as they went off. The ramp descended, and the noise increased. Two more guns were slung under two transports that landed as soon as the guns were unlatched from them. Troops came pouring out, and the two Wind Rider fireteams got in. One can of ammo for the coax machine gun was tossed into the Coyote along with two boxes of rifle ammo, then the ramp closed, shutting off some of the noise. Then Gerry accelerated out of the firebase and headed back to headquarters.

Brock dragged the coax ammo over to its storage rack and put it in, then joined Shandra and Marlene loading rifle ammo into empty clips. Once he loaded the first one, he climbed up and inserted it in the light machine gun mounted on the cupola, then came back down. It used the same ammunition the rifles used and could use the same clips once the belt-fed ammunition was expended.

"Guy on the back gun burnt out two barrels," he said. "That one up there probably is done, too. I'll probably have to change the coax barrel as well."

"Rather loose barrels and ammo instead of people," Marlene said. "Hope that stupid Echo kid learned his lesson. What are they teaching them over there? He was just out of training and on his first deployment."

"It was a quiet sector, Boss," Brock said. "Those guys were just patrolling. They probably would have left the next day. That stupid transport guy is more to blame."

"Ah, Boss?" Gerry said. "We've got a problem. I'm almost out of fuel."

"What do you mean we are almost out of fuel? Didn't you check it last night?"

"Ya." Gerry said. "I swear it was full last night."

"Okay, we are far enough away now," Marlene said. "Pull over and we'll fuel it up with the jerry cans. We could use the fresh air anyway."

The Coyote came to a stop, and the rear ramp came down. For the first time since they had started the action, Gerry opened his driver's hatch. He shut the Coyote off and clambered out, walking to the rear rack where the spare fuel was kept.

Marlene hobbled over to the side of the road and gingerly stretched out her cramped muscles. That's when she noticed the pool of fluid running from under the vehicle.

"Hey Brock, check that out, will you?" she said pointing.

Brock walked over and bent down.

"Looks like we got a hole in the tank, Sarge," he said.

Gerry jumped down from the hull, went on his back, and crabbed under the Coyote.

"Yup," Gerry said. "Got a 5.56 hole in the bottom left corner of the tank. You two ladies got a spare tampon?"

Marlene dug into one of her cargo pockets and pulled one out. She tossed it under the vehicle to him.

"Okay, now I need some gum, that roll of duct tape, and the rest of the tube of that medical glue."

Brock tossed him a stick of gum, and Shandra brought the tape and adhesive.

"Okay, that's got it," Gerry said a couple of minutes later. He wiggled his way back out from under the Coyote, then sat up, the front of his uniform and his hands stained with diesel fuel.

"What did you need the gum for if you had all the other stuff?" Brock said.

Gerry unwrapped the gum and popped it in his mouth. "Knew it was your last stick and you wouldn't give it to me," he said, then laughed. He started fuelling with the two spare fuel cans.

Three hours later, they were back at the main camp and headed to the vehicle maintenance area. Marlene asked to speak with the head mechanic.

"Hey Warrant," Marlene said sticking out her hand. "Master Sergeant Isabelle, Zebras."

"Holy shit, where you guys been? Warrant Black." He said shaking her hand.

The Coyote was drawing a crowd. It had scorch marks all around the hull and more than a few dents from where the machine gun rounds had hit it. The bluing was all gone from the machine gun barrels, and the stock of the pintle-mounted one was scorched. The paint was all gone from the main gun, and there were gunpowder stains and missing paint on the grenade launchers and auxiliary weapons systems. If it wasn't clear the vehicle had been hard used, Shandra and Brock came out of the vehicle kicking expended machine gun and main gun casings in front of them. Then his eyes dropped to Marlene's leg, seeing the blood-stained and duct-taped pants.

"Regular day at the office, Warrant," Marlene said before he could ask the question. "I wonder if you could tell me why a vehicle that is supposed to be armored to deflect a 12mm round is almost put out of action by a 5.56 round to the gas tank?"

"What?" he said. "No way. Those tanks are supposed to be armoured." He went down on his back and crawled underneath the Coyote. "No shit!" he crawled back out.

"Not only that, but they are supposed to be self-sealing fuel cells, not metal tanks," he said. "How the hell did that happen?"

"One of our teams got overrun, and the enemy used the squad gun against us," Marlene said.

"I wonder how long this has been going on?" the Warrant said. "There has been a lot of shady shit going on in the latest vehicles. Got two that had engine failures within a couple of days. Okay, leave it to me. I got a few spare fuel cells here. We'll swap out that main gun as well. There are a couple of brass hat chair warmers that use their LAVs for personal transport around the base. We'll slap a new coat of paint on yours and swap them. They'll never notice. We'll give your lady a good work over, don't you worry, Master Sergeant."

"Thanks Warrant," Marlene said shaking his hand again. "There are a couple of buckets of fresh local berries inside, Warrant. Enjoy."

The Zebras were drawing a lot of stares as they walked toward their barracks down the pristine streets of the base. Few of the rear area troops were armed, and those that were had pistols strapped on web belts around their hips. Their uniforms were starched, clean, and had sharp creases.

The four Zebras were walking abreast down the middle of the street. Their uniforms were dusty, wrinkled, and sweat-stained. The top three buttons of their shirts were open, and instead of berets, they wore dirty tan ball caps. Not one of them was showing any badges except for the camo pattern planet badge on their right shoulders, and that was small. They had their pistols up high, attached to the left side of their weapons harnesses. The two women had their long sniper rifles slung across their backs, Brock his crew weapon. All four of them had the rifles slung across their chests, barrel down, with clips installed and right hands on the stocks just behind the trigger guards, thumbs on safeties. Large knives were sown on the outside of their pant legs.

They were laughing and cracking jokes at each other as they walked and were almost at their barracks when a shiny military police vehicle stopped beside them and two troopers got out and approached them. They didn't even slow down as they walked up to the policemen, but the safeties were clicked off.

"Look guys," Marlene said. "We just got back to base. We haven't been home for four weeks and were in a firefight this morning. So unless you want to be laying in this street bleeding out, I would recommend you get the hell out of our way."

"Hey, no problem," the sergeant said. "Some chair warming major said some bad people were wandering his base disrupting everything. Not good for efficiency or moral he said. Me, I didn't see anything. Did you, Corporal?"

"Nope, nothing unusual around here," the corporal said. "You guys want a lift?"

"Nah, our barracks are just two doors down," Shandra said. "Thanks for the offer though, cutie. Rain check? Just ask for Sergeant Shandra of the Zebras."

"Who'd want to go out with you?" Gerry asked. "Christ, you're a mess. Don't you ever change that crappy uniform? It stinks."

"Like yours smells like roses," Marlene said.

The two MPs just shook their heads and smiled. Just as the Zebras were about to go in their barracks, another clean but not shiny G-Wagon pulled up. Carol got out of the passenger seat. The Zebras came to attention and saluted.

"Shit, you guys smell," Carol said, returning their salutes. Then her eyes dropped to Marlene's leg. "You three, go shower, get on some clean uniforms, and get over to the mess hall. You, Master Sergeant, get your ass in that backseat."

"Hey you, Mr. MP. I want a high-speed escort to medical!"

"What are you talking about?" Marlene said. "This is just a scratch. Shandra patched me up. It's all good."

Then Carol grabbed her under the arms as she collapsed.

"Shit, getting dark out here," Marlene said, then passed out. None of them but Carol had noticed the blood running down over her boot.

Her eyes snapped open, and her right hand reached for a weapon but was hampered by a bunch of tubes attached to it. Her eyes followed the tubes and saw one was attached to a blood bag and another to a bag of some kind of clear liquid. There was a clip attached to her index finger that had a cord leading to a monitor. She was in a hospital gown and lying on a bed. Her wounded left leg was free of the blanket, the thigh heavily bandaged and elevated on a pillow.

A nurse popped in, stuck a thermometer in her mouth, and checked the monitor and the fluid drips. She then checked the thermometer and wrote everything down on the chart hung at the foot of the bed. She filled a plastic cup with water from a jug and put a bent straw in it before giving it to Marlene.

"Sorry," she said. "It's just water. Doc is on his way."

"Nectar of the gods," Marlene said. "Just what I needed. Mouth was real dry."

"Well, well, super girl is finally awake," the doctor said, breezing onto the room. He took a look at the chart, then took out his flashlight and checked her eyes.

"You've been out for a day," he said. "That is your fourth bag of blood. You damn near bled out, my dear. That long walk you made from the maintenance facility to your barracks tore open all that good work your medic did. You've been given a complete workup of antibiotics, and we are just about to remove the bandages and make sure everything is still okay."

Marlene winced as they pulled the tape off and removed the pressure bandage.

"Shit," she said. "Now I'm going to have to wax both legs so they look the same."

The doctor chuckled. "That's the spirit," he said. He poked around a bit at the wound. "Okay, it's closed nicely and no infection. Can you lift the leg and flex the knee for me?" Marlene did as requested, although it felt more like an instruction.

"Not too much discomfort?" he asked. "Normally, I would let you out of here tomorrow, but I hear you like to run and don't like following orders. Plus, you were dehydrated. So, you get to be our guest for a week. You spend the rest of the day in bed, and if things look better tomorrow, we will unhook those IVs and you can start wandering the halls a bit."

"What about the trooper with the bad leg?" Marlene asked.

"Corporal Jensen has a badly sprained ankle," the doctor said, "along with a lot of bruises from the beating he took. He was released this morning. He kept stopping in to check on you."

"Good," Marlene said. "He'll be buying me a beer as soon as I get out of here, too."

"Ya, he mentioned it was his fault you were in here. Okay, try and get some more sleep. You were pretty worn out. Oops, she's out again."

It was dim in the room when she woke up again. The sun had gone down. The door to her room was closed, and only a dim light above her bed and the monitor still hooked up to her finger provided any illumination in the room. A water jug and plastic cup were sitting on a small portable table by her bed, so she gingerly dragged it over and poured herself a glass. She only had a half full IV of clear fluid hooked up now. The monitor must have been connected to the nurses' station because a nurse walked in almost immediately, leaving the door open, and again stuck a thermometer in Marlene's mouth, checked the monitor, then wrote in the chart.

"No pain in the leg?" This nurse was much older, about forty, and she had major's bars on her shoulder boards. "What?" she asked, noticing Marlene looking at the shoulder boards. "An officer can't look after the famous Zebra Master Sergeant?"

"Sorry, Ma'am," Marlene said. "I know all of you are officers. I just didn't expect one of such high rank working the nightshift. Ma'am."

"I always take the Friday and Saturday night shifts," the major said. "Gives the young ones time to party. Now, no pain in the leg? Any wooziness?"

"No. It's a little stiff and pinches a bit, but it feels okay," Marlene said. "I think I could eat a horse though."

"I have some in the fridge for you," the major said. "It's rubber chicken hospital food, but it's edible. I'll just warm it up and be right back."

"Oh God, heaven!" Marlene said after the first bite. "And it smells fantastic. I've been eating nothing but crap coming out of a tube or packet for so long, I forgot what real food tastes like."

"You must have been out there a long time calling this real food," the major said and laughed.

"Well, we had some fresh rabbit and deer, and a few fresh berries, but no real veggies," Marlene said. "Can I get up tomorrow and start walking around? I promise I won't overdo it. We are really short-staffed out there, and I need to be back on duty as soon as I can."

"I don't make those calls, Master Sergeant, the doctor does," the major said. "We want to make sure you don't reopen that wound. If you do, your stay with us will be much longer."

"I get it," Marlene said. "That's okay. I can catch up on my beauty sleep without those other noisy mugs around me."

"That's the spirit," the major said. "I'll be back in a few minutes, after I toss this garbage out and fill out some paperwork."

Marlene's eyes closed again as the major walked out of the room. She came back a couple of minutes later and saw Marlene was sleeping. She took her communicator out of her pocket and pushed a button.

"She woke up and ate a meal, my lord," she said. "She is stable, and the leg has no long-term damage and is causing her no discomfort. If she were anybody else, I would kick her loose tomorrow, but we both know she would overdo it the first day and be back in here. She still needs to fill out her after-action report and will probably have to testify at the board, my lord. Yes, it is very serious, my lord. Well, let's put it this way, my lord, the Black Shirts didn't have a lot of work to do when they got there. She and her gang had chewed them up pretty good. Yes, my lord, I will keep you informed."

She put the communicator back in her pocket and walked into the room. She checked the monitor again and then looked down at Marlene.

"You always were a tough one, love," she said gently stroking the scar on her cheek. Marlene opened her eyes and held the hand on her cheek.

"I thought I recognized your voice," Marlene said. "You were the one treating me before I was fully awake, weren't you? And you are the head surgeon, not a nurse."

"Yes and yes," the major said.

"Is he angry?" Marlene asked.

"Duncan? Mad at you? Never," the major said. "'Tell her to leave some enemy for the Black Shirts next time,' he said. He, and we, are concerned about you is all. I wasn't kidding. You are the most headstrong, stubborn person I have ever met. But this time, love, where this wound is, if you push it too hard, you will only hinder the healing. If you take it easy now, in a couple of weeks, you'll be almost back to normal."

"Almost?" Marlene said.

"Well, short skirts will probably be a no-go anymore," the Major said.

"The only guy I care about won't care," Marlene said. Then she was asleep again.

"I know, love, I know," the Major said.

Chapter Eleven

C arol came in the next morning with some tacky kids' balloons that she attached to the foot of the bed.

"How is the sick little princess today?" she said, playing mother by fussing over the covers and kissing her on the forehead.

"Okay, okay, rub it in," Marlene said. "Tell them to let me the hell out of here, will you? It's quieter and more relaxing out on a hillside than here."

"No can do, princess," Carol said. "Doc says a week, so a week it shall be. Besides, your Coyote will be in the shop at least that long. In addition to your shit fuel tank, you've got the same crappy bearings the other Coyotes have in their engines. Two of the LAVs that came to relieve you guys blew up their engines as well. Same thing, shitty main bearings. We are taking the engines out of the chair warmers' LAVs, swapping the bearings out, and reinstalling them in the wrecked units. Those yahoos should not have LAVs anyway.

"So it'll be a couple of weeks before your unit is ready. It just seems to be this latest batch of vehicles that are affected, all of them, of course, with this battalion of Black Shirts and our new Coyotes. Nobody would have noticed the fuel tanks if you guys hadn't taken that hit. Again, just this battalion and our new vehicles are affected."

"Somebody is getting a big kickback," Marlene said.

"Oh, ya," Carol said. "The boss is pissed. Big time. He's already canceled all the other contracts. Some firm in Ukraine is sending us a Coyote and LAV prototype to test. We have our own people working on the powertrain, but I think the boss wants to keep everything in house now.

"You really impressed the hell out of those kids, Marlene. All the rookies and your three malcontents are out in the boonies boning up on hiding in plain sight and bushcraft every day, even the kid with the sprained ankle."

"I hope you were not too hard on him, Carol," Marlene said. "I gave him enough shit already."

"Naw, I just gave him a dirty look," she said. "I'm really pissed at that supply major. He's the same jerk that was causing all the trouble on the transport."

"Ah shit, just what I needed, more tacky balloons," Marlene said as all the Zebras walked in.

Each of them had four helium balloons. Brock untied one from his string and inhaled a bit of it.

"Nothing but the best for the boss," he said in his helium-squeaky voice.

"Who are we?" he asked as the others took a hit of helium.

"Zebras."

"What are we born and bred for?"

"To run."

"What do we love to do?"

"Kick enemy ass."

"Zebras, Zebra, Zebras, Hoorah."

Even Carol had taken part and everyone was howling in laughter. A nurse gave them a dirty look as she walked by.

"Hey, come on, I need to walk a bit, and there is a lounge at the end of the hall," Marlene said as she swung her legs out of the bed and stood.

"Here," Shandra said taking a pair of uniform pants out of a bag and tossing them at Marlene. "You have a nice ass and all, but I really don't need it shoved in my face."

"Jealous?" Carol asked. "I am. Mine is not nearly as shapely."

"Maybe it would be if you got out from behind that desk more often," Marlene said. She quickly shrugged into the pants, and they walked over to the lounge. The doctor found them just before suppertime.

"Okay, I need her for a minute," the major said. "Why don't you comedians give us all a break and wait for her down in the cafeteria. I won't keep her long."

"Drop the pants, Missy," the doctor said after they were back in the room. She removed the bandage, poked and pressed a bit, then had her move the leg back and forth a few times while she looked at the wound. Then she bandaged it and tossed a shirt at Marlene.

"Okay, missy, off you go," she said. "But take it easy and as soon as that leg bothers you at all, back up here. Got it? No boots yet."

Marlene hurriedly dressed and walked out of the room headed for the cafeteria.

"This food is almost as good as that deer you shot, Boss," Gerry said.

"You what?" Carol said. "You shot a deer and gave that kid shit?"

"Deer was only twenty yards away," Marlene said. "I popped him with my Sig. Had the silencer on."

"Oh, that's okay then," Carol said.

Now they all had their Wind Rider and rank flashes on. Black berets laying on the table with the Wind Rider brass badge very prominent. They were sitting by themselves off in a corner, but everyone else in the canteen was looking at them. Carol left them after a few minutes, and the four friends stayed together until visiting hours were over.

Marlene was up at daybreak the next morning and walked ten laps of the hallways before she stopped at the nurses' station and told them she was going to the cafeteria for breakfast. After breakfast, her nurse changed the bandage, and Marlene headed to the small hospital gym and started pushing weights. She tried the stationary bike, riding slow and with no pressure. She only went a mile, then she went to the chin up bar and did twenty.

By then it was lunchtime and back to the cafeteria. Then she had a snooze. The major came in that afternoon, removed the bandage, and checked the leg again. There was no leakage, and she just put on a protective bandage this time. Then the Zebras were back, this time with some really tacky greeting cards. They all went down to the cafeteria until the end of visiting hours again.

This time, instead of going back to her room, she went back to the gym and worked out again. The major and the physio tech kept an eye on her as she worked out. In three days, Marlene was running on the treadmill, slowly at first. Every day she went a little further and a little faster. The same with the stationary bike, a little faster, longer, and with more tension. After five days, she was running five miles and doing the same on the bike. That night, the major let her out.

Her first stop was the barracks, where she composed a long and mushy text to Duncan on her laptop in their own secure code and routed through their own special accounts. Her next stop was the junior ranks. She was on her third beer when the rest of the Zebras showed up. All four of them staggered the two blocks back home that night.

The next morning, she was up before the rest of them. She took her weapons harness, made sure she had five full clips, inserted another in her rifle, and ran to the firing range. She was the only one there. There were no targets, but she found a permanent feature on the berm backing the range and used it for a target. As the designated marksman for her team, her rifle barrel was two inches longer than a regular trooper's and had a grenade launcher mounted under the barrel. This made the weapon longer and heavier, and not as easy to use in close quarters, but she was used to it.

The spot she was aiming at was two hundred and twenty meters away, instead of the normal two hundred, where the targets normally would be. She used the built-in bipod and the firing table for the first clip, firing single-round shots slowly until the clip was empty. Then she let the barrel cool down and picked up the expended cartridges, dumping them in the large used fuel barrel.

She lay on the ground for the next clip, using the bipod for the first half of the clip, then without it for the next half. Again. she let the barrel cool down and collected all the brass. The next clip, she fired with one knee on the ground, propping her left elbow on the other knee. She fired the first half of the clip single shot, pausing a second between each shot, and the rest of the clip she rapid-tapped three shots at a time until the clip was empty.

The next clip she fired five single shots standing up, then five rapid taps, and the final fifteen at three shot burst auto fire. This time, after she picked up all the brass, she put the new clip in the rifle, slung it across her chest, and ran back to the barracks.

After she ran off the range, Amanda, Ann, Megan and Carol walked out from among the shadows and to the berm. The hole in the berm Marlene had made with all one hundred shots was no bigger than the top of a beer can.

"Goddamn, she's good!" Megan commented.

The next morning, Marlene was back at the range. This time, she went to the long-range portion of it and had her big rifle with her. She went through the same routine, but only five shots at each position and she started from the standing position. This rifle was bolt action, so she could not fire automatic or semi-automatic bursts, but the shots were still quick. The spot she chose was six hundred and twenty meters away.

When the three women checked after Marlene had left, the result was the same as the day before.

"Damn," Amanda said. "Can you imagine what would happen if she and Duncan teamed up on a mission? They could probably take out ten of us before we even figured out where they were."

"More like twenty," Carol said. "Duncan took out ten himself from that distance using a 7.62, on his own, with no spotter and no backup. Using those fifties? We wouldn't even hear the shots. They'd hit us from a klick away."

Marlene was just pressing the bullet into her last casing when Carol walked into the barracks. Marlene made all her own sniper bullets.

"Duncan doesn't even do that," Carol said. "He has them custom-made for him."

"He has more money than I do," Marlene said, polishing up the brass on the bullet and placing it in a custom-made bullet case. There were a hundred bullets in it. She would only put them in the clips when she was on a mission.

"Remember that Black Shirt major that was causing all the trouble on the transport?" Carol asked. "He was the idiot that got you guys spotted. He was trying to save money. Said it was more efficient to fly them in."

"More efficient, eh?" Marlene said. "Cost us two G-Wagons."

"Acceptable losses, he said, considering we pretty much wiped out a whole enemy battalion," Carol said. "Oh, he has been arrested and is being shipped back home to face trial. It seems he was also the one approving all the changes on the vehicle specs. He tried to justify it, saying it was saving us money. What he didn't say was that he was pocketing more than he was saving us. His screw-up was with the engine bearings. We probably would never have found out about the fuel tanks if that enemy gunner hadn't put a hole in your tank."

"So, Tanya is off the hook then?"

"For that, yes," Carol said. "The vehicles from Ukraine didn't pan out, so we will still obtain the vehicle bodies from Oaken. But everything else and the final assembly, we will do ourselves."

"No biggie to me," Marlene said. "As long as the damn things don't break down on us in the field, I'm happy."

"You'll be a lot happier after your five years are up," Carol said. "Shelly invested half your money between the assembly plant and the power plant assembly factory. We already have a lot of orders for the power plants, mostly civilian use. The civilian version of the G-Wagons, with all our power plants and upgraded interiors, are commanding top dollar from the rich and famous. We have a big waiting list."

"Three years is still a long way off," Marlene said. "I'm only thinking day-to-day right now."

"Why don't you let me help you?" Carol said. "With all the evidence we have gathered, I can get your sentence annulled."

"No, leave it be," Marlene said. "I owe these kids. If I pull strings and use my relationships to get ahead, how am I different from the people in the system we are trying to replace?"

They were relaxing at the table they had claimed as their own in the junior ranks club. It was back by the front door and in the corner. As it was far from the bar, it was the least favourite of the patrons anyway. The place was usually populated by off-duty support troops of the Black Shirts, or those who were back at base for repairs or a week off from the lines. At rare times, enlisted Wind Riders would come in, but unless they knew the Zebras, they sat at their own tables, close by. The Zebras didn't mind. They were different from the other troopers, and they knew it.

Marlene had just finished telling the gang about the latest development. Echo and Foxtrot would be part of their section for the rest of the tour, bringing their number to twelve. The other two units would be bringing their personal gear over to the almost empty barracks the Zebras were using now.

Warrant Jensen, the vehicle maintenance foreman, and his sergeant came over and sat down. He motioned the waitress for a round.

"We mounted and did preliminary tests on your main gun today," he said. "The engine is purring like a kitten, and the fuel cell has been mounted and properly armoured. You can take her out to the range tomorrow and test her out. It's all set up."

"What about our replacement G-Wagons?" Marlene asked.

"Came in the day before yesterday," the sergeant said. "Four came in and you have been issued three. They all operate fine, and the electronics seem to be okay, but we really don't know how most of that stuff works. You can come and get them anytime you want."

"Seven tomorrow morning too soon?" Marlene said.

"Hell, I'm just getting out of bed at seven," Jensen said. "But the sarge here and a few of his guys will be there."

"Ya," the sergeant said. "We're working a lot of overtime, pumping through four LAVs and a Coyote every week, not including the regular maintenance and breakdowns."

"Well," Gerry said. "We appreciate all the hard work, Sarge. If our engine had crapped out there on that canyon, we wouldn't be here right now."

"Seeing all the burn marks and dents on your Coyote kind of brings it home for us," Jensen said. "Not to mention the spent shell casings and the blood and bandages on the floor. Most times, the vehicles come in dirty and muddy, and we clean them up, change the oil, stuff like that, and then bitch about how dirty they are inside and out. Then yours comes in, paint missing, guns burnt out, and a trooper bandaged up and limping away with a bloody uniform, and it gets very real."

"When was the last time you had your guys on the range?" Marlene asked.

"Just before we shipped out," Jensen said. "Why?"

"If that battalion had broken through," Brock said. "The only thing stopping them would have been the firebase full of support troops. What happens if one of your vehicle recovery teams gets ambushed? We have a lot of technology that the bad guys want. They took all of Echo's weapons and ammo. Right now, we have the advantage over everyone because of our weapons systems."

"Kind of hard to get my guys motivated," Jensen said, "being way back behind the lines, and this is not exactly the big war they were telling us it was."

"That's because the other side is regrouping," Shandra said. "Our side was not the aggressors. They don't want to go on the offensive. They are happy with what they have. It's not going to stay that way."

"Why don't you schedule one of your recovery teams to come with us?" Gerry said. "They can bring us back if we break down."

"Might be fun for us," the sergeant said. "That last major didn't want to spend the money on live fire training."

"Let me guess," Marlene said. "Waste of money?"

"Ya," Jensen said. "He was running it like the old corporations back on Oaken. Cuts all over the place, making his numbers look good, and forgetting the reason why we are here."

"And pocketing the profits," Marlene said. "I imagine he is looking for a new job and home right now."

"All the officers are worried," Jensen said. "The commander is supposed to be on the next transport. Good, I say. It's time they got their asses kicked. Ever since the last commander got railroaded, things have gone to shit. She was a hard ass, but she was a fair hard ass, and we got whatever we needed as long as we got results. She never would have put up with this shit."

"Ya," Brock said. "I heard she was a real fire dragon. Wonder what ever happened to her?"

"All kinds of rumours flying about," the sergeant said. "Some say she might be fighting over on the other side of this deal. Others say she is serving as a common trooper with the Marauders, or that she is working on some farm in the back and beyond. Ya, she was a tough one alright. Damn near killed lord Duncan himself once."

"Thanks for the beer," Marlene said. "I have to go make sure my two rookie fireteams are not destroying our barracks."

"Takes her job real serious doesn't she?" Jensen asked after Marlene walked out. "She's a lot older than you guys. They put the old vet in with you to season you guys up?"

"Don't know what her real story is," Gerry said. "We all went through PIG basic together. She showed up at the transport center in Oaken with just the clothing she was wearing. Didn't have a penny to her name."

The rest of the Zebras thanked the warrant for the beer and also left. The warrant looked at the sergeant.

"Big scar on the left side of her cheek? Tough as nails, shows up penniless right after? You don't think?"

"Nah," the sergeant said. "No way would the Wind Riders would let her anywhere near them, not after what she did."

The lights in the barracks snapped on full, and Marlene started to yell. All the Zebras were fully dressed and armed, hollering along with her.

"Let's go, let's go, let's go! You guys have slept in! It's five thirty and we have five miles to run to the maintenance shop and get our vehicles by seven! Combat loads! Move it, move it!"

Twenty minutes, later Echo and Foxtrot were lined up in front of the barracks. Marlene looked at the two designated marksmen in the fireteams. Neither had their sniper rifles with them. Marlene's and Shandra's were on their backs.

"You two forget something?" Marlene asked. "Go back and get them. You had better have caught us before we reach the maintenance depot." Then she turned and started running.

They ran into the maintenance yard at five to seven. Three lines of four, all their weapons and basic loads for them on their bodies. She had pushed them hard, and all were breathing heavy at the end, none more so than the other two snipers. They were bent over, hands on knees, and the Echo sniper vomited.

Marlene walked over to him and handed him her water bottle.

"Not bad, kid," she said. "Wait until you do that with one of these fifty cal monsters and a hundred rounds of ammo. Adds another ten pounds to the load."

"Jesus, Master Sergeant," he said. "I don't know how you do it."

"Practice, kid," she said patting him on the shoulder and taking the water bottle back. "Lots of practice."

"OK guys," she said. "We've got an extra G-Wagon. As a reward for catching us in time, the two snipers get to drive it. Load all your shit in the tin cans, and then follow us in our newly rebuilt Coyote to the firing range."

Everyone headed to their vehicles and stowed their weapons and gear. Brock opened the gunner's hatch and mounted his crew gun on the pintle, then dropped back down and began his main gun systems check. Shandra was already working on her electronics, and Marlene was checking hers. Gerry clambered into the driver's compartment and started flipping switches.

"*Check in,*" Marlene said on the Coyote internal comm system.

"*Two, three, four,*" came the reports. Then she clambered up to the commander's hatch and looked around. Everyone, including the two LAV recovery vehicles, seemed to be ready to go.

"*Zebra Section, Zebra One, comms check,*" she said.

"*Echo One, Foxtrot One, Echo Two, Tango One, Uniform One.*"

"*Zebra Section, Zebra One, crank 'em up.*"

Six starters whined, and blue exhaust came belching out as all six engines started. Turrets and guns on the coyote and the LAVs began to move as the gunners tested them.

"*Two, three, four,*" the Zebras checked in. If there had been a problem, they would have said so. All of Marlene's systems were working properly.

"*Echo, Foxtrot, Tango, Uniform, Zebra Junior.*" Marlene laughed at the last one. The kid has a sense of humour she thought.

"*Echo on point,*" she said. "*Foxtrot the rear, Tango after Echo, Zebra, Zebra Junior, then Uniform. Move out, people.*"

Marlene manned the machine gun, Echo's gunner was manning his, Tango had their turret pointing to the left, and their commander, like Marlene, was operating the machine gun. The Coyote turret swung to the right. Marlene looked behind her. Uniform was traversing its turret to point to the rear and slightly left, her commander pointing his machine gun to the right. Foxtrot's gunner was pointing to the left, but forward. Junior didn't have a gun.

Good, Marlene thought, they are taking this seriously.

The little convoy made their way about five kilometers out of the base, where a large flat area had been turned into a firing range for the heavy weapons. Old civilian vehicles had been planted from two hundred meters to two thousand meters across the area as targets. The vehicles came to a stop, and the G-Wagons pulled over to a parking area just at the edge of the range. All the troopers dismounted and congregated in front of the Zebra's Coyote.

The vehicle gunners and, in the LAVs case, the commanders, would each fire their main gun, the coax gun, and the mounted machine gun with half their stored munitions while stationary. The rest of the troopers would go to the far edge and fire their personal weapons, again using half their ammo. Marlene would supervise and spot for Shandra when she shot her sniper rifle.

The LAV crews had not been given a lot of practice time and were having fun putting holes in the old vehicles. Even the ten Wind Riders were enjoying themselves. It was always more fun to shoot an object rather than a target with bullseye rings . Too soon, they were all through the first half of the training and Marlene gave them time for a break, except for the three snipers and their spotters.

Where the rifle practice had been at two hundred meters, she started the snipers off at three hundred and moved them out in one hundred meter increments until they were at the eight hundred meter maximum effective range of the rifles. Then she told everyone to take a break.

"Just a little curious, Master Sergeant," Warrant Jenson said. "Don't you need some practice, too?"

Marlene wagged her finger at him, then walked over to the Coyote and pulled out her assault rifle, weapons harness with pistol attached, and the big rifle. Donning and adjusting the weapons harness she walked a hundred yards ahead of the firing line, put the big gun on the ground, and slung the assault rifle across her chest. Then she quickly drew her silencer-equipped pistol from its holster and fired the full clip at a car one hundred yards away. She holstered it, then fired the assault weapon. The first clip was at three hundred yards standing, then four hundred from a knee, the next five hundred laying down, and the last six hundred with the bipod extended.

Now it was the big gun's turn. She fired three shots at three hundred yards standing, three at four hundred kneeling, three at five hundred kneeling, three at six, and seven lying down. Then she changed clips and extended the bipod. The first three shots were at eight hundred, then she shifted to one thousand.

It took her some time to calculate the wind and dial in the scope. She chose a smaller car. She targeted through the scope, fired the first shot, ejected the round, and fired the second before the first had hit the car, then the third.

Both Wind Rider spotters and Shandra had been watching the car with their spotting scopes.

"Holy shit," the Fox' spotter said. "All three shots an inch apart in a perfect line."

"And that, my good man," Marlene said, "is why you are still a corporal and a master marksman and I am a master sergeant and a master sharpshooter."

She picked up all her sniper rifle shell casings and put them in a cargo pocket, then went back to the Coyote, loaded fresh clips in her assault rifle and pistol, and stowed everything away.

"Right," she said. "Back to work."

For the next exercise, they would simulate an ambush on the column. The spare G-Wagon would not be used so that Echo and Foxtrot could have full vehicles. They drove off a kilometer and came back to the range at convoy speed at a predetermined distance, Marlene yelled, "contact left!" All the turrets swung left, and Marlene and the other machine gunners opened fire. Then the main armament opened fire, still on the move. The G-Wagons swung in and to the side of the LAVs so the bigger vehicles covered them. The armored vehicles swung so their noses were facing the range, and the rear ramps thumped to the ground. All the dismounts deployed in defensive positions and began to fire. Then Shandra deployed the remote weapons pods on the Coyote and rippled off two rockets and a five-second burst from the fifty caliber chain gun.

"Not bad, guys," Marlene said. "Not bad."

The warrant told her he wanted to repaint the now scorched and bubbled paint on the Coyote's gun, so the Zebras unloaded their gear and surrendered the vehicle to the techs and took over the spare G-Wagon. Then, back in column formation, they returned to base, the G-Wagons to the marshalling area and the armoured vehicles to the maintenance bay.

The rest of the day, they cleaned their weapons, and Marlene reloaded her spent big gun ammunition. They had set up an unused part of the barracks for this purpose.

"So, guys," Marlene said, "everyone ready to go back out in the field? I'm getting a little bored sitting around here." Everyone agreed with her.

"You rookies are not going to screw up like the last time? Unseen and unnoticed until we have no choice. Right?"

Everyone agreed again.

"Okay, I'll let the Colonel know we are ready then," Marlene said. "Be ready, but you know the army. Hurry up and wait."

They were sent their mission orders ten minutes later. They were going back out in the morning.

Chapter Twelve

The Zebras ran into the maintenance yard with their full 60 pound combat loads, this time at precisely seven in the morning. All of the techs and mechanics who had trained with them the day before were lined up waiting. A huge tarp was draped over the Coyote, and, at a nod from Jensen, the tarp was pulled off. They must have worked all night. The Coyote was freshly painted and cleaned – not even the tires were dirty. On the slanted nose of the Coyote was the normal Wind Rider wolfhounds snarling head, but on both sides of the cupola, instead of the rider astride a wolfhound, this rider was firing rifle astride a zebra in full flight.

The inside was spotless. Mounted on the bulkhead over the loading ramp was a plaque made out of expended shell casings. It had a slogan on it.

Zebras: Born To Run, Trained To Kill Lions.

Marlene made sure she shook the hand of each tech and mechanic and thanked them.

"You didn't have to do that, Warrant Jensen," she said.

"Yes, I did, my lady," Jensen said. "Yes, I did. I wasn't always a maintenance trooper, Ma'am. I had the honour to serve as one of your assault troopers, Ma'am. I know what you did, how hard you worked to form this battle group. Don't worry, Ma'am, I'm the only one who knows and I'm not spilling the beans. Just do me a favour and bring her back in one piece, eh?"

Then he stood to attention and saluted her.

The new position was twenty kilometres north of the last one, but still on the banks of the big canyon, which was two kilometres wide at this point and not as steep. Their side of the bank was well-treed, and it was easy to conceal the Coyote and construct their hidden observation post. They could easily observe ten kilometres inside enemy territory, and the surveillance suite range extended to twelve kilometres on that side.

This time, their support and rapid response base had a full company of Black Shirt combat troops and three of the heavy artillery pieces. The Black Shirts conducted intermittent patrols with their LAVs, as did the enemy on the other side. Occasionally, either when heading out or returning to base, the LAVs would drop off rations or fuel if they called for it, which was not often.

The woods and surrounding area were full of wildlife, and the field rations were often supplemented with fresh game, fruits, and edible mushrooms. This time, the Zebras had brought a crossbow along with them so as not to waste valuable ammunition hunting.

It was hot in the day and warm at night. After the first month, one of Marlene's pairs of pants had worn through a knee, and instead of patching them, she cut them off to make a pair of shorts. She also cut the sleeves off one of the shirts, leaving her shoulders bare, and she normally wore it with only one button closed and the shirt rolled up to bare her abs. Shandra did the same, but the guys preferred their pants long and cut the sleeves off their shirts, but left them unbuttoned and untucked. The guys all had cropped short beards now. The women had let their hair grow out. It was almost shoulder length and kept in ponytails. However, when the Black Shirts' captain came by on an infrequent visit, they were all properly dressed.

The enemy also conducted intermittent patrols in section size, sometimes with just scout vehicles, other times with the larger armoured vehicles. Active peace negotiations were now being conducted, and nobody wanted to start anything. They were just going through the motions, letting each other know they were still around and ready.

Marlene had brought a camera with her this time and took candid shots of life around camp. One day, she brushed out her hair to hang the way she liked it, long on the side covering her scar and the other swept behind an ear, then had Shandra take a picture of her standing in front of a flowering bush. She sent that photo to Duncan that night.

Peace about to be signed and I can't wait to be back home. We are getting nice tans out here, and it is nice being out on our own and away from base, but seven months is a long time away from you, my love. I miss you like crazy.

Mar

A response came quickly: *Woah! Maybe I should change the uniform regs. You look awesome! I just showed Barb and Jane, and they told me to shut my mouth. I was drooling all over the floor!*

You guys are overdue for a rotation, but we knew the peace negotiations were about to conclude so elected to keep you in place. You will have priority to ship back home. The ships are leaving tomorrow, but you didn't hear that from me, and please don't tell anyone.

See you soon. Love You,

Dunc

Finally, peace was declared. The Zebras cleaned up and stowed all their gear, ready to head back to headquarters. All that was left was one final official act. A party had been planned. It would be held on a large island in the middle of the river that ran down the canyon, and both sides would be there. The Black Shirts were the first to the site, then the former enemy. After the initial greetings, everyone looked around and noticed the Zebras were missing.

"*Zebra One, Bravo Sierra Charley Echo One. You guys coming?*"

"Just waiting for an invitation Charley Echo One. It's not polite to crash a party."

"Zebras, it's time to party!"

Then to the astonishment of the enemy, the three Zebra teams broke cover, appearing out of nowhere and making their way easily down the canyon sides, linking up and heading into the party.

"You just brought them up to impress us," the enemy captain said. "We have had that ridge under constant surveillance. There was nothing ever there."

"Oh, I can assure you," the Black Shirt captain said. "They have been there for three months now."

The vehicles were covered in a thick layer of dust, equipment stowed all over the roofs and decks, aerials on each corner deployed to their full height. When the troopers dismounted from the vehicles, unlike the Black Shirts, they were not wearing body armour. Their uniforms were wrinkled, dirty, and sweat-stained, and instead of berets, they wore tan ball caps. The men had beards and the two women had long ponytails hanging out the back of the ball caps.

All twelve of them marched up, formed a line, and saluted the two captains.

"Wind Rider, Charley Company, Zebra troop, reporting as ordered," Marlene said. "All present and accounted for, Sir."

"Your captain tells me you have been up there for three months," the enemy captain said. "I find that hard to believe. We have had that ridge under constant surveillance the whole time."

"Nice fish you caught, Captain," Brock said. "I don't think I have ever seen a sturgeon that big."

"That number three scout vehicle had a bad rod right from the start," Gerry said. "I was amazed it lasted as long as it did."

"Want us to keep going?" Marlene asked. "Just because you can't see us, doesn't mean we're not there. You only spotted one of us the last time, and it cost you. Big time."

"That was you people?" the captain's eyes got narrow, his look stern.

"Now don't be like that, honey," Shandra said. "You were trying to kill us, too. Who do I have to kill to get a beer around here?"

"Don't mind her, Captain," Brock said. "She hasn't had a beer in three months and is a little bitchy."

"I've got a fresh deer in the back of the Coyote," Marlene said. "Who do we drop it off to?"

The Black Shirt captain spoke into his radio and four men ran over. He pointed at Marlene when they came up.

"There is a fresh deer kill in the back of the Coyote," she said, "also a couple of buckets of mushrooms and fresh apples. I'll trade them for a couple of bottles of beer each."

"What?" she said, seeing the look on face of both captains. "It got boring sun tanning all day everyday."

The beer was warm, but nobody cared. It was the first any of them had had since coming out to this remote area. It was also the first time all twelve of them had been all together. All contact, which was infrequent, had been by encrypted text. The three teams got reacquainted. All were tanned a deep bronze and badly in need of a shower and change of clothing. Their clothing was faded and had more than one patch, boot toes were worn off, showing the protective toe caps underneath. Despite the reinforcement, the knees had been patched and repatched. But, for the first time in three months, they could relax a bit. However, they were not home yet.

The Wind Riders were not exactly ignored by the clean, crisply uniformed regular troops as they made jokes and comments on their appearances, but they were left alone. They had just started the second beer when Marlene's ear peace crackled.

Zebra One, Bravo Charley Seven, copy?

That got all of their attention, as even the Black Shirt captain had received it. It came from the overall commander.

Bravo Charley Seven, Zebra One, copy.

Zebra One to proceed to embarkation point Alpha at once and provide ETA. Copy?

Zebra One, copy. To proceed to embarkation point Alpha. ETA four hours.

Bravo Charley Seven, copy. ETA four hours point Alpha. Bravo Charley Seven out.

Marlene looked around at the group and shrugged her shoulders.

"No rest for the wicked," she said and raised the beer bottle and drained it. Then she walked toward the Coyote. The rest following behind.

"Echo in the lead, Fox in trail," she said once she was in her commander's hatch. "Let's get the show on the road."

The three vehicles fired up and, twenty yards apart, made their way up the ridge and over the other side. For the first ten kilometres, they followed a rough dirt trail to the firebase, then sped up as they hit the gravel road that led from the firebase to the main highway. Although there was supposed to be peace now, they didn't leave their guard down, but they did stay inside the vehicles, buttoned up and letting the vehicle air systems filter out the dust kicked up on the gravel road. A half-hour later, they pulled onto the paved main highway, accelerated to the maximum speed allowed, and sped back to base.

Slowing down as they hit the town limits, everyone in the Coyote popped their hatches and clambered up to the outside air. They needed the visibility now that they were in an urban environment and closed the gap to Echo to five yards. Although it was nothing new to see military vehicles coming and going, this small group drew some attention due to the condition of the vehicles and the people in them and the Zebra painted on the cupola. This was even more evident when they reached the space port.

The rest of Charley Company was already in the process of loading into a transport ship, and all of them were in clean, crisp uniforms. Their vehicles were spotless. Zebra's three vehicles were directed to a smaller, faster transport by Black Shirts in immaculate uniforms, where they were told to load immediately. Everyone but the drivers disembarked, and, seeing Carol and her command party approaching, Brock took over from Marlene to guide their Coyote into the cargo bay of the transport ship.

"Hey, Boss," Marlene said after Carol had returned her salute. "A shower and a beer would have been nice."

"Hell," Carol said. "The rest of the gang only got in yesterday. These transports only came in a couple of days ago, and we thought we had at least a week to get ready. But oh no, this morning we get ordered to ship out. Look at it this way. This time tomorrow, you guys will be snug as a bug in a rug in your own beds, and we will still be stuck in that tin can for three more days."

"I guess another day in these crappy uniforms won't kill us," Marlene said. "At least we will have real food and a bunk for a change."

"Speaking of uniforms," Carol said. She brought out her communicator, hit a button, and passed it to Marlene.

It was a picture taken of Shandra and Marlene hamming it up in front of the Coyote with their cut-off shorts, shirts rolled up and tied in a knot just below their breasts, assault rifles braced on a hip, ball caps pulled low, and wearing dark sunglasses. The next picture was of the two guys, similarly posing, but with their shirts open, showing off their muscles.

"Anybody we know?" Carol asked. "Those are going viral, at least with the Wind Riders. I don't think they have hit the other battle groups. Yet."

"I'm gonna kill him when I see him," Marlene said. "Those were supposed to be private."

"Ah, come on," Carol said. "You got it, flaunt it, I say. Good for morale, too."

"Ya, I'm sure. If I can be excused, Ma'am? I have to make sure all our equipment is stowed properly." Marlene saluted and marched away, clearly upset.

"Uh, oh," Carol said. "Me thinks the Master Warrant is in a heap of shit."

Other than having a fast shower and going for one meal, Marlene kept to her bunk for the whole trip, sleeping for the most part. She had her personal communicator turned off, so a messenger had to be sent from the captain asking her to come to the bridge. She was told they would be in port in two hours and that they were to proceed directly to their barracks once unloaded. Further orders would be issued at that point, but that they were to have the next three days off to re-acclimate.

There was a crowd of spectators at the port and the gates when they came out. Another crowd was lined on both sides of the road on the other side of the base gates and more than a few people gathered around the barracks as they pulled in. While the rest of the gang revelled in the attention, Marlene just looked straight ahead.

"Unload my shit for me, would you?" Marlene asked briskly. She marched into the barracks and into the showers. She was in blue jeans, sneakers, and a polo shirt as the others finished unloading the gear and was driving away in her beat-up personal vehicle before anyone could talk to her.

She came back after dark, not saying a word to anyone, and by the time they woke up, she was gone again, then came back late that night. Shandra was waiting for her the next morning, grabbed her by the arm and dragged her to the bathroom.

"What the fuck, Boss?" Shandra said. "What the hell did we do wrong?"

"Nothing," Marlene said. "You guys didn't do anything wrong. I just need some time to think is all."

"What's going on, Mar?" Shandra said. "This isn't like you. All of your buddies have been calling, looking for you. So have we. You're worrying me."

"Why did they pull us all back so fast?" she replied. "Us in particular, on a fast transport. Something does not smell right, and I am afraid they are going to send us out right away again. Shit, we are not machines! And even if we were, even machines need time off for maintenance and repair. I can see them doing that to me, and I probably deserve it, but you guys don't deserve this shit. You all work so damn hard, never complain. Shit, this pisses me off."

"I did some digging, Mar," Shandra said. "There is a clause in our contracts. Time off-planet in a war zone is credited with an extra half of a day added to each day served. We can take the time in cash or time served. Hell, with all the time we have in hot zones, I'm gonna be rich. Or, I can be out of the Army with a full five years at the end of this year instead of two more years. No worries there. If they want me to head out again after a couple of weeks off, I'm all for it. I thought you were pissed about the pictures."

"That was the straw that broke the camel's back, Shandra," Marlene said.

"Oh, come on!" she replied. "Hell, we all think they are a hoot. The kickass Zebras showing off."

"That's not the point," Marlene said. "Those were sent as a private e-mail. Not to be spread around."

Then she dressed and took off again.

The next morning, they joined the regular run, and Marlene didn't play around that day, pushing them hard and leaving everyone behind. The Zebras were breathing hard at the end of it. Then they received a call to report to headquarters after lunch.

As they were still technically on off-planet duty, they reported wearing their tan uniforms and boots. Instead of ball caps, they wore berets and the men had shaved. Shandra and Marlene had their hair pulled back tight, and all of them had the proper rank and other required insignias on their uniforms. Everyone else in the headquarters complex and on the base itself was in the light green casual work uniforms. The twelve of them were ushered into a large room and lined up in two lines in front of a table. Duncan sat in the center, with Jane on one side and Dave on the other.

"Welcome home, Zebras," Duncan said. "Job well done. Once the rest of Charley arrives, you will be honoured with a formal parade and medals ceremony. After your leave period, Echo and Foxtrot will return to Charley squadron. Zebra will, on paper, be reconstituted to a squadron. Zebra will be augmented after the current training cycle by three more teams. Requests for volunteers for this augmentation will be taken from current Wind Rider members. Volunteers will compete in a competition designed and supervised by Zebra members and Master Sergeant Isabelle.

"Once again, good job, people. Top notch. Dismissed. Master Sergeant? A word in my office?"

Duncan let Marlene walk into the office before him and shut the door.

"Shit, have I missed you," he said coming forward arms out stretched. Marlene took two steps back and came to attention, raising her right leg high and stomping it to the floor.

"My lord Duncan has something to discuss with the Master Sergeant? My lord," she said almost at a shout.

"Come on Marlene, cut the shit."

"If my lord has nothing to discuss, the Master Sergeant requests permission to rejoin her troops, my lord."

Now Duncan took a long look at her. She was still at rigid attention, her stern gaze focused two inches over his head and no hint of a smile in her eyes, only defiance. He had clearly done something wrong but did not know what.

"You haven't returned any of my calls, texts, or emails, love. I was worried."

"The Master Sergeant was not aware that she had to respond or even to keep her personal communication devices on while off duty, my lord. Nor was the Master Sergeant aware that my lord would use her personal communication device to issue orders. My lord."

Oh, I'm definitely in shit for something, Duncan thought.

"Very well, Master Sergeant," he said. "Dismissed."

He punched the intercom button for his aide as Marlene left his office.

"Get Amanda in here ASAP," he said.

Jane and Amanda showed up at the same time.

"That was fast," Jane said. "We thought sure we wouldn't see you two for the rest of the afternoon."

"She's pissed about something," Duncan said. "I've got enough trouble figuring out normal females like you guys, but her? She's gone all ice queen on me again. I mean, I don't expect her to jump all over me, like I see you guys do from time to time. It's not in her. But shit, not even a hello, I missed you, how are you? Shit, you should see the emails she was sending me."

"She was out there a long time, Boss," Amanda said. "In some heavy shit too. Probably just some culture shock. I'll go talk to Zebra and see what's up."

"Thanks Amanda, I appreciate it," he said. "See if you can get her to the junior ranks this evening. Let me know if you can."

"She's not Karen, you know," Jane said.

"I know that Jane, dammit," Duncan said. "Karen would have tracked me down and damn near raped me coming back from that long a time away. Marlene, well, she would have quietly come over. We would go for a quiet dinner, then she would rip my clothes off after we got back home. But she hasn't called, texted, nothing. No, I did something wrong."

"Give her sometime, Duncan. Magdalene says she hasn't called her yet either. But she says that is kind of normal. She usually takes a week or so to call her."

Amanda texted they were all in the junior ranks and Duncan stood.

"Where are you off to?" Jane said.

"Junior ranks," Duncan said. "Last time I checked, I was still not an officer."

The club was about half full when Duncan walked in and nobody noticed him as he walked up to the bar. It wasn't usual for a Master Warrant, or any Warrant, to come in, but it wasn't unusual either. The bartender gave him his two beers, noticed the Wind Rider badging and, having never seen him in the bar before, pointed to the back corner where the Wind Riders hung out.

The Zebras were sitting apart from the few Wind Riders in the bar in the back corner by the door. They had dragged three tables together, and all twelve of them plus Amanda were sitting around the beer bottle filled tables.

"Hey guys," Duncan said, coming up to the table. "Mind if I join you?"

"Hell no," Brock said. He pointed to an empty chair next to Amanda and across from Marlene. "We got a rule though."

"Last one in buys," Duncan said and laughed. "Same rule all over." He got the waitress's eye and swirled his hand over his head.

"Look at you guys," he said. "All tanned up and relaxed."

"Hell, I feel bad taking all the extra money," Gerry said. "Almost. That first deployment was a real bitch."

"I heard that," Duncan said. "The pencil pushers were pissed at all the ammo you used, and you should have heard them howl at the loss of all that expensive equipment and the two G-Wagons. A guy would think the world was coming to an end or something. I take it the ankle healed fine, Master Corporal?"

"Yes sir," the Echo member said.

Duncan looked all around him at the bar.

"Somebody let an officer in here?" he said. "Asshole brass have their own club. I work for a living like you guys do."

"I'm sure my lord has better clubs with better people in them to associate with," Marlene said. The smile left everyone's faces.

"Amanda," Duncan said. "Did you here that? Now they let some stinking lord in here. No standards in this club."

"Ya, Dunc," Amanda said. "Not the kind of place for us lowlifes. I'm amazed these rookies let us sit with them. After all, they are the Zebras you know."

"Oh shit," Duncan said. "They're letting wildlife in here now? No wonder the place is half empty. So, despite the ice queen over there, I am going to force myself to be allowed to sit with you rookies and listen to all your bragging about glorious deeds of daring do."

Brock started a story and Marlene stood, making to leave.

"What?" Duncan said. "Too good for the ice queen to have a beer with the lower forms of life?"

"Outside!" she said. "Now!"

Amanda put her hand on Duncan's arm as he rose to follow her.

"If she wants to duke it out, it's going to be a short fight," he said. "Keep my chair warm."

"Why can't you just leave me alone?" Marlene said. "You didn't get the picture when I didn't return your calls?"

"Actually, no, I didn't," Duncan said. "Last week, the woman I love told me she couldn't wait to see me again and that she missed me and loved me dearly. Now, she not only ignores me but is damn-right hostile. So, no, I don't get the picture. It is a little fuzzy right now."

"I don't know what you have up your sleeve, my lord. We get shipped back priority, then we are getting three more fireteams. The only thing I can think of is you are shipping us out again. Those kids need some rest! You want to send me out again with another fireteam, fine. I don't give a shit. I'll get my mandatory time over with all that faster and get the hell out of the army and away from you finally."

Now Duncan was upset.

"You want me gone? I'm gone," he said. "Now get back in there with your kids. The next time you see me, you are going to find out what a real recon soldier is." He squared away his beret and walked away, head held high.

"Well, that's it then," Amanda said. She and Shandra had come out and witnessed the fight. "I don't know what you think he has done, kid, but now you have really pissed him off. We have been putting up with your Zebra shit for a long time. Let the rookies have their fun. Now you've pissed off the Ghost, and if the Ghost is pissed off, we are all pissed off.

"Good luck, rookies. We've been humping sixty pound packs and fighting much better trained and equipped enemies than you guys will ever see. You think your first deployment was a bitch? You ain't seen nothing yet."

Chapter Thirteen

It was a nice sunny day. The three G-Wagons with zebras painted on the hoods were driving with their windows down and arms out the windows. The Coyote's crew were all sitting on the edges of their hatches, except for the driver, who had his hatch open and was sitting high in the hatch.

It had been two months since they had come back home. First was the parade where they all received their participation medals and a unit mentioned in dispatch medal. Then, after a month off, they selected the three new teams. Well, one team was new. The other two teams were the old Echo and Foxtrot teams. Now they were to be trained in anti-guerrilla warfare. Somewhere on the training range were soldiers in groups numbering from ten to a hundred. Their job was to find and neutralize those groups. Most of them would be original PIGs, but it was rumoured that some Wind Riders would be involved as well.

Marlene had not seen Duncan since the evening at the bar. He had not even been at the award ceremony. There had been no calls or emails. He had just disappeared. They had had disagreements in the past, but usually one or the other would try to make contact of some sort, or one of Duncan friends would get a hold of her. This time, other than for official reasons, there was nothing. Even Carol had disappeared.

They were about a kilometre inside the designated area when it happened. The only thing they heard were the bullets slicing through the air just before impact. They were real bullets, not laser hits. Three of the first ones sliced across her turret in a row, splattering hot fragments all around. Then two hit just below Gerry's head on the armour in front of his hatch. Two tires were blown out of the Coyote, then the same high-powered rounds that had hit the hatch started blowing the antennas off the Coyote. At the same time, tires were being shot on the G-Wagons, as were the antennas.

As the G-Wagons came to a halt and the troops bailed out, the radiators and engine compartments were hit by the high caliber bullets. Smaller caliber bullets riddled the interiors, targeting radios.

Marlene and her crew dropped inside the Coyote, and the cupola turned to the right, which was where the shots were coming from. Shandra deployed the mast, and it was hit multiple times as it rose. Then everything stopped.

"They must be on the back side of that ridge," Brock said. "Other than residual heat signatures, I have nothing."

"They took out the array, Boss," Shandra said. "I have nothing."

"Run, Zebra, Run," came over their head phones. *"You is all dead, dead, dead. Have fun for the next two weeks on foot. We will be. I am the Ghost in the Wind and you have just experienced what a real pack of wolfhounds can do. Catch us if you can, rookies."*

"No fair Ghost," came Barb's silky-smooth voice. *"You didn't leave any for me to play with."*

Two shots splashed against Marlene's hatch as she opened it. They came from the other side this time. Other shots rang out, then they too were silent.

"Now me, love," Conrad's unmistakable accent came across the radio. *"Wild pigs are just as nasty as wolfhounds. You come into our territory, you pay the price."*

"Where the fuck are those guys?" Marlene yelled.

"The Ghost is in the wind, Zebra, and the wind is everywhere."

The rest of the week was a nightmare. They were attacked during the day, the night, and sometimes both. The bullets coming at them were real, and there was no doubt they were being played with. One time, they were attacked from every direction, flash bangs and smoke grenades simulating grenade hits. They actually saw some of the attackers that time, but only a few shots got off before they were all dead.

One morning, they woke up and found *Bang, you're dead!* stickers posted to five backs.

They had seen a line of nine figures on a ridge half a kilometre away, but by the time Marlene had her sniper rifle in hand, two rounds hit the ground just in front of her. Then the opposing sniper stood and all ten of the figures waved and disappeared behind the ridge.

The week was over, and the sixteen disheartened Zebras sat on their packs beside the road where they were to be picked up. They were tired, sore, and dirty. There was a shimmering in the tall grass along both sides of the road and one hundred figures rose like ghosts from the grass, split between the sides of the road.

Then a drone aircraft flew down the road, just over their heads, and disappeared in the distance. It had a machine gun and rockets mounted on it.

"*Ha, finally!*" Barb yelled on the radio. "*Bang, you is all dead!*"

"*Sure, rub it in, Voice,*" Duncan said. "*You would have had a stinger up your cute butt if this was for real.*"

"*Poor loser,*" Barb said. "*Tell the rookies they're buyin' tonight. Voice out.*"

"You guys were getting the hang of it at the end," Duncan said. "Against anybody else, you probably would have won. Unfortunately, you weren't. This is what all of us are trained to do and what we are normally used for. We operate in small groups and sabotage facilities, take out high profile targets, or once in a while provide overwatch and support for larger raids. So, now that you have seen it from the receiving end, we will be training you to do what we do.

"Party tonight and Conrad is buying. He lost the bet."

Conrad came up to Marlene.

"God damn Ghost," he said. "Don't feel bad. Those Wind Riders were kicking our asses when they weren't kicking yours. Look at them. They love this shit."

Now they were playing hopscotch on a hastily drawn course in the dust of the roadside. Yelling insults at each other and laughing like crazy. Everyone but Marlene joined in the fun. She just sat on her pack by the roadside, her eyes following Duncan everywhere he went. He was having a good time, talking and joking with everyone, but her.

Then the transport air cars arrived, and they all piled in. An hour later, they were in their own showers, getting rid of a week's worth of dust and grime. The Zebras would not listen to her protests, and made her come along to the bonfires set up in the Wind Riders' party spot. The Wind Riders kept their distance, but a lot of the PIGs kept her occupied, making sure she was not alone or feeling left out. But her eyes never really strayed for long from Duncan.

"He's not going to come over here while you are here," Conrad said. "You are the one who told him to leave you alone, not the other way around, dearie. You can't have it both ways, you know. I won't lie. We really need you people badly. All of us are getting a little too old for this stuff. We need some new blood, and you, my dear, are the best we have. Now the official reason you were sent back early was to set this all up. But I know, and, if you let loose the ice queen for five seconds, you know too what the real reason was."

Marlene shot him a dirty look.

"Oh, can it already," Conrad said. "I know who you are. I just never said anything. Do you know what happens when you mix fire and gasoline? You either have one hell of an explosion or, with the proper mixture, something very powerful. That's what you two are – fire and gasoline. You need to find the right mixture. Both of you are miserable right now. End it or fix it. It's affecting the rest of us."

Conrad got up, clapped her on the shoulder, and moved away. Marlene finished her beer, then quietly made her way back to her SUV and drove around aimlessly for a while. She eventually stopped and parked on a quiet residential street, laid her head back on the headrest, and let her mind wander. She didn't notice when the owner came home and went into the house a couple of hours later, nor did she notice him come out of the house and up to the SUV.

"Christ is this thing a piece of shit," Duncan said, startling her. He was crouched down and talking to her through the open passenger window. "You might as well come in. I've got some beer in the fridge, or I can make a pot of coffee if you want."

"Beer would be fine," she said.

She got out and followed him in. She had never been inside this house. It was spartan but clean, definitely a man's home. It had a large video screen on one wall and some trophies and awards hanging on walls or stored on shelves. There were framed photographs on the shelves, some with him in dress uniform getting some award or another, but most with Duncan and the original Wind Riders. They were young and in uniforms with a strange camouflage pattern, much like the one she had first seen them in, posed in front of an original G-Wagon, which was also in tan camouflage and had definitely been hard-used.

There were two pictures of her, one in her Black Shirt general's uniform receiving an award from Tanya and the other of her in her modified uniform rolled up to just below her breasts and held only by a knot tied in it. She had her hands behind her head and was turned slightly sideways.

"Grab a seat," Duncan said, putting a bottle of beer on the coffee table and sitting down. "You wanted to talk? That's a picture of a girlfriend I once had."

"She's kind of cute," Marlene said. "I saw a similar one plastered all over the internet. I wonder how she felt about that."

"Obviously not happy," Duncan said. "She hasn't talked to me since."

"Gee, I can't imagine why." she said, sarcasm dripping with every word. "Those were obviously personal pictures. Not meant to be blasted everywhere."

"I just sent out the one, Marlene," he said. "No names or units were mentioned and our recruitment numbers have been high ever since. I apologize. I should have asked first. Nobody has seen that one but me."

"I guess I kind of overreacted," Marlene said, "but I have been trying so hard to stay under the radar. To do the best I can. To make you proud of me."

"You have, Marlene, and you have done it on your own. Well, mostly. I pulled some strings and got you in the PIGs, sorry. But the rest was all you."

"Someone told me tonight you and I are like fire and gasoline and that we should handle this one way or another. That's why I am here."

"Good analogy," Duncan said. "One of my morons come up with it or one of yours?"

"Conrad, actually," Marlene said. "He also said to get our shit together because it was affecting everyone."

"Ya, I'll admit. I've been a bit distracted lately," he said. "So..."

"I don't know, Duncan," she said, looking him right in the eyes. "I won't ever be like Karen. I'm not the touchy feely type. I do love you, but I don't know if I am good for you or not."

"Ya, one of us is gasoline and the other fire," he said. "And who is which changes. But from what I have seen, it's more like smoke and fire. You can't have one without the other, and most of the time, Marlene, we get it right. It wasn't all apple blossoms and sunshine with Karen and me either. We both have our own personalities, Marlene. Shit, we have been apart more than we have been together for Chrissake. You make me whole, Marlene. It will never be perfect."

She saw the love in his eyes and knew he was right, but she was still scared and told him so. She was scared not of what he would do to her, but what she would do to him.

"I told you the last time we had a similar conversation," he said, "that you can only hurt me if I let you. I also told you to take your time and think all this over. I'm not going anywhere, nor am I looking for someone else. I'm a one woman guy. But shit, Marlene, the next time something is bothering you, will you please tell me? Otherwise, I'm scrambling around trying to figure out what is going on and then I get pissed off."

"Okay," she said and then stood. "Thanks for the beer."

"Anytime," he said as he escorted her to the door. He watched until she got in her car, then he closed the door and walked into the kitchen, trying to get her smell, the sound of her voice, and how she looked out of his head.

Ten minutes later, the doorbell rang. She was standing there, her shirt rolled up and only held closed by a knot in the front.

"You going to stand there ogling me, or are you going to let me in?" she asked. She kicked the door closed behind her and started to tear off his clothes.

Chapter Fourteen

All her teammates knew was that she was not spending her leave time in the barracks. For the first few days, they had noticed her beat-up SUV in town, but after that, it also disappeared. Carol and Megan had dropped by, but they had not seen her either. Asking Amanda at the club, they learned that Duncan was at work every day but disappeared on the weekends. However, that was nothing new. He always disappeared on the weekends. Eventually, the other members of the Zebras did what all young people do. They stopped worrying about it. It was time to party. No training, no stand to's, no inspections, and most of all, no sitting in an outpost waiting for something to happen. Their days were spent lounging around, the nights living it up to the max.

Duncan finally got tired of all the innuendos and hints and called a meeting in the boardroom with his closest friends.

"Thank you all for your concern," he said. "I can assure you that I am doing just fine. The last seven years has been incredibly difficult for all of us, coming to a new and strange place that is almost like home and building new lives for ourselves, then having that ripped out from under us and having to start again. But, we had each other and the tight bonds we've built. This new transition had been easier. We have trusted people to help spread the load now. We have people who share our vision of a better life, a freer life.

"For myself, as the local people begin to understand better how things should work, I have less to do and I can get back to doing what I like to do and what I do best. Some of you have opted to join me.

None of this is new to me. I enjoy a new challenge. I embrace change, and God knows, I hate working in the office. So yes, I am doing well.

"As for Marlene, of us all, she has had to endure the most. She was an outsider in her own home, a minor aristocrat in an unforgiving regime. We ripped that away from her. Then, recognizing her potential, we pushed her hard and she became a leader of her people. Her true nature came forward, a kind and caring person in a brutal and cruel occupation. She was only just learning our ways and a lifetime of obedience cannot be undone overnight, so, against her better judgment, she made a bad choice and once again lost everything. This time, she had to start right at the bottom, and once again, she has risen to the top.

"To say that I do not care for her would be lying. I care for her deeply and am very concerned about her. She asked me for time, and I gave it to her. Then I did something stupid, and both of us being who we are, it got out of hand. We both know that all of you are concerned for us, but I am asking you, please, let her be. No matter how much I care for and love her, she must make up her own mind in her own time. If it is meant to be, she will be with me. If not, I will still love and care for her, but from a distance."

Marlene was flying in circles over a tract of land. She had purchased the small four-place air car the second day of her leave. Unlike her banged up SUV, this vehicle was new, powerful, and had all the latest gadgets. She had paid cash for it, and now, after checking her bank accounts, she was checking out this land.

It was adjacent to the land her mother owned and was almost equally forested and open natural clearings. After seeing it, she put a down payment and arranged for a mortgage. Her military allotment had gone to her mother, but she had enough money in the bank for the down and the first six months of payments. After that, her pay would cover the monthly payments, just. She would have to be frugal. Her mother had agreed to manage the property, and Marlene would receive ten percent of the after-tax profit it generated.

A small, one-bedroom, prefab cottage had been placed in a clearing near the centre of the property. It had solar power and running water, and she spent her days sprucing it up in her style. She built a horse corral where she wanted her prefab barn to be. The best of her horse string had been brought from Oaken by her mother and were boarded there, but Marlene wanted to have the ability to board a couple here when she was home on leave.

Duncan spent the weekends with her, working hard during the day building the corral and clearing and levelling the area for the barn. This weekend, the barn would arrive, and they would fix it up the way they wanted it. Duncan never forced himself on her, letting her make the choice whether to be intimate. She was becoming more comfortable with him and her situation now, and the very deep love she felt for him was overcoming the guilt she felt. Sometimes she even forgot about it.

With one last turn around the property, she headed back to the city. Duncan would be waiting for her at the private landing port for his weekend away with her, and she found herself getting excited. After this weekend, she had one week left of her leave, and she wanted to make the most of it. Then it was back to the army for another year.

Duncan was an hour late but, as they had both agreed, did not talk about it or the goings on in the army on their time off. This time was all theirs, not the army's, not the government's, not the colony's. In an emergency, CT could easily find them, but he never intruded. In fact, now that he had some competent people under him, CT had taken to disappearing on the weekends himself.

Duncan asked if he could fly. He was becoming a good pilot, and Marlene handed control of the little craft to him. Once he was flying, he broke the surprise on her.

"I'm taking the week off," he said. "I found this cute girl, and I want to see if we are a good fit or not."

"Oh really?" Marlene said. "So weekends of hot sex with me are no longer good enough?"

"Nah," he said. "You're too civilized for me. Got your own one room shack and all. Nope, this new girl likes being in the bush and living in tents and all. Say, would you mind lending me a couple of horses for a week so me and this hotty can go romp with Mother Nature? Such a pain to bring mine all the way over."

"Let me get this straight," Marlene said, trying hard not to laugh. "Not only do you dump me for some cute bobblehead, but you want me to lend you my very valuable horses, so you can do it with her?"

"Well, you are a nice girl and all," he said, "but you have way too many brains for me. No, a nice bobblehead is what I need, all looks and body. I've got enough brains for the both of us."

"Suits me fine," Marlene said. "I found a no-brain hunk to hang around with in any case." Then she turned away and did not say anymore.

Duncan just chuckled. It was when they landed and she stalked off that he knew he had pushed it a bit too far. He sighed and took his gear over to a nice stand of trees, laid out his sleeping bag, draped a small tarp over it, and, making a small fire, cooked up a meal with army field rations.

He was up with the sun the next morning and fed the horses while his morning coffee was brewing. As he was just about to pour the first cup of coffee and start breakfast, Marlene stuck her head out of the shack's door and called him for breakfast. He kept his distance, and she acted like everything was normal, telling him about everything that had happened in the prior week and what she wanted to accomplish during her last week on the property, at least for a while. There was no mention of the conversation of the day before.

"Oh," Duncan said. "So, you are not coming with me then?"

"Where?" Marlene said. "I have a dinner with my mom tomorrow. What do you have planned?"

"Aw well..." Duncan said. "It doesn't matter. Would you mind if I tagged along for your dinner? I haven't seen your mom for a while."

"I suppose it will be all right," Marlene said. "One more shouldn't matter. You better bring your stuff over, it's supposed to rain tonight. You can have the couch."

The rest of the day was like every other weekend. The barn had arrived the week before, and Duncan spent all day setting up stalls and feeding stations. Marlene was busy painting it. It started to rain as the sun went down, and Marlene went back to the little house. Duncan was about to start a fire to cook his dinner when she called him in. She had prepared a simple meal, and they ate it together. Duncan helped with the cleanup, then Marlene went to bed.

Instead of sleeping on the couch, Duncan gathered his gear and went to the barn. He made himself a bed of hay bales in the combined tack room/office, spread his sleeping bag over it, and made a small fire in the wood stove, brewing a cup of coffee on it. He sat listening to the rain and the fire crackling for a while, then turned off the small lantern and went to sleep.

He didn't see Marlene at all the next day. She stayed in the house and he in the barn, fixing things up. The next morning, he would saddle one of the horses and head into the woods. He really needed some time. A lot was going on and this would most likely be his last time off for some time. He didn't need all this drama with Marlene right now. If she came along, she came along, but he was going regardless.

Duncan had just finished making sure the last stall gate slid open and closed smoothly when he noticed he was not alone. Marlene was watching him. She was dressed to the nines, wearing a short dress that showed off her figure. Her hair was up, she had on a bit of makeup, and she wore designer boots that reached mid-calf. She let him look for a second.

"We leave in half an hour," she said, then turned around and walked back to the house before he could say anything.

Duncan had not come prepared for a fancy party, but he put on his clean blue jeans and least wrinkled polo shirt and was waiting in the air car before the half hour had expired. He waited and waited and waited some more and finally she came out. Now she had on earrings and a neckless, and when she got in, Duncan smelled the perfume.

"Come on," she said as she buckled herself in. "We are late!"

It only took a few minutes to fly to Magdalene's place. Marlene put her arm through his and walked close to him into the barn that had been converted into a dance hall for the evening. She stayed draped on him until the music started. Then she was off dancing, with anybody but Duncan. Duncan had never had a problem socializing, and he moved around the room, meeting new people and reacquainting himself with old friends he had not seen for a long time. He sat down at a table by himself to have a quiet beer and watch Marlene enjoying herself. Magdalene sat beside him with a glass of wine, and he listened with half an ear. Marlene had latched on to one particular man and was definitely flirting with him. Once it went further than that, Duncan decided not to watch anymore, but when he caught them necking at the table of his friends, she sitting on his knee and his hands roaming, Duncan stood.

Magdalene saw where he was looking and then looked back up at him, expecting to see rage and preparing herself for an explosion. What she saw instead was sadness. He quietly excused himself and walked out the door. It was only three miles across country back to Marlene's house, and, while the trees were wet, it had stopped raining and was a nice night. He walked slowly through the dark bush, gathering his thoughts and controlling his anger. Really, he had no hold on her. They did not have a commitment to each other, and she was free to do what she wanted with her life. It hurt that she felt so little about him to do those kinds of things in front of him, but life is not kind sometimes.

She was not back in the morning, and he saddled a horse, packing the gear he needed on the saddle and putting his rifle across his back. He rode into the bush, alone and sad. On Sunday morning, he rode back into the yard. Marlene was standing on the porch watching him. She had already loaded her things in the air car and closed up the house. She wouldn't be back for a year.

Duncan unloaded all his gear, stacking it beside the horse, then unsaddled and brushed him down, before letting him loose in the pasture and putting the tack away in the barn. He then went over and tossed his gear in the air car.

"Ready to go?" he asked.

"I think we should talk," Marlene said.

"What's to talk about?" Duncan said. "You've made it pretty clear where I stand. He looks like a nice guy. I hope you are happy together. Now are we going back together, or do I have to call CT and have someone come get me?"

"But..." she said.

"Look, Marlene. I am not a slave owner. You are free to see or not see whomever you want, dance with, hang out with. I don't care. I draw the line at you making out with other guys. That shows me you really don't care about me. Now, you driving me back or am I on my own?"

Now she took him by the arm and made him look at her.

"I love you, Duncan, please don't be angry with me."

"This was my last week with you, Marlene," he said. "I wanted to be alone with you for the whole week. You made other plans. So be it. I should have stated my intentions better, but did not. I will not be around at all for the next year. There are much bigger things I have to worry about than some woman who can't make up her mind about what she wants out of life."

"But I want to be with you Duncan," she said. "I thought I made myself clear on that."

"Funny way of showing it," Duncan said. A military air car was making its final approach now for landing. "I never treated you with anything but respect, Marlene. I never chased other women, let alone what you were doing with that guy."

Then he took his gear out of her car and put it in the military one and he was gone. Leaving her standing alone in the yard.

Marlene drove from the private landing field right to the Wind Riders HQ. None of the regulars were around, but as she turned to leave, Jane saw her and called her.

"Is Duncan around?" Marlene asked.

"No, he is off-planet for a while," Jane said, "but you can still email him if you need him."

Marlene nodded her head and drove back to her own barracks and parked her SUV in a parking stall behind it. The rest of the gang was all there and heading for the bar, so she joined them. She kept up her end of the conversations and laughed along with the rest, but her heart was not in it.

They had a week to get back in the groove of things then were called to a training centre and given a brief. They would spend their mornings learning how to interact with drone aircraft, how to act on information given to them from the drones, and how to vector the drones to a target to destroy it. The afternoons would be spent learning how to deploy in small air cars. These were a bigger military version of her own private model and would hold all eight members of a section, with two crew members in the rear and two pilots up front. In addition to doing small or minor repairs on the air car, the two crew members would supply suppressing fire when deploying or withdrawing from contact.

The first three weeks were devoted to that. Then Marlene was told she was losing the Coyote and would be using a G-Wagon from now on. The Coyote wold be given to a new team that would be their electronics specialists. The commander was female and from Earth. The rest were from Oaken. All of them were Wind Riders. The female commander was a second lieutenant and the rest corporals. As Marlene was learning, the Earth tech specialists were slightly different from other people. CT had his long shorts and flip flops. This one had orange hair and holes in her nose and ears that spoke of jewelry not allowed on duty. Marlene offered her one of the separate office/bedrooms in the barracks, but she refused and took a bunk opposite Marlene's.

"Hi," she said, sticking out her hand. "I'm your new techy, Pigpen, but you can call me PG if you want. Everyone else does. And before you ask, yes, we can all run five miles with full packs and hit the kill zone with five rounds after. Maybe not as fast as you guys, but we can still do it."

"Welcome to the Zebras, PG," Marlene said. "I'll take your word on the running bit. So, you the boss now?"

"No way," PG said. "On paper, ya, but I am smart enough and been around long enough to know better than to get in your way. No, I'm just your eyes and ears and, if you need it, some backup with the heavy guns. Oh, we also handle all your logistics and paperwork and stuff like that."

"So," Marlene said, "I suppose we will be training with you guys next week then?"

"Not really," PG said. "They have some new aircraft, and you guys will be the first trained on them. They are like airborne Coyotes but without the guns."

The first day, the Zebras were familiarized with the aircraft and its systems and capabilities. It could easily transport all eight members of a full section and their gear, plus two electronics officers and two pilots. It was a conventional winged aircraft with a turbine engine powering a single propeller. It could transport a full load of almost two thousand kilos at just under three hundred kilometres per hour. During a mission, it could fly the whole team five hundred kilometres, land, let the team off, take off, and linger for eight hours. Its only armaments were electronic jammers and flares.

The electronics suites had long-range radio equipment, infrared cameras, high definition long-range cameras, and down-looking radar. The detection systems were, if anything, better than what the Coyote had, and the radios were definitely better. They would be the eyes and ears for the Zebras for missions where the Coyote was not feasible.

The next day, the Zebras were taken to the aircraft itself. Again, it was a militarized version of a civilian model, this time a corporate executive aircraft. The interior was spacious, and they were taken up for a short flight.

The rest of the week, they were broken up into their two sections and landed in a training area. The aircraft easily vectored the two teams to their separate targets, then vectored the smaller air cars to pick them up and take them back to base. Then it was the weekend and party time.

All that month, Marlene had not heard from Duncan, and she had not tried to contact him, thinking he was doing something important. As PG was an officer, the Zebras took over a back corner of the All Ranks bar. There were sixteen of them now, and PG could not go to the Junior Ranks. They were all bonding well, as young people all over did when they had something in common. The eight newcomers were a little in awe of the original Zebras, who had already shared in two engagements, but Marlene made sure they were never left out.

Chapter Fifteen

Monday's briefing told them why they were training on the new equipment and methods. A planet in a system at the edge of the Federation was experiencing attacks from outside. Small groups of troops were conducting hit-and-run raids, destroying infrastructure and local army and police commands. They were also not shy about killing local farmers or townspeople and destroying farms and successful businesses.

The Zebras were to be attached to a battalion of PIGs that had extensive training in operations like this and would be the eyes of the battalion, surveilling areas that the drones and satellites had identified as enemy camps. When they learned the enemy had projectile weapons similar to their own, the reason for all the recent training became evident. This was something new for all of them. They were used to outgunning their opponents. Now they would be facing an enemy with similar tactics and weapons.

When they arrived at the transport ship, there were a few surprises. This was a new type of transport – a bigger version of the small fast ones. Three air cars and the aircraft were already on board. The wings of the aircraft were taken off and stored beside it, but there was plenty of room in the cargo bay for the Coyote and four G-Wagons. Other than the crew of the transport and the aircraft, the Zebras had the place to themselves. It would take a week at high speed to reach the far-off planet.

It took a couple of days before Marlene got bored. She found the recreation hall and was playing a video game when she heard a familiar voice. It was Megan. She had three people with her, saw Marlene, and waved her over.

"Hey," Megan said. "So, you're not hiding from everyone then?"

All four of them were officers, and Megan and another had wings on their uniforms.

"Me, hiding?" she said. "Not likely. Us lowlifes are not allowed where you officer types hang out."

"Well," Megan said, "we're about to become real chummy soon. We are the ones tasked with babysitting you high and mighty Zebras planet-side."

"Oh, great," Marlene said. "The blind leading the blind, me and my rookies and you and yours."

"Speak for yourself, rookie," Megan said laughing. "I've done this a few times before. Had to pull Ghost's ass out of the fire once."

"Speaking of Ghost," Marlene said, "have you heard from Duncan lately?"

"Ya, every couple of days. You?"

Marlene shook her head. Megan saw her forlorn look, then jerked her head to her buddies, and they moved to the other end of the room.

"Duncan kind of implied you two were on the outs," Megan said. "He's not answering your e-mails?"

"I haven't sent him any," Marlene said. "I knew he was off-planet, so he must be doing something important, and I didn't want me to bother him."

"I don't think it is possible for you to bother Duncan, Marlene," Megan said. "If he was busy, he would still get back to you. You have to know he's crazy about you."

"No, not anymore, I think."

"What did the airhead do now?" Megan asked. "Men can be such idiots sometimes. I'll give him what for! You just wait."

"No," Marlene said putting her hand on Megan's arm. "He didn't do anything. I decided to play hard to get and flirted a little with another guy at a party, hoping he would get jealous."

"I could have told you that wouldn't work," Megan said. "Duncan is not wired that way. He went back home with you, right?"

"No, he left."

"He what?" Megan said. "That doesn't sound like the Duncan I know. You telling me the whole story?"

"Well, I was letting the other guy kiss me and get a little forward," Marlene said.

"Oh shit!" Megan said. "Did you chase after him when he left?"

"No, and before you ask, nothing happened. I spent the night at my mother's house. I was a little too drunk to fly home. The next morning, he saddled a horse and rode into the bush. I tried, but I couldn't find him."

"He's not called the Ghost for nothing, Marlene," Megan said. "If he doesn't want to be found, he won't be."

"When he came back, he hardly spoke to me, and before I could explain, he called CT and got someone to pick him up. I haven't heard from him since."

"Well, my dear," Megan said, "you have screwed up royally this time. I suppose you were in the same clothing and had not showered from the night before, right? What do you suppose he thought about that? Duncan could handle you flirting with another guy, but sex would be something else entirely. You didn't, did you?"

"No, God no," Marlene said. "He wasn't even that cute. What do I do now?"

"I don't know," Megan said. "Maybe mom can help you out. Shit, you really stepped in it this time. Leave it be for now. All of the original gang is on planet. This is a really nasty deal we are getting into. I'll talk to mom when we land, then I'll come find you. Like I said, everyone on this transport is part of the Zebras now. We need to stick together."

"He's out in the field, Marlene," Barb said. "They all are, and you will be soon. He won't be back for a while, and I don't want to bug him with this now. You should forget it, too, for now. The mission always comes first. You know that. We are sending you and Bravo team out in two days. We have identified a large camp and need you guys on the ground giving us up-to-date intel. A whole company of PIGs is going to hit them hard by the end of the week, so you better have your shit together or you, your team, and the PIGs are going to get hit hard."

Megan dropped off the section on a lonely stretch of back country road just after midnight. It had taken three hours to fly that far, and the section would be on their own the first day as Megan had to fly back to refuel. The drone would not be in place until daybreak. The eight of them hefted their full packs and weapons and headed into the countryside. The only sounds were the night animals scurrying in the undergrowth and the skies, their own breath, and muted footsteps.

It took the rest of the night to reach the base of the hill where they would set up to watch the enemy camp, which was a little over a kilometre away. Just after daybreak, the drone was overhead and providing basic data, such as where large groups of enemy were. The unit did not have the capability to take advantage of everything the drone could supply, and they were too far away and too low right now to receive radio transmissions from HQ. They would hole up at the base of the hill for the day and rest, moving to the top of the hill the next night.

The next morning, they mapped out the enemy camp, including its defences and the location of all the barracks and mess tents. The next step was to observe the enemy's daily activities, such as guard placements and rotations, where the major structures were located, and patrol patterns and duration. The data was sent to Megan's plane, which was rotating high and off to one side eight hours a day, as was one of the drones that kept in constant contact.

The attack took place at 2 a.m. Marlene first took out the heavy machine gun personnel with her big gun, then the sentries at the far end of the camp, while the other fire team's sniper with his smaller caliber rifle took out the near-side sentries. Once the attack company reported it was on final approach, Marlene took out the machine gun crew and started picking off sentries, as did the other sniper. The drone fired two rockets at structures in the camp, lighting the area up in fires just as the air cars holding the assault company hit the ground all around the camp. The fight was short and deadly, Marlene and her people supplying any sightings of enemy who had escaped the initial assault.

By daybreak, Zebra was called into the camp. They gathered their gear and trudged down the hill. The enemy looked human, not the exotic aliens they had speculated. The ground and the uniforms of the dead were stained red. The clothing was similar, but the weapons, except the machine gun, were all single shot rifles. The machine gun was large and cumbersome, not like their own.

A few prisoners had been caught and the PIGs were interrogating them. Marlene could not understand everything said, but knew it was a language called German. The Wind Riders talked in that language a lot, the original ones anyway, and Marlene had picked up a little of it from Duncan, but not enough to carry on a conversation. They had not even had time to shed their packs when Megan landed and ordered them to board. They were taken back to the main base, where they were briefed on another mission.

This went on for three months. Sometimes they were given a week between missions. Sometimes they were out for a couple of weeks. All the teams were deployed almost all the time, and it was rare that two teams were in base at the same time, and then only with a brief overlap. The enemy was being hit hard and becoming more cautious. Finally, all of Zebra was to be dispatched to a high, remote area. Two of the fixed-wing aircraft would be used for transport, as the small air cars could not operate at that altitude. The Zebras would do it all for this mission. They had a 20 mile hike from their drop-off point. This time, PG and her crew would accompany them, along with all the electronic gear they could comfortably carry. Other than what they could carry with them and the aircraft, the Zebras were on their own.

It was high and rugged going. The Zebras had to stop frequently the first few days to let their bodies acclimate to the thinner air. It was cool during the day and cold at night. Not wanting to alert the enemy, they used only small portable alcohol- tablet-fueled stoves to heat their meals to almost-hot. It took a week and a half of hard trudging up and down hills and ravines, following overgrown game trails and making trails of their own, to get close to the enemy camp. Then they had to find a way in without being seen. Megan and the other aircraft were a big help steering them away from the more obvious dead ends and cliffs, but they could not see them all.

Finally, they crested a ridge and saw the enemy camp laid out in front of them. It was a communications camp with numerous tall aerials, surrounded by a barbed-wire fence with a guard tower at each corner. Two-man sentry teams with dogs walked the perimeter, but otherwise they could see little security. The Zebras spent the next two days observing and developing an assault plan. There were only twenty of them and over a hundred and fifty of the enemy. They would have two drones for support, but until they had control of the camp, they were on their own. The only access was by air. There was an airstrip at the far edge of the camp, but any transport craft would be vulnerable during landing.

The attack was planned for dawn the next day. Four transport aircraft holding a combined company of PIGs would land after the assault started, so it was important that the landing strip be secured early. Echo and Bravo fireteams would take the landing strip side. Alpha, Marlene's team, Charley, PG's team, and Foxtrot would handle the camp itself. Shandra would be in command of their assault teams, and PG would spot for Marlene, who would take out the guard towers and targets of opportunity after that.

Their IFFs were all working, and everyone was in position when Marlene called the first drone in for its attack. As it came, she sighted in on the first guard tower and fired, just as the drone did. Then the assault teams attacked, first firing the four grenade launchers, then the crew machine guns at tents, and finally the assault rifles. By that time, Marlene had taken out all the guards in the towers and was looking for additional targets. The enemy was disciplined and fought back. But they were not having it their own way at all.

Then a hidden machine gun opened up as explosions rippled through the camp perimeter. A combination of Marlene's gun and the remaining drone put paid to the machine gun, but not before some Zebras had felt its sting. There was firing coming from the landing field side, but not as much as there should have been. The first plane landed and troops piled out even before it stopped, adding the fire of their weapons to the din. Green tracers reached out and touched anything that moved or had a weapon. Soon, enemy troops were tossing weapons away and raising arms in surrender.

The PIGs made their cautious way into the camp, directing the enemy to congregate together. There were fewer than twenty of them still walking.

"*Zebras, Zebra Alpha One*," Marlene said as she and PG were walking down the hill.

"*Alpha One, Alpha Two. Alpha Three and Four are down. Foxtrot One is KIA, Four is down. Charley Two is KIA. Three is down.*"

"*Alpha One, Echo One. Echo Two and Four are down. Bravo One KIA.*"

"Fuck!" Marlene said. She switched frequencies. "*Peru One, Alpha One. I have people down. Can you dispatch medics, copy*?"

"*Copy Alpha One, medics already onsite.*"

"*Bird Three, Alpha One.*"

"*Go ahead Zebra,*" Megan said.

"*Bird Three, Zebra has three KIA and six WIA. Status of WIA unknown this time. Mission completed.*"

"*Copy Zebra. Three KIA, six WIA, status of WIA unknown. Mission complete. Bird Three your location ten mikes for medivac. Bird One in twenty mikes, Bird Two in forty mikes. All Zebra to extract. PIG to consolidate position. Copy.*"

Marlene repeated the transmission and made her way to an aid station where she found some of her team. Brock had multiple shrapnel wounds, and Gerry had been hit twice by the machine gun. Shandra also had minor shrapnel wounds. All the rest had been hit by the shrapnel expended by the hidden mines. One of the Bravo was missing a leg and a Charley an arm. The medics were working hard to stabilize Brock and Gerry, the worst of the wounded. Marlene joined Shandra and the rest of the unwounded Zebras in helping out where they could. All six of the wounded were hustled into Megan's plane when it landed, along with two medics.

Eight Zebras, the ones with minor wounds or the rookies, were in the next aircraft leaving. Shandra, who refused to leave, PG, Marlene, and three others were in the last. PG was shaking and very white. It had been her team's first time in the field, let alone under fire, and she had lost two of them.

The PIGs captain walked up to them with an object in his hand.

"Anti-personnel mine," he said. "Nasty piece of work. Shaped charge, blows about a hundred ball bearings in a fan-shaped arc. Like an oversized shotgun. First time we have seen those things here. Would have chewed us up pretty good, too. We were not ready for this shit. They hid that machine gun well. You guys are damn lucky you all didn't get killed. Somebody screwed the pooch big time on this one. These guys were not your run-of-the-mill infantry troopers. They are as well-trained in this stuff as we are. If they had better weapons, this would have been a hell of lot worse."

The last plane landed, and the six of them piled in. Marlene shut her communicators off and looked at the three tarp-covered bodies laid out at the back of the plane, then pulled out her aid kit and began to clean and bandage Shandra. PG was looking at the floor, quietly crying, the other three looking anywhere but at the back of the plane.

"I'm sorry," Marlene said so everyone could hear. "I let all you guys down."

Shandra pulled Marlene's shirt open exposing the right shoulder and the big bruise on it. "How many rounds do you have left?" she asked.

Marlene checked her weapons belt, then popped the clip out of the sniper rifle. "Three," she said.

"Don't you dare blame yourself," Shandra said. "You had fifty rounds total. That means you killed forty-seven of those assholes. You did your job. We did ours. Like you say, sometimes shit happens. Well, today was the day, boss. At least we don't have to run home like the first time."

"We all did our jobs, Master Sergeant," an Echo trooper said. "Even them rookies back there. Even you PG. Nobody ran and hid."

Marlene looked down at her feet, then back up to Shandra and a smile hit her eyes.

"I say, Stewardess," she said to one of the electronics techs. "What does one have to do to get a cool beverage on this fine aircraft?"

"Got some top-dollar wine in the fridge up front," the tech replied and stood, making her way to the fridge and coming back with two six packs of beer in cans. "Vintage two weeks ago. Nothing but the best for our paying customers."

That broke the ice and loosened everyone up until they landed at the airfield adjacent to the main base. In addition to the Zebra walking wounded, four sections of Wind Riders were lined up along with three companies of PIGs. Three ambulances were waiting, and the last six Zebras waited in line with their comrades as the three bodies were loaded in the ambulances, every trooper saluting until the last body was loaded. Then Marlene marched up to Carol and saluted.

"Zebra Squadron reporting, Ma'am," she said. "Mission accomplished. All Zebra present or accounted for, Ma'am."

"Very well, Master Sergeant," Carol said. "You may return to your barracks."

"Zebras will form up and return to barracks," Marlene shouted.

They all shouldered their packs and weapons, then she led them off in column of four at a run.

"Zebras, what are we born to do!"

"Run!"

"What are we bred to do?"

"Run!"

"What are we trained to do?"

"Kill lions!"

"What do we love to do?"

"Kick enemy ass!"

"What did we just do?"

"Kicked enemy ass!"

"Zebra, Zebra, Zebra, Hoorah!"

They ran off the airfield toward their barracks. All the others lined up, saluting them as they went. Duncan, the rest of Alpha Team, and Bravo team were at the back of the formation.

Chapter Sixteen

R ight," Duncan said two days later. All the Wind Riders were in the aircraft hangar being used as a lecture hall. All the aircraft crews, drone crews, PIG Company, and upper brass were in attendance.

"This enemy is intelligent, resourceful, and deadly," he continued. "We messed up, people. Three of our people were killed and six badly wounded. Two of them might still die and, if they survive, will no longer be fit for duty. Zebra's intel section is no longer able to function, and the whole squadron is below minimum operating standard. Seventy percent casualties, people. Not good! So, now we analyze, dissect, and learn."

The rest of the day was spent going over everything step by step. They used drone and aircraft footage to help where possible, and each Zebra explained what their jobs were, where they were positioned, and what they did. The PIGs did the same. It took most of the day.

"Right," Duncan said after everyone was finished. "We will study all this, all of us, and we will learn from this. Those of us from Earth have seen this before and much more. This enemy is using similar methods. We need to train our new people so they know what to expect. If this enemy gets a foothold here, the rest of the Federation is in trouble. We are the only ones with equal technology. The rest of the Federation is hopelessly outgunned. It's up to us, people. We have to stop them and stop them here."

He stopped talking and looked over the crowd.

"Zebras, you did well," he said. "None of you had seen those types of weapons before or the tactics the enemy used. The follow on company said the Zebras had the situation in hand by the time they arrived. They just mopped up and consolidated. All further missions the division is involved with are being terminated. All Wind Riders and PIGs not currently here are on their way. Black Shirt and Marauder battle groups will be deployed here as well. We are sifting through the intel, and our techs are working out where the enemy is coming from.

"These guys want to play? Well, they are about to find out they are playing with the wrong people. Dismissed."

"Sounds like your boyfriend is pissed off," Shandra said. "I sure would not want Ghost pissed off at me."

"Me either," Carol said. "And I have been with him when he was. He meant what he said, Shandra. You guys did good. I think my team would have suffered the same casualties, maybe more, and we have seen this type of shit before. Mind if I steal your glorious leader for a bit?"

"Hell no," Shandra said. "More beer and guys for me. The boss, now that she is a free woman again, is a lot of competition for us normal-looking females."

"You okay, Mar?" Carol asked as soon as Shandra was out of earshot. "Come on, I'll buy you a beer."

"Ya, I'm fine," Marlene said. "I mean, I'm not happy about what happened, but I did everything I could."

"And then some," Carol said. "They tell me you only had three rounds left in that big gun of yours, and I know you never miss. At least that is what PG is telling everyone. She said she couldn't keep up with you. You were shooting targets faster than she could spot them for you."

"I don't know about that," Marlene said. "Fired, found a new target, and fired again. Shit, it was all so slow. I was going as fast as I could."

"From start to finish, it was only twenty minutes, Mar," Carol said. "I know it seemed like hours. It always does. You're going to need a new stock. Yours kind of burned up. Let me see your palms."

Marlene's left palm had heat blisters on it.

"That PIG captain said it sounded like a fifty cal machine gun on slow burst, you were firing so fast. I wouldn't wonder that your barrel is worn out, too."

"The Master Sergeant is my guest," she told the trooper at the door to the Officers Club. "Besides, she is going to be an officer soon anyway."

"I already told you guys I don't want to be an officer," Marlene said. "I am happy just the way I am. I don't want to be tied up in the office."

"A warrant is still an officer, Marlene," Carol said, "just not a commissioned one. As a Master Sergeant, you already classed as a Warrant First Class. All we are going to do is take away the stripes and give you a crown on your sleeve. Comes with a few more bucks per month, too."

"Maybe then she can afford a better set of wheels," Megan said. "It is so embarrassing driving around with her."

"Why should I when I can mooch rides off you and your fancy sports car?" Marlene teased. "A real hunk magnet that thing is."

"Speaking of hunks," Megan said, "have you talked to him yet?"

"No, your mom said to back off since he was in the field…"

"And the mission comes first," Both women finished for her. They all laughed.

"Well, he is right over there," Carol said pointing at a table where Duncan, Brett, and Scott were sitting. "Let's see if we can get moneybags to spring for a beer."

The three men were laughing at some joke when the women walked up. With Carol and Megan in front and being taller, the guys could not see Marlene walking quietly behind them.

"Making fun of my nice car again I see," Megan said.

"Well, if that thing was any smaller, you'd need a shoe horn to get in it," Brett said. "No, we were laughing at super trooper here and how he always has to bum rides because he is too cheap to buy his own wheels."

"Why should I buy one?" Duncan said. "I only own about a thousand or so G-Wagons."

"Then why do we keep having to drive you around?" Scott asked. "Oh, I know, you forgot how to drive. Hey Marlene, long time no see."

"Hey Marlene," Brett said, motioning for her to sit down. "Case in point, master mooch. The Master Sergeant there had her own set of wheels when she was but a mere corporal. Crappy as it is, it runs good."

"Miss Isabelle." Duncan said. "If I wanted a vehicle, I would have a bloody vehicle. Now if you will excuse me?"

He stood to leave, and Barb shoved him back down. She had walked up while this was going on.

"Alright you two," she said. Barb had the "I mean business and I'm the mom" look. She jerked her head at the other four and pointed to a table farther down the bar. "Sit your ass down there, young lady, and you two work out whatever shit is going on now. I don't care how you do it, if you make up or break up, but you do not leave this table until I see at least a handshake. For Christ sake, Duncan Kovaks, I have seen you treat enemies better than you are treating Marlene."

Marlene sat as Barb stormed over to the other table and sat down in a huff, pointing her finger at them and scowling. The waitress came up and Marlene ordered a vodka straight and a beer.

"So, Master Sergeant," Duncan began. "I apologize for you being put on the spot like this. I also apologize for what happened on that mission. In hindsight, I should have sent Denise and her section with you, but at the time, intelligence suggested only a small communications centre. I should have known better, and for that I am sorry. Not that it will bring your dead back."

The waitress came with Marlene's drinks, and she took a sip of vodka. Duncan was looking her right in the eyes, his eyes devoid of all emotion. She took a deep breath, shot the rest of the vodka down, and then took a fast swig a beer to cool her throat.

"I know, Duncan," she said. "That's all that camp looked like to us as well. We watched them for three days. Perhaps sending PG and her crew out with us for their first mission was a mistake, but we all have to go through it at one point in our careers. They caught us flatfooted, and we paid for it. That's what happens when we get it wrong. People get killed. I will have your people teach me and my people how to look for those, what do you call them, claymores? Then, maybe next time, it will not be so bad."

They sat in awkward silence for a while, and Duncan extended his hand.

"Friends?" he said.

Instead of shaking his hand, Marlene gripped it with both of hers.

"Yes, always," she said. "I love you, Duncan. I messed up. I know what it looked like, and I do not blame you, but I would like you to hear me out. Then, I will leave, okay?"

Duncan nodded his head and made to withdraw his hand, but she would not let him. She was looking him dead in his eyes, and he tried hard not to lose himself in them.

"I wanted to have fun at the party, Duncan, and I know you do not like to dance," she began. "Then I had a little too much to drink, and I wanted to draw your attention, so I started to flirt with that guy. Then I let things get out of hand. That was my fault, not his and not yours. I came to my senses and walked away, but you had already left. I was too drunk to fly home, so I stayed at my mother's house, and, stupid me, I didn't shower or change my clothing before I came home. I know what it looked like, Duncan. I searched for you in the bush but couldn't find you. I swear to you that nothing happened between me and that guy, or any other guy. There have been no other guys since I first met you, and there will be no other guys, ever."

He didn't say anything, but his eyes had softened and his demeanour was no longer rigid. He was caressing her hand with his thumb.

"I know I disrespected you, Duncan," she said finally. "I will understand if you want to break up with me. I just wanted to clear the air. I like the friends I have made with your people, and I want to know it will be okay if I come around and hang out with you guys."

"Marlene," he said finally. "What would you do if you saw me flirting with another woman?"

"Right now? Nothing. You have every right. We are not tied together."

"No, really," he said. "Cut the "I am a nice girl and will live and let live" routine. What would you do?"

"Nothing Duncan," she said just over a whisper. "My heart would break, but after a while I would get used to it and try to get on with my life."

"In my experience, Marlene," he said. "A man opens up to a woman and tells her his deepest thoughts and fears, and the first time the woman gets upset with him, she uses those feelings against him. It usually hurts the man deeply, and after a while he will stop confiding in the very person he should trust the most."

"My mom and dad fought like cats and dogs at times," he continued, "but they never used those kinds of things against each other, ever. They never deliberately set out to wound each other that deeply. Do you understand what I am saying?"

"Yes, I think so," Marlene said. "My father would say the most vicious things to my mother. She really did love him at the beginning, but then just stopped telling him things, anything at all in the end."

"Now, I am going to ask you again," he said. "What would you do if I flirted with another woman?"

"Nothing Duncan, honestly, nothing," she said looking at the floor. Then she looked up and had fire in her eyes. "But I would want to claw your eyes out and yank your balls off, and I would definitely cut you off for a month or maybe two."

He turned her palms over and stroked the heat blister on her left one, then took his other hand and stroked her right cheek where there was a heat rash from the heat of the barrel and stock.

"That's my girl," he said, "full of piss and vinegar. When I heard the first casualty report, Brett and Scott had a hell of a time holding me back from going to you. I was so goddammed worried."

She held the hand on her cheek with one of hers and kissed the other one.

"Some jerk-off chair warmer told me once," she said, "the mission always comes first."

"Ya, I know," he said. "Somebody should kick him in the ass."

She leaned over and kissed him on the cheek. "No, I think this is better," she said.

Then he pulled her to him and kissed her on the lips. After a few seconds, ice cubes were hitting them, tossed from the other table.

They shot them the middle finger and kept kissing until finally they both started to laugh.

He took her head between both his hands and looked deep in her eyes.

"Please don't do that to me again, Marlene," he said softly. "Please? Next time, nobody will ever find me."

"I know," she said.

All the battle groups were now on the small frontier planet. The remaining enemy had been quickly destroyed or captured. The few prisoners who spoke the common tongue were interrogated by the Black Shirts, and the few who spoke Russian were handled by the Marauders. The majority spoke German, and the German speakers of the PIGs were busy.

All the Wind Rider electronics specialists were working day and night, and none more so than Duncan and CT. Both had to be constantly reminded to eat and a few times physically escorted to their bunks to sleep. PG had recovered from the raid and had thrown herself into the work, even more than Duncan and CT had.

Capturing the communications centre had given them the enemy frequencies, but most of the communications were in Morse code and then coded further. Cracking the code was taking a long time. The enemy's computer systems seemed simple and archaic. This was what was consuming most of CT's and Duncan's time. They first had to crack the language, then they could design a Trojan to infect it.

After four months of nonstop work, Jane exercised her position as the overall commander and ordered all Wind Riders and everyone involved in the interrogations to take three days off. Tempers were growing short, stupid mistakes were being made, and the lack of sleep and bad eating habits were all contributing to a general degradation of everyone's efficiency.

At first, the local merchants and vendors had been extremely happy. They had never been so busy or made so much money. But as prices rose, it became cheaper to bring in supplies, and business began to drop off, especially once all the battalions started opening their own mess clubs and the local establishments no longer had long lines to get in.

Also, being who they were, the Wind Riders had stills up and running, and demand was high for their high quality vodka. Not to be outdone, the Black Shirts had two breweries, which produced better beer than the locals' breweries. The PIGs and Marauders travelled across the planet and dealt directly with the agricultural producers for fresh meat, fruit, and vegetables, cutting out the middlemen.

Having an army made up as theirs was, doing all the butchering and food processing was not a hardship once the necessary equipment was installed, and soon the division was producing more of everything than they could consume. Shops were opened in the towns the battalions were housed in, and locals were hired to staff them.

Electronic and mechanical repair shops were opened as bored troopers with a lot of time on their hands started repairing local broken-down equipment. Once again, they took on local people to perform the day-to-day operations. They paid better, treated the workers better, and produced better products than the local shops, and for substantially less money. It did not take long before the locals started losing money. The smarter, smaller business owners rapidly matched what the Division's people were doing and stayed in business, but the bigger companies refused to change and were soon on the verge of bankruptcy.

It didn't take long for complaints to be filed with the Federation trade commission about unfair trade practices. A delegation of investigators, filling two transport ships, descended on the planet. It took three months to complete the investigation, and just when things were reaching the most critical point in the work of the Division's intelligence people, the Federation people and local government and business leaders demanded a meeting.

All the battlegroup generals and their staffs, and all the battalion commanders and their staffs, were summoned for the meeting. All showed up in their dark green official uniforms in all their braids and badged glory. No one paid much attention to the lowly Master Warrant Officer, and Duncan was able to effectively disappear in plain sight as the four generals took most of the questions and provided most of the answers. Their colonels provided the answers the generals could not. Not once were the locals asked to justify themselves, and finally, after the fourth day of the inquisition, Duncan stood and approached the Division officers' podium.

"Good morning, everyone. My name is Duncan Kovaks. I am the overall commander of the Division and majority shareholder of Wind Rider Enterprises, which runs all of our businesses Federation wide. We have shown that we employ fair market practices. Like every business, we pay competitive prices for our raw materials and utilize recognized profit margins to establish our selling prices. We pay our workers a fair wage and provide the best benefit package anywhere in the Federation, let alone this planet, which does not seem to have any benefit packages at all. This, I must remind the Federation trade commission, is against Federation policy. I will admit that our profit margins are slightly higher here than on other planets, but that is more a case of high demand than anything else. In any case, they are well below the maximum allowed by the Federation, which again, I suggest is not the case for the local businesses.

"Now, my people and I really have better things to do than waste our time sitting here being treated like common criminals. I understand that to you, this is the most important thing in your lives, but I would like remind you of why we are here in the first place. I can assure you that if we were not here, this new invader would quickly overwhelm not just this planet, but the whole Federation.

This business activity of ours is just a sideline, something that keeps our troopers from being bored.

"Good day. This inquisition is over."

The Divisional officers rose together and walked out of the banquet hall.

"CT," Duncan said.

"No problem, Boss, way ahead of you," CT said. "Shelly was just awaiting the go-ahead. She has sent all the documents to the Federation Council directly, plus all the evidence we have uncovered outlining the collusion and corruption of the delegation. They have also been given a warning that we will suspend our military affairs in this sector now that the emergency is over and go back home if they continue this witch hunt."

"Did we learn anything from that transport ship we captured?" Duncan asked.

"Pretty primitive," Bishop said. "Solid fuel rocket propulsion using hydrogen as the fuel. It looks as though it can hold about four hundred troops and their equipment. They were refuelling when we picked them up."

"The major in command of the troops that just landed spoke fairly decent standard," Leblanc said. "Had a haughty, superior attitude, almost condescending. One thing of interest, he saw a group photo of us in our dress uniforms and commented on how similar they were to his. Showed me a picture, too."

"Oh, shit," Duncan said when he saw the photo and showed it to Jane, who whistled.

"How fast can that transport and its crew be ready to go, Bishop?" Duncan asked.

"Tomorrow easy," Bishop said. "Why?"

"Leblanc, set up a meeting with this major for this afternoon," Duncan said. "There will be five of us coming, so make it a boardroom. Then we will ship our friend back home to the Fatherland, and he can explain some facts of life to his commanders."

The group had grown to seven by the time the meeting started. The major walked in, came to attention, and gave them a Nazi salute. Duncan nodded at him in return.

"Have a seat, Major," Duncan said in German. The man was over six feet tall, had short-cropped blond hair and blue eyes. His uniform was an old pattern green camouflage with lightning bolts on each collar.

"We will be shipping you home tomorrow morning on your transport ship," Duncan said. "I want you to listen carefully to everything I say and report it back to your commanders. I do not require any information from you. You have given us enough already.

"None of us sitting across from you have any love for the National Socialist Party or their policies. Your revered leader is degraded and mocked for the coward he was. Your movement has been outlawed everywhere on Earth. Even the people of Germany react with disgust at the mention of your party and its leaders. Most of the SS were tried for crimes against humanity and hanged or shot.

"On my far right is Major Benoit of the French Foreign Legion, next is Colonel O'Donnel of the Australian Army, then General Jenson of the United States Army. On my far left, Major Conrad of the British Army, Colonel Rostov of the Russian Army and General Kaufmann of the army of the Republic of Germany. I am Lord Kovaks, Canadian Army.

"The Canadian Army fought against and defeated the Waffen SS in France and Holland. We have no love or respect for you people because you have no respect for anyone else. The Third Reich is long gone and destroyed. The people of Germany, with the help of the rest of the world, have recovered from the horrors and destruction you people forced them to endure. All of Europe has been at peace since the end of the war in 1945.

"What you see before you are representatives of the very countries that defeated you, and you have attacked us once again without provocation. Go home, and tell your commanders what I have just told you. And one more thing. It may take us some time, but we are coming. There is no place for you in modern society. Make peace now, or you will face the same as before. Unconditional surrender."

Duncan and the other six rose, frowned at the young Major, and left him sitting there. CT was reporting to Duncan as they walked out of the building.

"Okay, Boss," he said. "Now that we know what we know, it was too easy. They are still using the old Enigma machines to do the coding for them. We have two scout ships on standby to shadow the transport when it leaves. Once in orbit around wherever it lands, they will seed orbital satellites everywhere. We will have blanket coverage, and then we can start getting real intel."

The group walked down the block to the Black Shirt HQ where Bishop and the Black Shirt General were waiting.

"We know these people," Duncan said. "At least we knew who they were. At the time, they had advanced military technology, but the combined countries of the Earth defeated them anyway. They could not keep up with the technologies our countries were developing. We will find out what capabilities they have currently and how ours compares. It does not appear that they have advanced much in the last seventy years, but they will have the advantage over us in air power if they conform to past practices. Again, we will monitor the situation and come up with something to even the odds. I have ordered enough transports to deploy two of our four battlegroups at a time. Hopefully it is not too far away."

Once the Nazi spacecraft took off, it was easy to pinpoint where it was going. They immediately started to broadcast and receive messages, on which CT and his team were able to triangulate, fixing the location of the home broadcasts. At the speed the spacecraft was traveling, it would take three months for it to reach that location. The two scout ships could make it in two days without much effort.

The two scout ships were ordered to proceed to the targeted location, and by midday of the third day, the intelligence team was receiving data from high orbit satellites. The planet was not large but very Earth-like. It had one city with about one hundred thousand people in it and two more with around twenty thousand. All the cities had airports, and the largest hosted a military base and the spaceport. Only the airports and a two-lane highway linked the cities together and the distance between the cities was large. The planet was completely forested where there was land, but most of the planet was water, with only the one continent.

Areas across the continent were cleared, and the main industry seemed to be farming. While there was some mechanization, most of the farmwork seemed to be done with horses and oxen, much as it had been on 1930s Earth. The farms were no bigger than eighty acres.

As predicted, a number of FW 190 fighter aircraft were tied down at the main city's airport. This could prove a problem. They could fly as high as their four surveillance aircraft and were faster. In addition, the FW 190s were excellent ground attack aircraft, and their armament package would mount a challenge. In this aspect, the enemy had the advantage. The only armed aircraft the division had were the transport ships with their lasers, and the Hueys with their machine guns.

Also as predicted, there were twenty Tiger tanks with 80mm cannons. These were not expected to present much of a problem. The modern armor-piercing rounds from the 40mm guns of the Coyotes and LAVs, and their superior speed and handling, would outclass the tracked opponents.

Interrogations of captured enemy troops back on the frontier planet, verified the armaments. Each section had two MG 42s and the rest of the troops used STG44 assault rifles, comparable arms to what the division was using but with a larger caliber bullet and heavier construction. There was no body armor and no troop carriers beyond soft-skinned trucks. Artillery consisted mainly of 88mm multipurpose guns and a few short-range antitank guns.

With their armoured troop transports, the division expected to have the advantage in the ground war. They could track and eliminate targets on the move at a far distance. The enemy had to stop to aim and fire, and their cannon only shot slow, one-at-a-time shots, whereas the automatic cannon the division used could fire rapidly. The division's 105mm artillery was also superior to the enemy's in firepower, range, accuracy, and speed of fire. Even with the inclusion of the fighter aircraft, the division had the advantage.

Chapter Seventeen

The trip to the planet had taken a day and a half. It had been cramped in the small, fast transport as four companies of recon troops had been squeezed into the interior. All the vehicles were packed to overcapacity with personal gear, food, water, fuel, and ammunition, mostly ammunition. They would be on their own for a week. For the last two hours, they had been sitting in their vehicles as the transport slowed and entered the atmosphere. The lights were off. It was night, planet-side. The only light was dim and red so as not to affect their night vision.

The Zebras would disembark first, one hundred kilometres from their target town. Then the transport would take the other three companies of Wind Riders and drop them off a hundred kilometres from the main city. There was another transport that would drop off four more companies of Wind Riders on the opposite side of the main city and the other small town on that side. After that, the transports would return to the staging planet, returning a week later with the main assault transports. They would have a company of PIGs each, which would assault the airports in the two small towns.

The Zebras and other recon teams were to establish positions to observe the enemy, fixing numbers of troops and locations of barracks, armouries, supply depots, and communications centres. At initial assault they were to provide cover and eliminate threats at the airports.

The Zebras were given the heads-up five minutes before landfall and turned on their night vision goggles and vehicle engine. The transport came to a hover and started to descend, opening the rear hatch as it did so, the fresh air clearing out some of the vehicle exhaust. By the time the ramp was fully open, the transport touched down and the four G-Wagons and the Coyote roared out of the transport and down the two-lane paved highway the transport had landed in the middle of. In less than two minutes, the Zebras were clear and the transport taking off once again.

They had three hours of darkness to reach the abandoned farmyard in the trees that had been selected as their initial camp spot. They would spend the day there and then spread out around the town and set up their observation posts. PG had the sensors of the Coyote focused in the front and would spot any traffic on the road, but none was expected. They drove at full speed, ninety kilometers per hour, even loaded down as they were.

To look at the Coyote, there was not much an outsider could tell between it and its cousin, the Kodiak. The differences were mostly internal. The Kodiak was the primary fighting vehicle of the battle group. It held seven troopers in addition to the three-man crew. The Coyote held only four in total, a commander, gunner, driver, and electronics specialist. The interior of the Coyote was crammed with radios, monitors, and sophisticated electronics that, when the three-meter high mast was fully deployed, gave a visual of the surroundings, both infrared and color, plus the ability to detect and pinpoint radio or other electronic signatures from a distance. All this data would be correlated and processed, then sent back to the regular Kodiaks, who would act on the information. They would also collect all the data given them from the G-Wagon teams, who could be deployed tens of kilometres away.

For defence, each vehicle was armed similarly. The standard Kodiak had a 35mm chain gun cannon as the main gun, with a 7.62 machine gun mounted coaxially. There was also a 7.62 machine gun mounted on a stand that the commander could use outside the hatch. A few Kodiaks were equipped as anti-armour vehicles and had anti-tank rockets mounted in a remote weapons station mounted on the rear. Others had a remote with a 12mm heavy machine gun mounted in it. There were also eight grenade launchers mounted four to each side of the cupola housing the cannon.

The Coyote had the same main gun and grenade launchers but utilized a machine gun using the same ammunition the troopers' rifles used instead of the larger 7.62 ammunition. For this mission, the Coyotes had two rocket launchers, one on each side of the cupola. Each launcher held four antitank rockets. Also for this mission, they had an extra electronics person, who would be operating an unarmed aerial drone vehicle. It was a fixed wing aircraft that had a small propeller attached to a small internal combustion engine that used the same fuel the Coyote used.

The policy was to deploy four G-Wagons and a Coyote on a mission of this type. They had four-man crews – a driver, automatic weapons specialist, designated rifleman/sniper, and a spotter for the sniper. Each was issued what was called a C-8. Unlike the normal C-8s, these had 16 inch barrels, not the normal 14 inch, with the designated rifleman having a 20 inch barrel, a bipod, and a grenade launcher mounted under the main barrel. All weapons used the same 5.56 ammunition, except for the designated rifleman, who also had a dedicated long-range rifle. These were bolt action single-shot rifles that used a special 7.62 bullet made to exacting specifications rather than the mass produced 7.62 machine gun bullets. In addition, each trooper had a semi-automatic pistol that held eight .45 caliber bullets in the butt. All the weapons had flash suppressors and could be fitted with sound suppressors.

The most impressive of the crew weapons was the sniper rifle Marlene carried. Whereas the normal sniper rifle, under ideal conditions, could hit a range of 800 meters, her rifle could reliably reach 1,000 meters in normal conditions and more if conditions were optimal. It fired a massive 12mm bullet that could penetrate even a Coyote's armour. Against a human being, a hit anywhere on the body usually meant death.

For this mission, they had also been issued with four hand-operated antitank rockets. These had a maximum range of two kilometres.

Each G-Wagon had two remote electronic detection monitors, much like the one mounted on the Coyote. These would be mounted on a tripod and could be placed a maximum of two hundred meters from the vehicle.

Also, for the first time, each G-Wagon had been given a small unarmed surveillance drone. It was roughly square, with four electrically operated propellers. It could take off and land vertically as well as hover if required. It could fly as high as 4,000 meters, as fast as 60 kilometres per hour, and be operated as far away as one hundred kilometres. The internal battery could power it for up to six hours. Another battery powered the two onboard cameras, one of which was infrared. They were two meters long by just under two meters wide and painted a dull grey. The small size, low noise, and camouflage color would render them almost invisible.

It had been decided to add a fifth crew for this mission. Its members would act as a security team for the Coyote and were troopers who had passed the Zebra selection process, but who were not yet fully qualified to operate as Zebras.

A hint of grey was dawning as they reached the turn-off point for the clearing in which they would spend the day. By the time the sun peeked over the horizon, all six vehicles were spread out at the perimeter of the clearing. The new dark green and tanned striped paint scheme blended with the dark green trees, but netting was spread over the vehicles anyway. Half of each crew would stand watch for four hours, while the other half slept under cover of the trees, close to the vehicles. The Coyote deployed its mast fully and launched its drone. The drone would cover their back-trail and look for a fallback position should they require it. The other four G-Wagons deployed their smaller drones to survey the positions they wanted to deploy to the next day.

Brock had a big grin on his face as he placed the small drone on the ground, took up the remote control, and started flying it. He loved the little gadget. Marlene shook her head and smiled, then made her way to the back of the G-Wagon, unlashed a fuel can, and topped up the fuel tank. Then she took up Brock's normal position manning the machine gun mounted on the vehicle's roof. All the other crews did the same, except for those in the Coyote, who placed its weapons on automatic, the two crew members awake monitoring the electronics.

Just after ten, Shandra and Gerry came out of the trees. Shandra took the controls from Brock and Gerry the gun from Marlene, and they walked under the cover of the trees, laid down, and in seconds were asleep.

It was mid afternoon when Marlene woke up. Brock was already gone, and he had their two-burner camp stove set up at the rear of the vehicle with a coffee pot perched on top, steam escaping the spout, telling her the coffee was ready. Brock poured her a cup and then one for himself. He filled another mug and handed it up to Gerry. Shandra put down the remote and walked over to them, holding out her cup.

"The little beastie should be here in ten minutes," she said. "I put it on auto return."

The built-in electronics would return the small drone back to its launch site on its own.

"I have already calculated a route and found a good overwatch position for us," she continued.

"Gerry, come down from there," Marlene said. "We all need to see this, especially you."

The town they were to observe was in a floodplain at the junction of two small rivers. The position Shandra had found was located roughly in the centre of the town and 800 meters from the far edge of it. It was at the top of the large ridge overlooking the town and was mostly bare of trees, except for a large patch of brush that covered a small ravine. This was where they would conceal the G-Wagon. While they were too far away from the airfield and barracks to provide direct support, that was not their job for this mission. They had the perfect position to observe the whole town and would cut off any troops escaping in that direction.

Except for the last three kilometres, the route chosen to reach the position was under cover of trees. It was a barely cleared track through the trees, a firebreak really, not a road. In any case, they would travel by night. Marlene transmitted the information to the Coyote so they could input it into the Coyote's database.

"Well, big guy," she said to Brock, "it's your turn to cook. Make mine medium rare, please."

That drew a bunch of laughs. They would be eating freeze dried goo for the foreseeable future. Then she made her way over to the Coyote and rapped on the side of it.

"Get your butt out here and into the sunshine, PG," she said. PG would never leave the Coyote if they let her. She got lost in her electronic and computer world.

"I've got all the team's data, Boss," PG said. She was the ranking officer of their little group, but Marlene was the overall commander. "I have also plotted a fallback position and routes to it for each of you, should we need it."

"Good stuff," Marlene said. "Now get some food and some shuteye. Get all the sleep you can tonight and tomorrow. Other people can handle your stuff. I am going to need you sharp once we get going, so make sure you get rest, okay? My team has the farthest to go, so we pull out tonight. The rest of you take it easy here tomorrow."

"I'll keep an eye on you guys tomorrow with the drone," PG said.

"Thanks, but under no circumstances are you to come to the rescue if we get into trouble," Marlene said. "That goes for all of us. We need to keep the enemy in the dark for as long as we can. If you are discovered, give them hell, then run like hell. Understood?"

"Roger," she replied, then looked down at her feet and took a couple of swallows. Marlene clapped her on the shoulder.

"This time we are the eyes and ears, Pigpen," Marlene said. "Others do the shooting. Until the time the assault craft are inbound, nobody sees us or hears us. Got it?"

PG was still looking at the ground but nodded her head. She had taken the loss of her teammates hard. They had all been training hard for the last few months to get ready for this mission, especially PG. She had no intention of missing anything this time.

"Go see Brock," Marlene said. "He has a pot of tolerable coffee."

The other electronics tech came out of the Coyote as PG walked toward Brock.

"Make sure she gets a lot of sleep the rest of the day," Marlene said. "Keep anything unimportant until she wakes up. Send important shit to me if any comes up. And you make sure you spell off with the other tech regularly. Maybe bring one of the security team in to help you out. We are going to need all of you in top shape for this one."

PG had a cup of coffee and a tin plate of the mush they called rations and was just plunking herself down beside the G-Wagon as Marlene came up and accepted a plate from Brock.

"There you go, my lady," Brock said. "One filet mignon, medium rare, as ordered."

"Ewe," PG said with a grimace after tasting a forkful of the goo. "Everyone knows filet mignon is to be eaten rare, not medium rare."

PG was sitting cross-legged, her back against the front tire, and Marlene sat beside her, leaning against the fender. She also took a bite and sighed.

"Well, I guess it's better than starving," she said. "But not much."

They finished their meals in silence, the others in the team sitting at the rear of the vehicle. PG took a look around the little clearing. Her eyes took on a faraway look, and her face went sad. A tear slowly made its way down her cheek, and she looked down for a moment, then brushed the tear away and took a deep breath.

"It's a lot like this back home," she said finally. "The trees are a little different, but not much. My family used to spend the weekends and our two week summer holiday in a spot very much like this one. We would load up our big SUV, drive an hour west on paved roads, then an hour north on a gravel one, and finally, the last twenty kilometres or so on a small forest road, just like the one we are following now. It was always so peaceful and quiet, away from all the hustle and bustle of the big city, with its constant buzz of activity and underlying hum of traffic. Only the wind rustling through the trees and the sound of birds and squirrels disturbed the surroundings. A little stream running through the meadow provided us with clear, fresh water. An animal called a beaver had built a dam across the stream, making a small lake, and we would take fish from it each day. My mother did not much like roughing it in the woods, and my father would split up the yearly holiday, sometimes two weeks in the woods and one week in some tourist trap, then the next, two weeks at the tourist trap and one in the woods. But my brother and I, well, we loved the woods. The tourist traps with their ice cream and water parks were nice, but they were always jam-packed with people. A person might as well have stayed home. Out here, well, it is so peaceful, so quiet."

"So, you come from a place similar to where Duncan grew up?" Marlene asked. "He never talks about it much."

PG gave a little laugh. "No, Duncan grew up in a place very much like this one. I grew up in a city of a million people about sixty kilometres to the south. My mom and dad were both city people, but my dad's family were farm people, and he would spend the summer months on the farm. He loved being outdoors, so he exposed us kids to it as much as he could. My mom, well, her people were city people and rarely left, even for holidays, if they took those. They were always money hungry, never having enough."

"So, you were poor then?" Marlene asked.

"In the sense of what you call poor, Marlene, I guess we were," PG replied. "We didn't have a big fancy house with servants or big fancy stables with grooms and fancy horses. My mom worked, but I think mostly because my dad let her. He had a good job as a tradesman and was well respected. He paid all the bills, and my mom spent all her money on clothes and knick-knacks. My brother and I went to good schools. My brother followed dad into his trade, and I went to university. We never wanted for anything. If we wanted to play a sport, my dad made sure we did. We traveled some, to different parts of our country and others."

"You did not have mandatory military service?" Marlene asked.

"No, heck no," PG replied. "Our country had a population of thirty-two million, and I think our armed forces numbered around fifty thousand in total. When I was growing up, there had been no major wars for over seventy years. Our military people were all volunteers, and only the best ever made it through the qualification process. When we did get involved in a small war, everyone wanted us. Our people were that good. Only Duncan's mother's family and Carol's people had mandatory military service like we do here. In some ways, I think it's a good thing. I mean, how many eighteen-year-old kids really know what they want to do with the rest of their lives anyway? The way this is set up, you don't have to serve if you don't want to. But the long-term benefits are a lot better if you do."

PG had finished her meal by then and rose, gave the eating utensils back to Brock, and thanked everyone, before heading back to the Coyote, grabbing her sleeping gear and bedding down.

"Did you hear that?" Marlene asked. "She comes from a city of over a million people and a country with thirty-two million. Duncan tells me he comes from a small part of a small country."

"You know Ann from the Wind Riders?" Shandra asked. "She told me she comes from a country just to the south of the one Duncan comes from. The city she comes from has twenty million people, her country three hundred million, and that their two countries put together have only a quarter of the population of their world."

"No, I think it is less than that," Brock said. "I overheard one of the original PIGs say there were three billion people on that planet."

"And we thought Oaken was big," Marlene said. All of them grew quiet while they thought on that.

Chapter Eighteen

The G-Wagon was concealed under netting fifty meters from the crest of the long ridge that overlooked the town. The remote monitors had been set out on the crest as far as the cables would allow, angled to give almost one hundred and eighty degrees of coverage along the front and sides of the ridge. Marlene and Gerry had crawled to the top and were observing their side of the town with binoculars and the high-powered spotting scope, while Brock and Shandra continued to set up their small camp. The vicinity was basically treeless, but the area they had chosen for camp had some scrub brush about a hundred meters square and rose almost three meters high. Tonight, they would work on creating a hole into the center of it, just as they had done before. For now, what they had was good enough, but as they had learned the hard way, one week could easily turn into six weeks and they wanted to be prepared.

The side of the town they were observing was eight hundred meters away across a small bridge. While the streets inside the town and leading to the bridge were paved, the road was gravel after that and led to farmlands and the beginning of woodlands. The opposite side of the town was open farmland for as far as they could see, which was about thirty kilometres from their vantage point. After a distance of five kilometres, the other two sides were heavily forested.

The town itself was laid out in a square grid pattern. The airfield opposite them had two runways that formed a V pattern, with the hangers and other buildings closest to the town. Adjacent to the airfield was what looked like a barracks complex and depot, with repair shops and several other large buildings with an outsized paved open space to one side. Both the airfield and barracks complex were surrounded by ten foot high barbed wire fences in two rows, spaced eight feet apart. Unmanned guard towers and defensive positions were placed all along the perimeters of the fence, and anti-aircraft guns were mounted in several places. They also were unmanned.

The town appeared to be like any other town. In the centre was a large square with a park and fountains and what looked like administration buildings. Ranged around that were shops and small office buildings, none higher than three stories. There were four schools and grounds, one located in each quarter of the town, and every few blocks, there was a small green space with a children's apparatus and benches.

The houses were all two-story, long and narrow, with large back green spaces and the fronts close to the street. The streets were narrow. Two G-Wagons could pass each other, but the Coyotes or Kodiaks would take up most of the street. All of the houses were neat and tidy, and while the doors and trims might be of a different colour, the roofs were all red tile and the walls all cream. Yards had lush grass and trees with large patios, and most had stables of some sort and buildings that held farm implements.

It must have been a day off, because after the initial feeding of animals and cleaning of stalls, neighbours and families began to congregate in the yards and parks. Several families loaded into horse-drawn wagons piled high with food baskets. The children and adults alike were laughing and singing as they headed into the woods. Others went for strolls or congregated at two of the schoolyards where soccer matches of all age groups went on all day.

As the afternoon progressed to evening, most families congregated at someone's house and ate meals together at large tables. As the sun went down, those who had gone for outings returned home and joined the other gatherings. Soon the beer and food were flowing and laughter and singing filled the air. It was the very picture of a stable and happy society.

Night fell. Before midnight, everyone was back in their own homes, lights were off, and except for two policemen who casually wandered the streets. The town went to sleep.

"Shit," Gerry said as he and Marlene came back to their tiny cramped camp. "What the hell are we doing here? No war-like whooping and ranting and, except for the airbase, no guns or weapons anywhere. I have never seen anything like it. Have you?"

"Not what we were expecting, that's for sure," Marlene said, then she switched frequencies to contact PG.

"*Delta One, Alpha One, copy.*"

"*Copy Alpha One.*"

"*Uh, are we sure we are at the right place, Delta One? This hardly looks like a hostile environment.*"

"*Complex next to the airfield is definitely a barracks and armoury, Alpha One. Looks like it's big enough for a battalion of armoured troops. SOP for peacetime is to have weekends off.*"

"*Roger Delta One, Alpha One Out.*"

Brock and Shandra had made decent progress making the camp in the bush. Camo-coloured tarps were ringing the sides and across the top, and they would be out of the wind and rain. Marlene would take the first watch on the sensor arrays and the rest rolled up in the sleeping bags and went to sleep.

The next day, things began to fall into a routine. Two hours before dawn, bakers went to their shops and started baking. At dawn, cows were milked, horses fed, stalls cleaned, followed by breakfast, then men harnessing horses to wagons or other farm implements and heading into the fields. Workers began to walk to their shops or the local brewery. Uniformed men went to the police station or fire hall, while others in brown uniforms walked to the administration offices.

School-aged children headed off to school, and mothers began to hang bedding to air out of opened windows. Then they would sweep the front walks and the portion of the road in front of their homes. After lunch, they made their way to the shops in the centre of town, most of them riding bicycles with large baskets, where they would pick up fresh bread, produce, and meat. Few women appeared to be in the workforce, as most of the women seemed to stay home. Mid afternoon, the school children were home and men trickled back in from the fields. By early evening, all the workers came out of shops and the brewery, stopped for a beer in the local neighbourhood pubs, and went home. For all appearance, it was a peaceful society.

Two flights a day, one in the morning, one in the afternoon, by the FW190s: the only things military.

What they had first thought was another armoury turned out to be a kind of prison. The prisoners were brought out each morning after dawn, lined up, and counted. Then they were marched off to work. The prisoners wore black-and-white-striped uniforms that had seen better days. Many of them were barefoot, and, for those that were not, the shoes were in bad shape. They were escorted by ten guards armed with rifles, trailed by a truck with work tools, a water jug, and an armed machine gun mounted and manned in the back.

Even a minor mistake was punished aggressively by, at a minimum, beatings by hand or usually by rifle butts slammed into backs. The work was hard, removing large rocks from fields, and no breaks were given except for a short water break at noon. At dusk, they were roughly herded back to the prison and shoved back inside and the doors locked. The crews were rotated daily. On the second day, the guards were more brutal. One guard raped the same woman out of sight of the town. Both groups of guards were tough on one particular man, and when Marlene focused her spotting scope on him, he was a mass of bruises and open sores.

All of the guards had lightning bolts on their collars and death heads on their caps. On their off days, they went to the same tavern. Any townspeople who crossed their paths lowered their heads and avoided eye contact, and the policeman rendered salutes and scuttled out of the way.

This was the only indication that something was not quite right. Nowhere in the Federation were prisoners treated in that fashion, not even the most hardened of criminals. Marlene took videos of all this and had PG send them back to HQ. All the Zebras desperately wanted to do something but could not. Yet.

"Whiskey Romeo Zebra Alpha One, Whiskey Romeo Alpha Foxtrot One, sit rep."

This was the HQ communications squadron asking for Marlene. They should almost be in planetary orbit by now.

"Whiskey Romeo Alpha Foxtrot One, Whiskey Romeo Zebra Alpha One, status the same. Minimal Tango at this time, copy?"

"Whiskey Romeo Zebra Alpha One, copy minimal Tango. Sierra green, sierra green, copy?"

"Whiskey Romeo Alpha Foxtrot One, copy sierra green, over."

"Whiskey Romeo Zebra Alpha One, Whiskey Romeo Alpha Foxtrot One, out."

"Zebra Alpha One, Zebra, sierra green, I repeat sierra green, out."

The invasion and assault timetable was still as planned, three days from now.

"Shit, a little overkill for this place," Brock said. "We could take these guys down ourselves, easy."

Half a battalion of PIGs had been planned to assault and control this town.

"Every male has to have two years military training," Marlene said. "For all we know, they all have weapons in those houses or in that armoury over there. A half battalion might not be enough if they fight as hard as that last group we hit. Stick with the plan,

Brock. The first bullet I fire is reserved for that asshole guard, I can tell you that."

The next morning all started off the same, but by noon, things changed. Several large red Nazi flags were hung from windows of the main administration building. Children were sent home from school, and there was much scurrying around. Nazi flags started appearing on one house per block. Men came hurrying back in from fields, and a large dust cloud appeared above the woods near the road on that side of town.

"Alpha One, Echo One, uh, you see what I see?"

"Roger Echo One, any visual?"

"Negative, other than the first motorcycles and about four armoured scout vehicles. Everything else is under the dust, but it is at least a couple of kilometres long. Too far away for infrared as yet."

"Roger. Zebra, Alpha One, get the drones airborne and let's see what we can see."

Within minutes, Brock had the little beastie up and headed for the dust plume, and Shandra was monitoring it.

"Oh fuck!" Shandra said ten minutes later. "Multiple Tangos. We got tanks Mar, lots of them, and armoured personnel carriers. Looks like a whole Panzer battalion."

"You got enough to send to Division Echo One?"

"Roger Alpha One. Sensors pick up target-rich environment. Twenty-plus Panzer fives, one hundred plus half-tracks, one battery of arty and half a battalion of support vehicles. Sending info to Division Alpha One."

"Copy Echo One. All Zebra, invisible, people, invisible."

"Where the hell did they come from?" Shandra asked.

"Must have been on some training exercise," Marlene said. "Coms dark, people."

Brock brought the small drone back, and the remote systems started picking up and transmitting the vehicle signatures approaching. Brock came up to their overwatch position with his crew weapon and two antitank rockets.

This day, the prisoners were herded back to their cellblock early and made to jog as the guards piled into the back of the truck. Once they arrived, the prisoners were shoved harder than usual and locked up, and the guards hurried over to their barracks.

By then, the lead scout elements of the Panzer battalion were hitting the town, and the air was full of engine and tank tread noise. School kids and their escorts were hurried to line the streets leading to the barracks, wearing colourful clothing and waving miniature red flags as the dust-covered vehicles made their noisy way down the street leading to the barracks.

An awesome display of military might and firepower made its way into the marshalling areas, where, with last blasts of engines, they were shut down. Troopers began to dismount and make their way to a parade area where they lined up, were counted, and dismissed to barracks.

"Holy Fuck," Brock said. "Two thousand easy. Shit, now that half battalion is no way big enough. You see the size of those tanks?"

Marlene's communicator vibrated, letting her know she had just received a message.

"Surprise," Marlene said. "Hold and monitor, they say. Things just got a whole lot more interesting."

A couple of hours later, the barracks emptied as black uniformed troops went into town and took over all the pubs. PG relayed a message from division that it was an SS Panzer battalion. The town got rowdy that night, and the locals kept to their homes.

The next morning, even more cautious than they had already been, Marlene and Gerry were in their observation post and her communicator buzzed again. The main assault was still on, but their part of it was on hold for now, with the usual hold and report tacked onto the end.

The townspeople went about their normal day, but the air was noticeably more tense. When the people moved about, they did so with a purpose and did not linger as they had previously. The few black-uniformed men off-base were greeted respectfully, with downcast eyes. Those on duty showed up at the vehicle assembly area and started unloading supplies and cleaning the dust and mud off vehicles. Several of the tanks were sent over to a repair area and engines and power train units were pulled out of them.

Everywhere, engine oil was being changed, tracks cleaned and checked for wear, and bearings greased. Then, the work done, each vehicle was inspected by an officer and the troops sent off, only to reappear shortly in their black uniforms and head off-base to the pubs and taverns once again.

Marlene and Gerry were in place three hours before dawn the next morning. Ten minutes after the main assault hit the airfield in the capital city, sirens went off all over the town and every light on the base turned on, turning the dark into the light of day. Troops poured out of barracks, all armed, some heading to defensive positions, others to the armoury, and the majority to their vehicles.

Men spewed out of houses, pulling on grey uniforms, some with weapons, while others headed to what was now definitely their armoury. Camouflaged defensive positions were manned and high-power spotlights were turned on, scanning the air and ground around the town.

"Fuck!" Gerry said. "These guys don't fuck around."

Within a half-hour, all approaches to the town and all the bridges had at least a section of troops with two MG 42s guarding them. The town's anti-air defences were fully manned, as were all the concrete bunkers. A short-range antitank gun was pushed into place to guard each bridge and camouflaged, while four more were placed in the city centre.

The airfield was a hub of activity. The six aircraft were pushed out of hangers and fuelled. Trucks pulled up, belts of machine gun and cannon ammunition loaded, and finally two bombs strapped under each wing. Then the pilots, parachutes banging under their rear ends, ran over and climbed into cockpit. With blue coughing roars, the big engines came alive, and all six aircraft taxied to the active runway. In staggered pairs, they took off, headed for the capital just as the sun came over the horizon.

Munitions were trucked over to the tanks and half-tracks, and fuel tanks were topped off. Spare fuel cans were loaded and personal gear strapped to the vehicles' sides and tops. Exterior MG 42s were loaded, belts hanging freely. Within an hour, the scout vehicles were headed down the road leading to the capital city, leaving the town empty except for the four Panther tanks that had their power trains removed, and their crews. The tanks were being repaired at a feverish pace.

Marlene's communicator vibrated again.

"Main assault progressing well. Original timetable your location re-established. Panzer battalion will be greeted on route. Expect minimal return aircraft."

Marlene sent a confirmation and then a message to her troops to proceed as planned.

Once the tanks were repaired, two were left to guard the airfield, while another two took up position in the town square. Only two fighter planes returned, both badly damaged and hurriedly shoved into hangers. After a preliminary once-over, work on one was halted and a major effort was made to repair the other.

After confirming the night positions of the section facing them, Marlene and Gerry made their way back to their camp. While Marlene shovelled her supper goo down, she went over the data PG had sent her and was developing a plan of attack for the next day.

PG's main task was to take out the four Panther tanks with her rockets, then the remaining aircraft and the anti-air and antitank guns on the airfield. Once the airfield was secure, she was to start taking out bunkers. All the other teams were to use their antitank rockets to take out bunkers, but only after the four tanks were confirmed kills. The machine guns were to be taken out first, then the antitank guns, and finally the troops opposite them.

Marlene was not much worried about the antitank gun facing them. It only had an effective range of five hundred meters, and they were at eight. Even the MG 42s would have trouble reaching them. She was pissed off and intent on making a show the next morning.

They were up before dawn, pulling down the netting from the G-Wagon and retrieving the remotes, stowing them along with their other gear. Then they cleaned and readied weapons and made sure they had full ammo loads. Marlene brushed her hair and pulled it severely back and had Shandra braid it tight to hang to just above her shoulders. She did the same for Shandra. Marlene soon pulled out her camo paint and, using the G-Wagon's mirror, painted black stripes on her face, making sure she highlighted the scar she normally kept concealed.

Shandra followed suit. Brock and Gerry shaved clean and painted their faces as well. It was not for camouflage. It was a war statement, and each of them looked fierce. Then Marlene ripped the sleeves off her shirt, undid her buttons, and rolled the shirt up to leave her belly bare. Then she applied the black paint in stripes on her arms and midriff.

It was well past dawn by the time preparations were complete. The three transports were in orbit, and the rest of Zebra was waiting. Marlene shrugged on her weapon harness and hung her rifle across her chest. Gerry had attached their small battalion flag on one of the rear aerials, and they all took their positions in the G-Wagon, Brock standing in the open roof hatch with his C9 loaded and mounted on the roof pintle. Marlene nodded, and Gerry fired up the G-Wagon and began the climb to the top of the hill.

"*All Zebra, Zebra One*," Marlene said, breaking radio silence. "*All Zebra hold in place until my go. Sierra, wait my clearance.*"

Gerry crested the ridge line slowly and drove down a hundred meters before turning the G-Wagon sideways. Then all of them but Brock dismounted. Gerry and Shandra went to the back and unloaded the four antitank rockets, while Marlene placed her high-powered rifle on the hood of the vehicle and glassed the enemy position.

"*What the fuck are you doing, Alpha One?*" PG yelled into her comm.

"*All Zebra hold until my go,*" Marlene said.

The troops in front of her were scurrying about trying to get into firing positions. An officer was glassing Marlene, and she waved at him. To make things even more intimidating, all of them wore different coloured sunglasses. Then Marlene walked back behind the G-Wagon and shouldered her weapon, opening the breach enough to hand load a single round, then closing the bolt.

Snicks from rifles being cocked came from the other Alphas as she sighted.

"*All Zebra, on my mark,*" she said as she slid her sights on the officer still glassing her. "*Five, four, three, two, one…*" At one, she took up the slack on the trigger, and as the big gun went off, all hell broke loose all around the town.

All four tanks were hit seconds apart, and all were taken out, two with catastrophic secondary explosions. Then the Coyote's main gun opened up, raking the aircraft hangar and blowing up the airplane inside, shifting to the air and tank defensive guns. Shandra let loose with her first rocket, taking out the nearest bunker. Brock was firing three round bursts, and Marlene had already killed the two machine gunners and their assistant gunners. Anything that had a rifle was fair game, and, in minutes, there were no more targets at their location. Marlene started looking farther afield.

"Sierra, Zebra Echo One, airfield secure. Initial Tango neutralized. Panther neutralized. Secondary Tango deploying. Make it quick boys, target-rich environment and we only have so much ammo."

The Coyote broke cover and was firing as it came. Marlene put the sniper rifle across her back, and the four of them made their way down the hill. She was headed for the prison compound and had murder in her eyes. Shandra walked beside her and three meters behind. Gerry had his door open as he slowly drove behind them, his rifle angled out the window, and Brock was in constant motion scanning all around.

Ten brave men found out how outgunned they were when first Marlene let loose with a grenade from her launcher, and then she and the rest of her section hit them with their more powerful and longer-range weapons. By then, two transports were on the ground, Kodiaks driving at full speed, main guns engaging anything that moved or looked like a threat, as were the commanders' roof-mounted machine guns. Another transport landed on the opposite side of town from Marlene, and its troops soon joined the fun. As the Kodiaks reached their preplanned positions, dismounts poured out of them and fanned out, first forming defensive positions around the airfield, then fanning out and assaulting any strong points left. Four 105mm howitzers were wheeled into place, and the last remaining concrete bunkers were flattened.

Now dazed troops were throwing down weapons and placing hands behind their heads. White sheets were being draped outside the windows of houses, but still the odd brave man died trying to defend his town.

All this time, Marlene and Alpha made their way to the prison complex. Loudspeakers were blaring surrender instructions to the town. The prison guards were standing in front of their barracks, weaponless, with hands behind their heads and eyes very wide as they saw Alpha approaching, the scowls on their faces enhancing the war paint.

Marlene stopped in front of the trooper who enjoyed rape and came nose to nose with him.

"Give me an excuse, asshole," she quietly said in German. "I'll gut you first, then cut your balls off, and shove them in your mouth before you die. Come on, asshole, give me an excuse."

Her voice was calm, but the man was shaking in fear, as were the rest of them.

A G-Wagon and a Kodiak screamed up and troopers came piling out.

"Watch these fuckers," Marlene said. "If they move a muscle, waste 'em. Alpha, with me."

The PIG captain just looked at the Zebras in the war paint and the sunglasses with his mouth open as Marlene walked up to the gate and shot off the lock. Then she marched up to the prison barracks and gagged at the stench before she even opened the door.

"Everybody out!" she yelled in German. "Everybody out now!"

Prisoners came bolting out of the building, some staggering and some even crawling. They lined up as best they could, then Marlene took a deep breath and walked inside. She came back out and vomited.

"*Get a medical team out to the barracks complex on the west of town now!*" she yelled into her com. "*Multiple wounded and sick. Malnutrition and dehydration. Water and fluids stat!*"

Now she did bring her weapon to bear as she approached the former guards. Shandra knocked the weapon aside, and Brock pinned her arms to her sides.

"Let me at the bastards!" she yelled, kicking and squirming. Four more troopers came over and helped Brock take her to ground and keep her there. The PIG captain and his sergeant ran over to the building and went inside, coming back out gagging.

"Get those people some water!" the sergeant yelled out. A Kodiak and two G-Wagons with red crosses on them entered the compound, and medics piled out of them, headed for the prisoners.

"No," the captain yelled. "There are worse inside. Bring stretchers and set up a triage. *Hotel One, Charley Four, all available personnel to my location stat.* Leave the enemy wounded where they are."

"Get those fuckers out of my sight and to the assembly area. Keep them separate and shoot the fuckers if they so much as sneeze.,

"Warrant Isabelle, if I let you loose, can you control yourself?"

Marlene looked over to see the two lines of former guards being jogged off, none too gently, between six heavily armed and definitely pissed-off troops, and she nodded her head.

"Let her loose, boys," the Captain said, and Marlene stood, grabbed her ball cap from the ground, and plunked it back on her head. She left the sunglasses hanging on the cord attached to them.

"Sorry, Captain," she said. "We have been watching those assholes for over a week now. Christ, did you see what was in that building?"

Stretchers with people on them were being hurried out of the building, and medical staff was busy prioritizing treatment. IV bags were being hung, and, as word was getting around, medics from all over came at the run with their kits. The prisoners who had walked out or crawled out were the fortunate ones. The ones still alive inside were way worse off.

Forty had made it outside, and troopers were passing water bottles among them and sprinting back to vehicles to get more. Shandra was already beside the woman who had been repeatedly raped and was giving her water, and Marlene made her way to the man who had received all the beatings. He was refusing any water, making sure everyone else got some before he did.

"No," he said as Marlene handed him her water bottle. "No, the others first."

"Look at me," Marlene said. "Am I going to have to shoot you to take this bottle?"

He looked up at her face and swallowed as he saw the fierce face paint, but that was then softened by her smile, which went to her eyes. When she saw he didn't have enough strength to open the bottle, she took it back and opened it for him.

"Take it easy," she said. "One mouthful at a time."

He nodded his head. "Yes, I know," he said.

Marlene made him sit down, then she undid his shirt and took it off. The man was covered in bruises and open sores. She pulled out her personal first aid kit and took out an alcohol swab.

"This is probably going to sting a bit," she said. As she started wiping the worst of the sores, the man hissed slightly and grimaced. She noticed he did not have a tattoo on his arm with his blood-type on it, which would have meant he was SS. But he did have a number tattooed on his right bicep.

"So, what despicable crime did you commit to be in here?"

"I told an SS sergeant to go fuck himself," the man said.

"Ah," Marlene said. "A truly horrendous offence. If one of my troops told me to go fuck myself, I might have to punch him out. Isn't that right, Master Sergeant?"

"Yes, and send us to bed without din-din," Shandra said. "And no dessert for a week. Oh wait, isn't that what just happened last week?"

"Well, trooper," Marlene said to the man. "I think it's a little harsh, but hey, it's your army, not mine. A trooper should not tell his sergeant to go fuck himself."

"He wasn't a trooper," the man next to them said. "He was a captain of our reserve battalion."

"Oh my," Marlene said. "Well sir, I am just a lowly warrant officer and am privileged to be allowed to work on an exalted officer. So, what happens with the real bad guys? I am assuming that all of you here are in kind of the same boat, more or less."

"They just shoot them," the former captain said. "There is not much anybody can do about it. What the SS and the party hacks want, they get."

"Well, that's about to change," Marlene said. "You the only officer-type here? What about all these other folks?"

"Not many soldiers here, maybe half a dozen," the former captain said. "The rest are all civilians who ran afoul of some party rule or other. Or some jealous neighbour turned them in on some trumped-up charge. The woman your friend is helping is a nun and one of her students turned her in for saying bad things about the party. The student had been given a bad grade and her dad is a big-shot party man."

"A nun?" Marlene asked. "What's a nun? Hey, any of you guys know what a nun is?" She yelled out in Standard.

"Ya," the PIG captain said. "There is a religion back home, Catholics they are called. Men are priests, but women are not allowed to be. But if they devote themselves to God, they are allowed to be teachers or nurses."

"Religion?" Brock said. "What the hell is that?"

"Where are you people from?" the former captain said in German-accented Standard. "You talk a funny English."

"Well," Marlene said. "Us four Zebras are from Oaken. Where you from, Cap?"

"A country called Canada on Earth," the PIG captain said. "These people have no concept of religion, Sir. You are?"

"Captain Eichmann, formerly of the Das Reich regiment," he said. "Not the stinking SS or a party member."

"Decent regiment in the old days. I'm Captain Johnson, formerly of the Royal Canadian Rifles, now the PIGs. And yes, that's who we are, and we like the name. Most of us are from Earth originally. A lot has changed since you people left. For one, the Third Reich is long gone, as are the Nazis. Yo, doc! Give the sister there a look over, will you? She's a Catholic nun. He's a German, but not too bad of a guy for a square head."

"Ya, like you Canadians are all sweethearts," the doctor said. "Okay, why don't you Neanderthal Zebras get the hell out of here? You're scaring all the patients."

Chapter Nineteen

The worst patients were being loaded on ambulances to be transported to the local hospital. The Zebras loaded back into their G-Wagon and slowly made their way toward the airfield. Bodies were laying where they fell, and locals were helping walking wounded toward the hospital, while others were bandaging the screaming and moaning where they lay. Another transport landed at the airfield, and more medical teams poured out and started collecting wounded lying in the streets and pointing the helpers toward the airfield.

Gerry drove them into the airstrip. Bunkers and tanks were still smoking. They parked beside other Zebras and sat on the tailgate of the G-Wagon to watch the goings-on.

Conrad walked up to them with a case of beer in his hand.

"Wow," Conrad said. "Bloody red Indians you are, all painted up in war paint. All you're missing is the feathers and the loincloths."

"Red Indians?" Marlene asked. "What's a Red Indian? You Earth people are very strange. You've got something called religion, and Catholics, too, we just learned. Thanks for the beer, Captain."

"Oh no dearie," Conrad said. "Major Conrad now."

"Oh excuse me *Major*, Sir," Marlene said. "My, my, higher and higher we go."

"I'd rather be a sergeant with you guys," Conrad said. "No fun, this officer shit. A full battalion of Marauders hit that SS battalion about half an hour ago. Not much left of them. The Panther armour barely stood up to the Kodiaks' main guns, let alone the rockets.

From what I heard, the tanks never even got a round off. The half-tracks were absolutely no problem. Long-range engagement. The dismounts had little to do."

Loud speakers came alive and issued orders to separate the civilians from the soldiers, then the regular army and air force from the SS, and finally the death's head SS and brown-uniformed people off by themselves. Street-by-street house clearings then began. After three houses from which diehards sniped at the troopers were swiftly levelled by Kodiak main guns and 105 rounds, men all over town who had hoped to hold out tossed out weapons and surrendered.

After the first ten blocks were cleared, the residents of those blocks were called by name. If they were not brown-uniformed people, Party members, or their families, they were sent home. By evening, all the civilians had been mustered out. Then they began to clear the regular soldiers, most of whom were sent home as well. The same for the air force, but not so for the SS or Party members and their families. They were separated and led to easily guarded buildings, all except the death's head people. Marlene had special plans for them.

She marched them back to the prison complex and lined them up in front of it. Then she brought in all of the civilians from the houses of the blocks bordering the prison and made them go through the squalid prison, now cleared of prisoners. There had been over two hundred prisoners in that building, which should only have held sixty at most. Eighty were dead or close to it when they had been pulled out.

After the civilians came back out, many vomiting and all very pale, she lined them up and walked up and down the lines, her sunglasses on and a scowl on her face as she looked each civilian in the eye and then moved to the next one.

"How could one human being treat another like this?" she asked. "I don't even treat my farm animals this badly. Now, you people will find some proper clothing for these people. They will be taking over the guards' barracks for now until we can get all this mess sorted out."

Some of the PIGs had gone over to the former guards' barracks, and they brought back mops, buckets, brooms, and other cleaning supplies and dumped them in a pile in front of the former guards.

"That, gentlemen, is your new barracks," Marlene said. "The sooner you get it cleaned up and our medical people say it is safe to inhabit, the sooner you get indoors. Maybe in a couple of days, we might find some blankets for you. I think it goes without saying that all of us look forward to you trying to escape."

All of the Zebras and PIGs had grins on their faces and were stroking their rifles.

Relatives of the prisoners heard the news, and quickly came at the run with clothing and food for them. They were crying as they hugged their relatives and threw curses at the former guards. Then, as dusk was approaching and the dusk-until-dawn curfew came into effect, all the civilians hurried back home.

A tablet computer had been left on every home's kitchen table with instructions on how to turn it on. It showed them the end of the Third Reich, the death camps, devastated cities, what had happened to the Nazi leaders and to Germany after the war. Then they saw modern-day Germany, a free and democratic country that had risen from the ashes and taken its proper place among the leading Earth countries. Finally, they were told about the Federation of planets and shown how far advanced the Federation was compared to their society. They were also told what the Federation had decided. Duncan then came on the broadcast and described how things were going to be on this planet from now on: That the Nazi party leaders were going to be held for trial, charged with crimes against humanity, and punished. That all people on the planet who were free of guilt could stay as long as they followed the new laws and the new government and that any who did not wish to stay were free to leave. They had a week to make up their minds.

No one was allowed to leave the town the next morning, but they were allowed to leave their houses. Schools were closed. The dead had been collected overnight and sent to a temporary morgue. The worst of the wounded were being treated in the local hospital and the others in huge tents. Names of the dead and wounded were posted on the walls of the town administration office, listed by the blocks they lived in. Not many families were unaffected, but the wounded outnumbered the dead, and some were already being released.

Local medical staff were busy helping the conquering military. Anyone with medical knowledge was welcome, including dentists, vets, nursing assistants, and students. Another transport of medical supplies arrived and another with wounded SS Panzer men aboard. The unwounded or lightly wounded SS men were sent to the airfield and placed under guard with their comrades.

The Zebras took over a barracks to themselves and tossed all the SS gear out in the street. Then they had showers and, finding washing machines, wore clean uniforms the next day. Alpha had just finished unloading and storing all their equipment from the G-Wagon and were in the process of cleaning it up when two spotless G-Wagons drove up escorted by two Coyotes. All had the wolfhound emblazoned on the hoods and sides.

"Well, the Warrant and her gang of ruffians actually do have the proper uniforms," Duncan said as he came up to them. All four of them snapped to attention and saluted. He returned the salute, then came toward Marlene with his arms outstretched. She hugged him as hard as he hugged her, both of them with their heads on the other's shoulder and with eyes closed for several seconds.

"Dammit Duncan," Marlene said. "The boss is supposed to be up on a transport supervising, not on the ground in a firefight!"

"Wasn't much of a fight," Duncan said. "You had a bigger one here. We didn't have any fanatic SS to deal with and had the element of surprise. The rest of the division will be on-planet by the end of the week. Take me over to that prison complex, Mar, then to the hospital. The rest of you mugs stay here. She won't need any bodyguards."

He jumped in the driver's seat, forcing Marlene to take the front passenger seat, and as soon as her door was shut, he leaned over and kissed her, then looked in her eyes.

"God, how I've missed you," he said.

"Me too," she replied and kissed him again. They looked at each other for a minute, and then Duncan sighed.

"Work first!" he said, starting up the vehicle and heading off toward the prison. Everywhere, townspeople were busy cleaning up the streets and performing repairs where they were needed. The four demolished houses were being cleared of belongings and the four bodies brought out. At the prison, they were escorted by ten PIG troopers. Duncan and Marlene entered the yard, and the SS men were mustered outside. Duncan just glanced at them and spit on the ground at their feet. He didn't even break his stride or return their salutes.

The men had been very busy, but the building still stunk and the walls remained filthy. After Duncan inspected the guards' prison building, he made his way to their former barracks to meet the former prisoners, who had clean new clothing.

"As soon as the medical people give the okay," he told them, "if you want to, you may return to your families. If not, we will make other arrangements for you." Then he walked over to the medical officer and talked with him.

"Who was that?" Captain Eichmann asked Marlene.

"That is my lord Count Duncan Kovaks," she said. "He is the new head of state for this planet. My lord Kovaks, a moment? This is Captain Eichmann of Das Reich Battalion."

Eichmann came to attention and saluted. Duncan returned the salute.

"I am but a lowly Master Warrant Officer, Captain. I, like Warrant Isabelle, actually work for a living. Master Warrant Officer Duncan Kovaks, Wind Rider Regiment, at your service, Sir."

"But Warrant Isabelle just told me..." Eichmann blurted out.

"Well, yes, I am," Duncan said smiling, "but not today. You see, Count Kovaks is not allowed to play, but Master Warrant Kovaks is, and I do like to play. Sorry about that, but we are very good at what we do. The Warrant there was up on that ridge for over a week, and I was on a similar one for the same time at the capital. I have generals and other high mucky mucks who do all the general and high mucky muck stuff for me. So, what did you do in Das Reich besides tell SS sergeants to go fuck themselves?"

"I was a company commander of a reconnaissance company," Eichmann said.

"Ah, well I just might have a job for you later if you are interested. What do you think Eichmann, should I alter the women's uniform code? Didn't she look hot yesterday or what?"

Marlene smacked him on the arm hard while both men laughed.

"I think the body paint was a bit much," Eichmann said. "But I agree with the uniform shirt."

Marlene punched Eichmann on the arm after that, but softly.

"Now Warrant, do try not to scare the captain too much. We might need him later," Duncan said. "Alright my dear, next stop and then tea I think, what?"

"He's English?" Eichmann asked as Duncan strutted off head up in the air.

"Duncan? Hell no," the PIG captain from the day earlier said. "He's a Canadian like me. I say, Warrant, you do clean up nicely. Perhaps you might save me a dance at the ball?"

"In your dreams, Conley. You'd better hope I don't have you in my next training class." Then she pecked him on the cheek and flounced out the door after Duncan.

"She's as tough as they come," Conley said to Eichmann. "She took out half that section guarding the bridge with that big gun of hers by herself."

Eichmann had seen that as it happened. "How many of them were out here?"

"Twenty-five," Conley said. "They had things pretty much in hand by the time we arrived but were reporting their ammo was low."

"Are you not worried about that Panzer battalion? They have a lot of fire power, much more than we had here."

"They have been taken care of," Conley said. "They are no longer a factor. Ninety percent causalities." Then he, too, walked out.

By midweek, the PIGs and Zebras were helping the cleanup effort. While armed Kodiaks were keeping watch, life in the town was slowly returning to normal. As each family had their records reviewed and were cleared, men were allowed to return to work in their fields or shops. Some families were segregated pending further investigation, but most were not.

The regular SS men, Nazi officials, and segregated families were escorted under heavy guard to a transport ship and sent to the capital for further investigation and possible charges and trials. The death's head guards were not. They were still cleaning the prison building and sleeping outside, but they had been issued small tents and blankets and were fed and watered. Once the medical officer cleared the building as fit for human use, the guards were marched over to the airfield and shipped to the capital, never spending a night in the building they had worked to clean up.

It had been a busy month. The Federation had agreed the big threat was this system and had authorized a full deployment. All four battle groups were now on-planet. The Marauders were stationed in the capital city, Black Shirts at the other satellite town, and the PIGs in the same town as the Zebras. The barracks were nowhere big enough to hold the whole battlegroup plus the one-third of the Wind Riders allotted to the town, so they were under canvas or in modified shipping containers.

The town was called Cologne, and all of the remaining inhabitants had elected to stay. As required, they had quickly organized themselves into groups of thirty households or families and had elected representatives. Today, a meeting was being held for all of the representatives. Duncan and the command group would be chairing the meeting, and the Zebras had been chosen to provide security.

They were arranged around the hangar that was to be used for the meeting, dressed in crisp, clean uniforms, boots and beret badges gleaming. Not a hair or decoration badge was out of place on their forest camo uniforms. Weapons consisted of rifles draped across chests and pistols on left hips. While they were vigilant, they did not look or act intimidating, merely professional. As with any gathering of almost seven hundred people, the hum of conversations was quite loud, but as Duncan and the command group walked in, it quieted. You could hear their feet as they walked up to the raised platform where table and chairs were set up. The crowd rose as the command group arranged themselves at the table, Duncan in the middle. As he sat down, so too did the crowd.

The command group was dressed in forest camo uniforms like the Zebras, but with only pistols on their hips. Unlike in a social setting, they all had their berets on their heads for this meeting. Duncan adjusted the microphone in front of him while the crowd settled itself.

"Thank you all for coming," he said. This conversation would all be in German. "My name is Duncan Kovaks, and I am ruler of this planet. Temporarily, my counsel and I will be handling all of the affairs here. The system of government will be a constitutional monarchy. That means that I, and my descendants following me, are the head of state. Once your elected officials become more experienced, more and more power will be delegated to you, but the ultimate authority will still sit with my office, and I may overrule anything that I feel is not in the best interests of the people as a whole.

"All of you have been elected to represent the people. This is a great honour and a great responsibility. Sometimes, you will have to make rulings that may not be popular, but you must make them. All of us, including me, are trying to build a better life for our families, and as every parent knows, sometimes the children do not appreciate what the parents want them to do. I know I sure did not."

Duncan went on to tell them that negotiations with the mother planet and the other satellite planet in the system were ongoing. The mother planet had recalled all the SS divisions on the satellite province, along with any battalions of their regular army units, leaving only local reserve units. The satellite planet had asked for terms, and they had been sent. It was hoped by both sides that the negotiations would be quickly concluded and that the planet would be joining them. The mother planet had flatly refused to negotiate.

Investigations of the previous establishment were ongoing, Duncan went on. Many charges had already been laid, and trials were being scheduled. Others, including family members of those charged, had been cleared and would be returning shortly.

Duncan stated that he was aware that the school year would conclude in a few weeks. All graduates would report for mandatory military duty two months after graduation, just like they already did, with two differences. The mandatory commitment would be for five years instead of two, and both sexes would report instead of just the males. Volunteers between the ages of twenty and thirty-five would be accepted. Those currently in their two-year service would continue in service with a credit for time already served. Priority for volunteers would be for those already serving, then single people of both sexes or married ones with no children. Term limits would be the same as the mandatory terms – five years full-time, five years active reserve, and ten inactive reserve. Anyone who wanted to stay full time would sign five-year commitments for each term.

Starting this year, any children reaching the age of thirteen by the end of the school year would be enrolled in a military cadet program. All school-aged young people over thirteen would be enrolled at the beginning of this year. For now, this program would be administered by members of a battlegroup from off-planet until enough qualified locals could take over. The expectation was that the planet would field its own completely trained and equipped battle group within five years.

Duncan's comments seemed to go on forever. Taxes would begin to be calculated at the beginning of the next school year and would be due the following year. Until that time, the Crown, or Duncan in other words, would pay for all government spending, such as schools, roads, water and sewer, police and fire, and medical costs. After that, the taxes would pay for them.

As this was largely a farming community, agricultural specialists would soon be arriving to instruct farmers on the latest technologies and practices. A demonstration farm would be established in lands that would soon become available, where techniques would be taught, and results compared with the methods currently being used. This would be turned over and used as an agricultural college as soon as possible.

"Now, as anyone who has been in any army can tell you," Duncan continued. "Troopers have a lot of time on their hands when they are not on duty or deployed. My people are no different. Some are young and dumb, like those Zebras hanging around the walls here. They do what most other young and dumb people do, party a lot and spend money foolishly. I am sure none of you ever did those kinds of things when you were young and dumb. I certainly didn't."

The head table was snorting and laughing and some of the crowd as well.

"What?" Duncan said looking at both sides of the table. "I'll have you know I was only tossed in jail once for being drunk, and I save a whole five dollars a year from my salary. Not like you guys."

Now the whole room started to laugh.

"That being said," Duncan said. "We have a zero-tolerance policy. Any transgressions against the laws or rules will not be tolerated and will be severely punished. That includes those Zebras over there, and if you ask them, they will tell you that no one is above the law. No one. Not even me. We will not repeat what I saw when I arrived here.

"Now, my not so young and dumb troopers are very creative. We encourage that. You will soon start to see shops opening up offering goods you've only ever dreamed of. Where one of our businesses directly competes with an already established local one, we encourage and actually require our members to seek out the local establishments and hammer out a partnership arrangement. As our methods are, in many cases, more advanced than yours, I would recommend that the locals accept. Other than that, we believe in free enterprise.

"So, that is all we have for you on this, your first yearly meeting. Once again, I thank you for your service and commitment to your people. I hear that the local brewery has the best beer in the planetary system, and I mean to find out if it is true.'"

Carts full of fresh beer were wheeled in at that point, and the rest of the afternoon was spent socializing. Except for the Zebras, who were still on duty.

Chapter Twenty

The Zebras were just finishing up their preparations for a night out. All the weapons and uniforms were put away, and they were dressed in casual civilian clothing. They would stand out from the locals anyway because of their clothing and PG's hair colour, today a shimmering blue violet, but at least they were not in uniform and were trying to appear normal. PG had started copying Marlene's hairstyle, the left side down, but where Marlene swept the right side behind her ear, PG had hers shaved short. She had given up on the facial-piercing jewelry, as it was to prone to infection in the field. Her fingers were loaded with rings, several types of necklaces hung on her neck, and she had multiple bracelets on her wrists and arms. Some of the others had wrist watches, and some of the women wore earrings, but that was it as far as decorations went. Marlene wore no jewelry.

It was the start of the local soccer summer season, and the PIGs had formed a team and joined a senior's league. The Zebras, coolers of beer and vodka in hand, were heading off to watch the game.

"Ten-hut!" somebody yelled out, and automatic reflexes kicked in, everyone lining up at attention in front of their bunks. Duncan was standing to the side of the bunk closest to the door, also at attention and looking around the room.

"I don't see no stinking officers around here," he said. "Oh, sorry, Lieutenant Ma'am." PG was the only officer in the Zebras.

"What? Who me?" PG said. She didn't consider herself an officer either.

"I keep telling you guys, I work for a living," Duncan said. "Besides, I'm in civvies today."

He had a polo shirt tucked into blue jeans, which were draped over a pair of cowboy boots. A battered black and red ball cap with a white horse was on his head.

Marlene walked up, gave him a peck on the cheek, and grabbed an arm.

"We are headed to the game," she said. "Coming?"

"Well, if I'm gonna spend time with my girl, I guess I have to," he said and gave her a squeeze. "So, who's driving? I don't have any wheels."

"When do you ever have any wheels, Mr. Cheap?" Brock said. "We are all on foot here. Damn commander won't let us use our wheels for personal reasons."

"Damn officers," Duncan said. "I sure as hell am not running over there like you guys do. Not in these boots."

"No running today," Marlene said. "There is a cute guy I have my eye on, and I don't want to be all sweaty and stinky." She folded herself into him and kissed him.

"Make sure you leave the room in one piece, you two," Gerry said, and the Zebras filed out the door.

Duncan eyed Marlene's bunk and raised his eyebrows.

"No damn way, Kovaks!" she said. "Don't even think about it."

Duncan laughed, gently turned her around, and shoved her out the door. They stayed at the back of the skylarking gang, walking close together and holding hands.

"How much time do we have?" Marlene asked.

Duncan sighed. "Just the weekend. Too much shit going on. I told them I would shoot anyone that bugged me for the weekend though."

"When are we going to hit the mother planet?" she asked.

"No work talk this weekend, okay?" he said. "I just want to be with the woman I love and be normal for a while."

"Can we ever be normal?" she put her head on his shoulder.

They walked on in silence for a bit, and the others kept on laughing and joking, while the two of them held back, in their own little world.

"I am going to have to move here full time, Mar," he said finally. "Bishop will be the governor of the other planet. The Federation is giving me this whole system, not just this planet, so I have to stay."

Marlene didn't say anything for a block, just walked with her head on his shoulder. Then she kissed him on the cheek.

"Like you said, no shop talk. Now, are you buying me dinner tonight or what?"

"I bought the last time," he said.

"Well if you want in my pants tonight, you're buying tonight, too," she said and laughed. "If I like it, I might buy tomorrow."

Duncan spent a lot of time explaining the intricacies of the game to the Zebras. Soccer was not played in their planetary system. The locals outplayed the PIGs, handily winning the game. Most of the PIGs had not played for many years, and while they did have their moments, they were definitely outclassed.

The rest of the gang headed off to the local pub they had begun to call their own, while Duncan and Marlene slowly walked hand in hand through the quiet streets. Their clothing identified them as strangers, but nobody recognized out of uniform. They were just a couple in love going for a walk, not that much different from others in town. They never did get dinner that night.

Marlene woke up to Duncan running a finger on the scar on her inner thigh. His eyes were far away, not seeing the wall of the bedroom. He had taken a suite on the top floor of the best hotel in town. He looked down to see her watching him and smiled.

"Morning," he said.

"Morning yourself," she said and pulled his head down to kiss him.

"I love you," she whispered. She didn't often say that to him.

"I know," he said. "Almost more than I love you, but not quite."

She kissed him again, then gathered her clothing and headed to the bathroom. She finished her shower, dressed and came back out, still towelling her hair dry. Duncan was fully clothed and looking at a small box in his hand. He looked up at her and made to speak.

"No," she said. "Before you ask, no. I will not marry you. I will love you always. I will bear your children and raise them with you and live with you, but I will not marry you. I will not dishonour Karen's memory like that."

"But..."

"But nothing," she said. "I have my own legacy to hand down, you know. My family's lands and titles and my own. Our children will want for nothing. I will love them, as will you. You have set up our laws that it does not matter if we are married or not. Before my father, the Isabelle name was old and honourable, and next year, once I have finished my five-year term and received back all that I lost, it will be again."

"Well, the Kovaks name is also old, Marlene," Duncan said. "Just not aristocratic."

She took his face in her hands and kissed him.

"It is now, my love," she said. "And I wouldn't care if it weren't. Your first love was Karen, and she was your wife. I will be your wife in all but name. Does it matter otherwise?"

He shook his head and kissed her back, then made to put the little box back in his pocket.

"Oh no you don't," she said, holding his hand. "You are still going to give me that engagement ring. I will wear it with pride and honour, just not the wedding band that goes with it. But not yet. Carol tells me her people have a ritual that bonds two families together. Go ask her what it is. We will do it, and then you can give me the ring."

Duncan put his communicator in his ear and tapped it.

"Whiskey Romeo Charley Alpha One, Whiskey Romeo One, copy?"

"Copy, Go Ghost."

"All Whiskey Romeo on planet to assemble in Hangar One no later than sixteen hundred. It's party time, so make it happen. Everyone in uniform, if you please."

"Roger, what's the occasion?"

"Since when do we need an excuse to party?"

"Roger, out."

Duncan took the communicator out of his ear and stuffed it in his pocket, then opened the door to the suite, and, with an elegant gesture, ushered Marlene outside, closing the door behind them and offering her the crook of his arm.

"Why thank you, my lord Kovaks," she said, slipping her arm through his.

"Not at all, my lady Isabelle. It is the least I can do for the lady who will be buying me breakfast like she promised."

"Not at all my lord Kovaks, the pleasure is all mine."

They made their way down the stairs and sashayed through the main floor lobby to the dining room, like the aristocrats they were but seldom acted. Then Marlene came to a sudden stop just before the entrance.

"Wait a minute," she said. "You were supposed to buy dinner last night."

"Indeed I was," Duncan said. "It's not my fault you didn't want to stop and eat."

Marlene was trying to decide whether she should be mad or not, then looked up at his innocent face with his laughing eyes, and she laughed instead.

"Ya, I know. You snooze, you lose. You just wait until tonight, buddy."

"Are you going to ask Carol about that ceremony like I asked?" she said as they were finishing the last cup of coffee.

"Don't have to," he said. "My mother came from her people, remember? I know what has to be done."

After breakfast, they walked out of the hotel, and he steered her toward the camp. He changed the subject and took her hand as they walked. It was a nice sunny day, and many people were walking about, it being a day off. The couple smiled and greeted any who crossed their path, but although some thought they looked familiar somehow, nobody put it together.

"We won't be able to get away with that for much longer," Marlene said as they entered the camp.

"Most people only see what they want to see," Duncan said. "They expect to see me in a big fancy uniform, not wearing blue jeans and cowboy boots. It mostly worked for us in Oaken. It should work here as well.

"Now my dear, grab your buddy Shandra, and both of you guys get your hair done nice or whatever you females do at big parties. You two especially will be needing nice crisp uniforms. Can't have you showing up at your engagement party looking like a bum, now can we?"

They had just walked up to the Zebra barrack, and Shandra and the rest of Alpha were lounging in lawn chairs out front.

"Engagement party?" she said. "Who's getting engaged?"

"Why, my lady Isabelle, of course," Duncan said. "You didn't know? I thought BFF's always knew everything? Anyway, I must be off, always more beans to be counted."

Shandra was hugging Marlene at that point, and Duncan took off in the direction of headquarters.

"Who you getting engaged to?" Brock said.

"Are you that dense?" Shandra said. "Nobody could be that dense."

Others came out of the tent to see what the commotion was all about, and Marlene was soon in the centre of a ring of people, being congratulated.

"Come on, come on," Shandra yelled after putting her fingers in her mouth and letting loose with a loud whistle. "We have no time to lose! The party is at sixteen hundred, and we ladies have much work to do."

Transports were landing all day, and reunions were cropping up all over the Wind Rider part of the base. Many had not seen each other for a couple of years, and there was a lot of catching up to do. The Zebra ladies came back by fourteen hundred with hair and nails all done up. Brock stopped one stunning brunette from entering.

"Nobody but Zebras in here," he said.

"Well, if the sergeant doesn't get the hell out of my way, this lieutenant is going to kick his ass so hard he won't sit down for a week," PG said. "And I don't want to hear any comments from any of you other yahoos either."

The Zebras walked into the hangar a half hour early and found a table at the back by the door. The place was filling rapidly, and the locals hired were busy bringing beer and vodka bottles to the tables. Once again, the raised platform was in place at the front of the hangar with tables and seating for twenty in a long line.

Someone yelled *Attention!* over the intercom, and everyone rose and did as bid. Ten dark green formal uniforms rose to the platform. They were all Wind Riders, original Wind Riders, and Duncan was at the head, Jane was next, then the rest of Alpha, including Dianne, Megan, Carol, Barb, Dave, and Amanda.

"Zebra Alpha! Front and centre!" Duncan yelled out. Marlene grabbed PG and shoved her to the front of the line, and the five of them marched up and spread out in front of Duncan on the podium. Marlene nudged PG with a foot after they had stopped.

"Lieutenant Walker and party of four, Sir!" she belted out.

"At ease, Lieutenant Walker," Duncan said. They had stopped the regulation two paces away from him, and he waited for them to assume parade rest.

"Warrant Isabelle, two steps forward!" he barked.

"Left face!" she turned facing the assembly at attention. Then she felt two hands take hold of her shoulders.

"I am Duncan, House of Kovaks. This is Marlene, House of Isabelle, my love, my life. What is done to her and hers is done to me and mine, so say I in front of God and man."

"So say we all!" all thirty of the original Wind Riders belted out.

Then Duncan came in front of her and placed the ring on her ring finger. She put her hands on his shoulders and looked into his eyes.

"I am Marlene, House of Isabelle. This is Duncan, House of Kovaks, my love, my life. What is done to him and his is done to me and mine, so say I in front of God and man."

"So say we all!" the Zebras belted out.

Then he kissed her, and the party was on.

It was Monday morning, a week after the engagement party. Alpha company of the PIGs and all the Zebras were in the old SS drill hall standing around in small groups. Eventually, they were called to attention, and Duncan, with Jane and the PIGs' general and Alpha's colonel, marched in and stood in a line in front of them.

"On Wednesday morning on the mother planet, a war council meeting will be held in its main conference room. We will be crashing the meeting, people," Duncan said.

"You will be transported by the same method we were brought to this system. You will not, however, be asleep this time. Alpha will be going with their Kodiaks. At the appropriate time, you will all be inside the Kodiaks and buttoned up. When you are given the word, you will dismount the vehicles, form a defensive perimeter, and engage anything that engages you. That includes the main weapons systems. There are two Panthers and four half-tracks with dismounts in two locations. They will be neutralized immediately. Your commanders will give you the locations of those units and whose responsibility they will be.

"Zebras, you will be transported directly into the conference room. You will find yourselves spread out around the walls facing inward. You will be a little disoriented, but get control quickly, because there are four personnel with automatic weapons stationed at the entrance to the conference room. Once those guards are neutralized, you will block the doors from opening. You will be shown how to do that. After that, you are to neutralize any threats that appear. Everyone, Alpha and Zebra, will have full weapons loads. Long rifles will not be required.

"Address any questions to your commanders. Dismissed."

"What kind of transport was he talking about, PG?" Marlene asked as they were walking back to their part of the base. PG's hair was back to her normal radical self. This time a shocking pink.

"I'm not sure," she said. "I went to bed one night and woke up on the barracks floor in Oaken along with twenty-five other people. I thought we had destroyed that thing when we hit Arial. They could only transport thirty people and equipment max and then the thing was out of action for a week after."

The rest of the day, the Zebras, using the floor plan CT had sent over, planned their positions and who would do what in the opening seconds. The next morning, they practiced. In the afternoon they cleaned and oiled weapons and loaded clips.

Marlene was up early, but she was not the first one. PG was. She was washing the dye out of her hair when Marlene entered the washroom and started her shower. After Marlene had dried her hair, she pulled it back and made a tight braid that came just above her shoulders. Once again, she started putting thick black stripes on her face, making a fearsome mask. Then she started on her arms and hands. She went to her bunk and methodically started to dress in the alternating dark green and tan striped cammo battle fatigues, instead of the forest green and mottled light green ones. Next came the calf high combat boots, a fighting knife scabbarded on the left one. The pants had a scabbard sewn onto the outside of the right leg to hold a six inch combat knife. Next, she took out her pistol, once again stripped and cleaned it, loaded a full clip into it, and holstered it. Four spare clips for the pistol and six for her rifle followed, two of which went into her large cargo pockets on her pants. Her personal combat first aid pack was placed in one pocket and a spare comms battery in the other. Four spare grenades for her launcher were placed in pockets on her weapons harness along with the spare rifle and pistol clips. Then two smoke grenades and fragmentation grenades were attached to it.

Next came the rifle itself. Once again, it and the attached grenade launcher were stripped, cleaned, and oiled. The two-powered optical scope was checked along with the open iron sights. The laser designator was turned on and checked, then the sound suppressor was attached and a full clip inserted in the rifle and a fragmentation grenade in the launcher. She put her small comms unit in her ear and the accompanying radio in her right shirt pocket. She strapped her combination watch/GPS unit on her left wrist and checked its functionality, then made sure her IFF unit was also functioning properly. Now came the time to don the weapons vest and adjust it so it was comfortable. The final act was attaching all the unit and rank badges to the appropriate Velcro patches and donning her battered and sweat-stained desert tan ball cap with the Wind Rider crest in the centre.

Finished with her preparations, she looked around the room. Everyone had their personal rituals they went through before deployments, and most had finished. Everyone had the same dark-stripped war paint on arms and faces. Some wore black berets, others tan ball caps. Some had coloured lens sunglasses perched on their faces or dangling from cords on their necks. Some had armoured tactical vests on, but most did not. All but one of the women, like Marlene, had pulled back their hair into tight braids, some hanging to the side, the others, like Marlene, to the centre of the neck. The only exception was PG. She had gelled her hair to stand up like a Zebras main and had coloured her hair alternating black and white. She wore no head gear. All of them looked fierce, even though some were smiling.

Marlene checked her watch, took up her rifle and clipped it to the front of her weapons vest, barrel pointing to the right and down. Everyone went to their positions and stood facing inward, except for Marlene and Shandra, who faced to their left.

"Who are we!" Marlene belted out.

"Zebras!"

"What are we born to do!"

"Run!"

"What are we bred to do!"

"Kill lions!"

"What do we love to do!"

"Kill Nazi Ass!"

"Zebras! Zebras! Zebras! Hurrah!"

Bolts were pulled back, arming weapons. Marlene and Shandra brought theirs up to their shoulders, fingers on the trigger guards just outside the triggers and crouched down. Then there was a shimmer in the air, and they were gone.

One second, she was crouched down in their barracks, the next she was facing a machine-pistoled soldier in a black SS uniform.

Marlene tapped her trigger twice, and the man was blown off his feet, She sighted on her next target as Sandra's weapon went off beside her. The four guards stationed on the inside of the doors were down and dead before they knew they were being attacked. Next, Marlene and Shandra knocked out the four stationed outside the open doors, and Marlene fired her grenade down the hallway to explode at the guard post at the end of the hall.

Gerry pulled the two doors on Marlene's side shut, but not before setting up a claymore mine outside it. Bob from Bravo did the same at the other two doors. Then they tightly wrapped heavy chains through the panic bars of the double doors and padlocked them shut. Only then did Marlene turn around and survey the room, sweeping it with her rifle to her shoulder and eye on the scope, looking for targets.

One SS uniformed officer was lying on the floor, a hole in his forehead and the back of his head blown off. The men beside and behind him were covered in blood and brains. The others in the room had panicked looks on their faces, and most had their hands up, but a few were cowering under chairs. An SS-uniformed man bolted out of the side room, pistol extended and ready to fire, but was almost cut in half as Brock let him have it with a three-round burst from his crew gun, and he was hit at least six times by other rifles. Another brave but stupid trooper actually got a shot off, hitting one of the Zebras in the chest, knocking him back against the wall and knocking the breath out of him. The Zebra was wearing an armoured vest.

That was the end of any resistance in the room, and Duncan, along with the rest of Alpha and Bravo troops from Alpha Squadron, appeared behind the man who had been speaking at the podium. Brett grabbed the man by the suit jacket collar and frog-marched him off the stage. At that point, another SS trooper, this one with a machine pistol, came from behind the stage, and without seeming to even look, Duncan raised his rifle and tapped the trigger twice, hitting the man in the chest with both shots. The reports from his unsilenced weapon were loud.

"Anyone else want to play?" he asked. "Then, everyone, sit down!"

One SS General refused to sit, but then his aide pointed at his chest, which had six red dots on it, and then to the six corresponding rifles, and the general sat down.

"My name is Duncan Kovaks, and I am here to accept your unconditional surrender."

A series of sharp cracks, followed by loud secondary explosions were heard from outside. A set of doors rattled as there was an attempt to open them, and shouting was heard from the other side. Gerry hit his button, his claymore exploded, and there was silence outside the doors after that.

"If you are hoping for rescue," Duncan said. "those explosions outside were your two Panzer tanks, four half-tracks, and all their troops going bye-bye. There is a battalion of armoured troops and their vehicles surrounding this building. We have taken complete control of all telecommunications on this planet and are broadcasting what I am about to say to you here in this room, complete with actual footage of the events and the aftermath.

"In April of 1945, the borders of Germany were breached on the west by two million American, British, and British Commonwealth troops. Six million Russian troops had crossed the eastern border and were advancing on Berlin. They had crossed the Austrian border and were closing on Vienna. Hitler, Goebbels, and Himmler committed suicide. Other top Nazi officials were fleeing anyway they could, but most were captured. Berlin and most of the large German cities were piles of rubble, and Germany unconditionally surrendered on May 1st.

"On the Pacific front, Japan was pushed back and surrounded, her navy destroyed as well as her air force. In August, a bomber dropped a single bomb and destroyed the city of Hiroshima. A few days later, the same thing happened to the city of Nagasaki, and Japan surrendered.

"The leaders of Germany and Japan were arrested. Some, like Goring, committed suicide, while others were found guilty of crimes against humanity and hanged. Others got life in prison or other long sentences. Any SS or party officials in charge of death camps or who had taken part in the extermination of the Jewish people or others were executed or imprisoned. Several hundred thousand German prisoners captured by the Russians were never heard from again.

"Germany was partitioned – half to the Russians and the rest split between the Americans, British, and French. The Third Reich was renamed the Republic of Germany after the partitions were eliminated in the 1980s, and the Nazi Party was outlawed.

"You are fighting a war that was lost seventy years ago for a cause the German people no longer believe in and now abhor."

Duncan let them think about that for a moment.

"Russia now has 175 million people, America 350 million, China and India over one billion. The solar system of that planet you just decided to take over? It has over one hundred planets, each of them much more advanced than you are. While their weapons systems might not be as long-range as yours, they have, combined, about 100 million troops. You have what, forty, fifty thousand?

"I defeated your two thousand troops with half a battalion, and we don't have main battle tanks like you do. I invaded your secondary planet with two battalions, no air cover, and no heavy tanks, and you suffered 100 percent casualties to my four percent. Using conventional transportation methods, I now have forty thousand combat troops and their vehicles on that planet, and, again, using conventional transportation methods, I can have them all here in less than a week. Using unconventional methods, well, this is a demonstration of that.

"My weapons systems are superior to yours. We can fire faster and on the move, and have better systems that can track, target, and kill targets at longer ranges than yours. Our ground troops have better weapons, training, and skill levels than yours do. You will lose any war, gentlemen. The planet I invaded has already agreed to join our Federation, and the other planet is voting on it right now.

"You gentlemen have ten minutes to make up your minds. Your options are unconditional surrender or not. If not, we kill the lot of you and negotiate with the next bunch. Feel free to talk among yourselves,."

More commotion was heard outside in the hallway, and Bob triggered the other claymore, once again killing whoever was out there.

As Duncan had thought while planning this raid, it didn't take but five minutes for the leaders to surrender. He had the documents of surrender with him and they were willingly signed. He handed orders to the civilian leaders and others to the military ones.

"All troops are to report to their barracks, disarm, and stay there. All Nazi party members and political leaders are to report to the nearest military barracks and stay there. Don't try to hide or change your names. We know who everyone is and what they look like. Anyone suspected of committing atrocities like we witnessed on the other planet we invaded, or of corruption of any kind, will be arrested and held for trial.

"The Federation of Planets has awarded me this whole system. I am the absolute ruler at this time. Your people are being told of the new system of government and can opt out if they choose to do so. Any of you in this room, not charged or found not guilty of charges, will also be given the opportunity.

"Now then, gentlemen, my time is running short and I have a tea party to attend."

Marlene blinked as the air shimmered, and she found herself back in her barracks facing her bunk. Shaking her head, she took the clip out of the rifle and tossed it on the bed, leaning the rifle against it, then unloaded the pistol, putting it back in its holster, and started taking the pieces of equipment off the weapons vest, emptying her pockets and removing the vest itself. Now came the boring task of unloading the bullets from all the clips into a large barrel, to be used at the practice range, and storing away the clips, grenades, and weapons vest into her locker. She quickly cleaned her weapons and put them back in the locker, then tossed her ball cap on the top shelf, grabbed two towels, and walked to the showers, undoing her braid as she walked.

She was blow drying her hair and wearing only a towel when Duncan walked in.

"Typical man," she said. "Invites me to a party, I spend hours getting ready, then he gets bored and we go home after half an hour."

Duncan kissed her behind the ear, then went over to the Bravo trooper who had been shot and admired the dark bruise on his chest.

"Get over to the docs and get checked out," Duncan said. "You might have a broken rib or something."

"Great job, everyone," he continued. "The only casualty was to super trooper here. You used a minimum of munitions, which will keep the bean counters happy, and we accomplished the mission in a professional manner, with minimal casualties to the enemy. The PIGs destroyed both Panzers and four half-tracks, killed about fifty troops, and shot down two FW 190s. So, once you are cleaned up, I have rented the main ballroom at the big hotel for an old fashioned whoop-up. No uniforms, okay? But more than just a towel, Warrant Isabelle, if you please."

She stuck her tongue out at him and raised her right index finger. Duncan laughed and headed back out the door, ears ringing from all the laughter that followed him.

Later that night, he lay on his back staring at the ceiling, his arm around Marlene's shoulder as she slept snuggled up to his side. He had accomplished his purpose. Finding a home for his people. Now they had to make it their own.

Don't miss out!

Visit the website below and you can sign up to receive emails whenever R.P. Wollbaum publishes a new book. There's no charge and no obligation.

https://books2read.com/r/B-A-DWJC-JJFFC

BOOKS 2 READ

Connecting independent readers to independent writers.

About the Author

R.P. Wollbaum and his faithful companions Lady and Baron, live in the foothills of the Rocky Mountains in Southern Alberta Canada.

When not busy composing a new novel, he can be found exploring North America in 'Da Buss'.

Read more at www.bearsandeagles.com.